Libby Ashworth wri[...] [...]
she was born and brought up. Libby still lives in Lancashire and is passionate about its history. She can trace her direct ancestors back to the village of Whalley in the Middle Ages. Many of her ancestors worked in the cotton industry – first as home-based spinners and handloom weavers, and later in the mills of Blackburn. It is their lives Libby has drawn on to tell her stories.

By the same author

The Rag Maiden
The Market Girl

The Widow's Shillings

LIBBY ASHWORTH

PENGUIN BOOKS

PENGUIN BOOKS

UK | USA | Canada | Ireland | Australia
India | New Zealand | South Africa

Penguin Books is part of the Penguin Random House group of companies
whose addresses can be found at global.penguinrandomhouse.com

Penguin Random House UK,
One Embassy Gardens, 8 Viaduct Gardens, London SW11 7BW

penguin.co.uk

First published 2025

001

Copyright © Libby Ashworth, 2025

The moral right of the author has been asserted

Penguin Random House values and supports copyright.
Copyright fuels creativity, encourages diverse voices, promotes freedom
of expression and supports a vibrant culture. Thank you for purchasing
an authorized edition of this book and for respecting intellectual property
laws by not reproducing, scanning or distributing any part of it by any
means without permission. You are supporting authors and enabling
Penguin Random House to continue to publish books for everyone.
No part of this book may be used or reproduced in any manner for the
purpose of training artificial intelligence technologies or systems. In accordance
with Article 4(3) of the DSM Directive 2019/790, Penguin Random House
expressly reserves this work from the text and data mining exception.

Set in 12.5/14.75pt Garamond MT
Typeset by Falcon Oast Graphic Art Ltd
Printed in Great Britain by Clays Ltd, Elcograf S.p.A.

The authorized representative in the EEA is Penguin Random House Ireland,
Morrison Chambers, 32 Nassau Street, Dublin D02 YH68

A CIP catalogue record for this book is available from the British Library

ISBN: 978–1–405–96206–3

Penguin Random House is committed to a sustainable future
for our business, our readers and our planet. This book is made from
Forest Stewardship Council® certified paper

For Ralph, who always does his best to help.

Summer 1852

I

Kitty Cavanah pushed her barrow into the back alley behind the houses on King Street. It was very early in the morning and she and two of her children, Maria and Peter, were amongst the few people who were up and about. As they searched for any items of value, the sun crested the top of the tall buildings with the promise of a hot summer's day to come. It brought welcome relief after days of incessant rain when their clothing had been soaked every morning and barely dry by bedtime.

Kitty poked her stick into a pile of rubbish that had accumulated in the gutter that ran down the edge of the cobbles and was pleased to feel something solid. Wondering if it might be bones that she could weigh in at the rag warehouse for cash, she eased the tangle of weeds and sodden paper aside to take a better look. Seeing what looked like a small hessian sack, she bent to retrieve it.

The sack was much heavier than she expected when she lifted it, dripping, from the ground. She held it at arm's length to put it in the barrow to inspect it more closely. As she laid it down, she heard what sounded like coins chinking together and eagerly pulled off her gloves to pick at the tight knots in the string that held it closed.

Kitty gave a sharp intake of breath as she caught sight of the money. She glanced up to check that no one was watching her, then cautiously withdrew one of the coins from the bag and stared at it as it lay on the palm of her hand. It had a picture of the young queen stamped on it, bareheaded with her hair curling down at the back as if it was coming unpinned. Some Latin words were stamped around the edge, but Kitty had no idea what they meant. She turned the coin over. On the back, surrounded by a wreath of leaves and the queen's crown, there were two large words. Kitty could read these. They said ONE SHILLING and the numbers below were the year the coin had been minted — 1850. Two years ago, although the coin looked shiny and new as if it had just been made.

She opened the bag a little wider and began to count the shillings. There were maybe a couple of dozen or more. A lot of money — all seemingly lost in a back alley.

Someone must have dropped the bag. Though who would be in the backs behind King Street with so much money? Possibly one of the businessmen who lived here. She looked up at the row of tall terraced houses and considered whether to try to return it. She could begin with the Andertons. They knew her and wouldn't accuse her of stealing, but she wasn't sure if they would be out of bed at this time and she didn't want to disturb them if they were still asleep.

She made her way towards their back door to see if there was anyone in the basement kitchen. Even if Mr and Mrs Anderton were still abed, their maid Dorothy might be up and kindling the fire ready to make breakfast. But when she reached the top of the steps, Kitty could see no movement from inside the house and she was reluctant to go and knock at such an early hour. Perhaps she should call back later to ask if they knew anyone who had lost some money.

In the meantime, Kitty tucked the bag of coins underneath the pile of rags she'd found to take down to Mr Reynolds at the rag and bone warehouse. It would be safe enough there until she could return it to its rightful owner.

Calling quietly to the children, who were at the far end of the alley, to follow her, she continued on her rounds. They gathered what they could here and there as they scoured the streets and ginnels for cast-off clothing, unwanted pans, even lengths of twine and lost nails from horses' shoes. It was all of some value and every farthing they could earn was important.

'I think it's time to finish,' she told the children as doors began to open. Maids brought out rugs and hung them over the front railings to beat them clean. The sound of hooves echoed on the cobbles, and carts rolled past delivering milk and fresh vegetables to the gentry, and cotton to the mills. Before long the hooters would sound and the workers would come rushing from their cottages to file in through the mill gates to spend long hours working at looms and spinning machines. Kitty didn't envy them. She knew the men earned good money, but she preferred to be outside even if it did mean she was sometimes drenched. And even though many people regarded the rag gatherers as beneath them, Kitty was proud that she'd managed to keep her family fed and clothed in the years since she'd arrived here, bereaved and bewildered and seeking help from her cousins.

'Let's go home to sort these out,' she told Maria and Peter. 'We'll have some breakfast and then go down to the warehouse.'

She wheeled the barrow back towards Mary Ellen Street as the sound of the mill engines began to pound and smoke rose from the chimneys to sully the clear blue of the morning sky. The streets which had been silent when they set out at dawn were now filled with noise and Kitty had to dodge around the workers as they pushed past, rubbing their bleary eyes and yawning – not just mill hands, but clerks and shopkeepers, apprentice boys and street sellers. The town had burst into life and it was time for the gatherers to retreat to their cellars and houses.

When they reached their home, Maria and Peter carried the finds inside and Kitty manoeuvred the barrow in through the door. Her elder daughter Agnes was getting ready to leave, pinning on her cap at the small mirror propped up by the kitchen sink.

'Has Timothy gone?' asked Kitty. Her elder son worked as a letter carrier for the post office.

'He went about five minutes ago,' Agnes told her. 'And I'm off now. I'll see you later,' she called as she hurried out of the door.

'Your shawl!' Kitty called after her.

'I won't need it. It's going to be hot today!' she called back before shutting the door behind her. Kitty heard her eager footsteps pass the window as she went on her way. She was so proud of what Agnes had achieved. It still amazed her when she walked past the cheese shop and saw the name on the sign outside – *Marsden and Cavanah, cheesemongers*.

It hadn't come without a cost, though. Kitty's greatest wish was to see her daughter married. Life was hard without a man and Kitty wanted Agnes to enjoy the security that had been lost to her when her own husband, Peter, had been drowned on the voyage from Ireland. She'd been so disappointed when Agnes had turned down Patrick Ryan, the son of a family who worshipped with them at St Alban's Church. Eligible young men from their own community were few and she despaired that Agnes would ever find a suitable husband – especially since she'd opened the cheese shop with Jonas Marsden, a local farmer's son. It worried her, because Jonas wasn't a Catholic, like them. And although she knew that Agnes had grown close to Jonas, she didn't think a marriage between them was possible and she was anxious about Agnes being hurt.

Kitty was glad to see that her daughter had brewed some fresh tea before she left. She poured it out for herself and the younger children and spread a smear of lard on to the last of the bread for them. She'd eat any that was left over herself later, or maybe she'd treat them all to a pie for their dinner if they got a good price for the rags today. For now, the hot drink was enough to revive her.

'What's this?' asked Maria curiously as she lifted the hessian sack from amongst the rags she was sorting into whites and coloureds. 'It's heavy.'

'I found it behind King Street,' Kitty told her. 'It must belong to one of the men who live there. We must take it back this afternoon.'

'Is it money?' Maria asked when she heard the jingle of the coins. She put it down on the table and began to pull the strings apart.

'Leave it!' Kitty told her. 'It isn't ours.'

Her daughter looked disappointed but did as she was bidden and went back to her sorting.

The bag remained on the table, taunting Kitty. She couldn't help thinking of all the things that she might buy with so much money. Just one of those shillings would make such a difference to their lives. She could go to the market and buy bread and potatoes and even some meat to feed them for a week or more. She could buy lengths of material to stitch new clothes. She could buy candles and coal, tea and sugar – the temptation was huge. And there were so many coins in the bag that surely just one of them wouldn't be missed?

No, thought Kitty, she mustn't allow such thoughts to intrude. It would be stealing, and she knew that stealing was wrong. She must find out who the money belonged to and return it to them. The best she could hope for was a small reward when she gave it back. That would be more than enough.

But first she must take the morning's finds down to the warehouse and get paid for them so she could buy food for their dinner. Maria had bundled the cloths into two piles and these were put back into the barrow at the door, then all the metal objects were put into a wooden box beside them. There had been no bones today, but there were some from yesterday that Kitty had boiled to make a soup. Scraped clean of any scraps of meat, they were added to the haul and Kitty set off towards Clifton Street with the children.

She had wondered whether to leave the bag of shillings hidden in the house, but she was so worried about someone breaking in and stealing it that she'd decided to take it with her. As soon as the rags had been weighed in and the shopping done, she would leave Maria and Peter to rest at home and she would go back to King Street with the money.

Mr Reynolds greeted her with a smile.

'Better weather today,' he observed. 'Ye all looked like drowned rats when ye came in yesterday.'

'Yes. I'm thankful for a bit of sun,' agreed Kitty as she lifted the pile of white cloth on to the scales.

'Tuppence ha'penny,' Mr Reynolds told her.

Kitty weighed in the coloured cloth, the bones and the nails. It came to fivepence altogether and Mr Reynolds counted the coins into her hand.

'There's work at the tables for Maria if she wants it,' he said. 'Same wage I paid your Agnes.'

Kitty glanced across to where her elder daughter used to help sort out the finds – the clean cloth for the paper mill, the bones for the glue factory. Even though Maria had often watched with fascination as her sister had worked there, Kitty wasn't sure she would be keen to do it all day. When Agnes had started here it had been to save them from starvation, but things weren't quite as hard now and she was hoping that her younger daughter might find cleaner work at the cheese shop. Agnes had promised to take her on as an assistant once she and Jonas could afford to pay her a small wage.

'Thanks,' she told Mr Reynolds. 'I'll bear it in mind, but she has her heart set on shopwork, like her sister.'

He nodded. 'Agnes is doing well. I called for some cheese yesterday and her shop was busy with customers. She and Jonas Marsden make a good team.'

'They have done well, much better than I expected,' Kitty admitted.

'He's a good lad, and a hard worker,' went on Mr Reynolds. 'It can't have been easy for him to take on the farm and the dairy after his father died, but he has stalls on most of the local markets now and probably more shops to come. I daresay there'll be a place for young Maria before long. Do you not fancy it yourself?' he asked.

'I'm happy gathering rags,' Kitty told him. The truth was she would find it odd to work for her daughter. The rags might not bring her in a fortune, but she was beholden to no one but herself and she liked the independence.

'What have you got there?' Mr Reynolds asked, spotting the hessian sack that Kitty was still holding.

'Oh, this isn't for weighing in. I found it in the backs behind King Street. Someone must have lost it so I'm going to walk up and try to find the owner.'

'What is it?'

'Money,' she told him. 'It's shillings. I would have given

it back straight away, but it was so early that everyone was still abed.'

'Let's have a look.' Mr Reynolds held out his hand and, reluctantly, Kitty teased open the strings and took out one of the shillings to show him.

'They look new,' she said. 'But the date says 1850.'

Mr Reynolds weighed the coin in his hand then studied it thoughtfully, turning it over to examine both sides. He looked concerned.

'What's wrong?' asked Kitty.

'I don't think it's real,' he told her.

'What do you mean? Not real? It's a shilling, isn't it?'

'It looks like a shilling,' he agreed. 'But I think it might be a counterfeit – a shilling made to look like the real thing to trick people.'

Fear struck through Kitty. She knew what a counterfeit was. She'd heard Agnes talk about them and how careful they had to be at the shop not to accept a coin that was worthless – and how much trouble they could be in if they were found to have any on the premises.

'Are they all like this? Shiny and new?' Mr Reynolds asked her.

'Yes.' Kitty showed him the rest of the bag.

'Give it here,' he said, holding out a hand for it. 'We can soon find out if they're real or not.'

She watched as he counted out ten coins and put them on one side of the balance he used for weighing in nails and other scraps of metal. Then, rather than a weight, he fetched ten real shillings from his safe and put them on the other side.

'See?' he asked as the real coins fell and the ones Kitty had found rose. 'They aren't heavy enough. They aren't made of silver. They're probably cast from some type of pewter.'

Kitty stared at the scales. She was suddenly afraid. She knew she must get rid of these coins before she got into trouble for having them in her possession.

'What do you think I should do with them?' she asked. She wondered whether she should just go back to King Street and throw the bag back into the alley where she'd found it.

'You should take them to the police station,' Mr Reynolds advised her. 'It's up to them to investigate a crime.'

The thought of the police frightened Kitty even more. She shook her head. 'I can't get involved with the police,' she said. 'What if they don't believe me? I could be sent to prison or transported back to Ireland.'

'Well, what else can you do with them?' he asked. 'You can't keep them.'

2

Kitty hurried home with the hessian bag of coins. She felt as if they were red hot in her grasp and she glanced about her as she walked, terrified that she might pass one of the police constables walking his beat.

'Stay here and watch your brother,' she told Maria when they reached Mary Ellen Street. 'Don't open the door to anyone.'

'Where are you going?' Maria asked anxiously. 'What are you going to do with the money?'

'It isn't real money,' Kitty explained. 'I have to get rid of it because I could get into trouble for having it.'

Maria looked worried. 'They won't lock you up, will they?' she asked.

'No, of course not,' Kitty reassured her. 'I'm just going to put it back where I found it. Then we can forget that we ever saw it and nobody will be any the wiser.'

She closed the front door behind her and with the bag of coins hidden in the folds of her shawl she walked briskly in the direction of King Street. When she reached the back alley, panting with exertion and fear, she looked about for a place to hide the bag, but before she could, she heard a door open behind her and the Andertons' maid, Dorothy, called to her.

'Mrs Cavanah!'

Kitty felt her face flush and she was overcome with guilt even though she knew she'd done nothing wrong.

'Where are thy little ones today?' asked Dorothy.

'I've left them at home resting. They were tired.'

'Would tha like to come in for a cup of tea?' Dorothy asked.

Kitty was reluctant, but she didn't like to refuse. It had taken a while for Dorothy to trust her and she didn't want to damage their fragile friendship, because she liked the woman and knew that she was kind-hearted.

'I can't stay long,' she said.

'Well, I've just brewed a pot. Come and take the weight off thy feet for a few minutes.'

It was tempting on such a warm day and Kitty went down the steps to the kitchen door and into the shade.

'I'm glad of the sun to get a few things dry,' said Dorothy, 'but it's too hot now. We're never satisfied, are we?'

'That's true,' agreed Kitty, glancing at the washing line filled with shirts and shifts that stretched across the backyard, lifted high by a wooden prop.

'Sit down,' said Dorothy. 'I'll slice some fruit cake for tha to take home for the children. I know they like it.'

'Thank you. That's very generous.'

'Well, I know they'll be disappointed if tha says tha's been in and then go home empty-handed.'

Kitty sat down on one of the wooden chairs that surrounded the scrubbed table. The heat was oppressive in the kitchen, where the fire was lit so that the oven would be ready for cooking. She wouldn't light her own fire when she got home, she decided. The children could eat a cold tea, especially if there was cake to follow.

Suddenly, the hessian sack slipped from her grasp and hit the floor with a jangle of coins. 'Oh!' she exclaimed as she bent to retrieve it. She had hoped to keep it hidden from Dorothy so that she wouldn't need to make any explanations.

The maid looked curious. 'That sounded like money,' she remarked, handing a cup of tea to Kitty.

Kitty felt her cheeks flush and hoped Dorothy would think it was the heat.

'It's just something I found earlier,' she said. 'I thought it was money and I intended to return it, but Mr Reynolds said the coins are worthless because they're fake.'

Dorothy stared at the bag that Kitty had put on the table. It was clear that she was curious and wanted to see what was inside, so Kitty teased apart the strings and took out one of the shillings to show her.

'Mr Reynolds said it was the wrong weight.'

'Aye,' Dorothy agreed as she looked at it closely. 'It's well done, though. It would have fooled me. What do you intend to do with them?'

'Well, Mr Reynolds suggested the police, but I'm wary of getting involved with the law,' Kitty confessed. 'I thought I would just put them back where I found them.'

'Is that what you were doing outside?'

'Yes,' she admitted.

'Do you think someone had hidden them in the back alley?' Dorothy asked. 'Why would they do that?'

'I don't know.'

'I've never seen anyone hanging about,' said Dorothy, 'and I'm down here for most of the day.'

'They must have hidden them in the night. I'm sure they weren't there yesterday when I scoured the alley for rags.'

Dorothy sat down at the table and stirred sugar into her tea. 'It gives me the shivers, to think of men skulking about out there when we're all asleep,' she said. 'I thought these new policemen were supposed to be walking the streets to keep us safe, but it seems they don't see everything.'

'They probably don't walk in the backs,' said Kitty. 'You can't blame them,' she added. 'It's pitch-black there after nightfall.'

'Aye,' agreed Dorothy with a frown. 'I think I'd best mention it to Mr Anderton, though.'

'Must you?' asked Kitty. She was worried now that simply hiding the coins wasn't going to be an answer to her dilemma after all. She suspected that Mr Anderton would insist on her going to the police station when he found out about it.

'I think I should,' said Dorothy. 'He's not in at the moment – or Mrs Anderton – but he deserves to know if there's goings-on behind his house.'

'I suppose so,' said Kitty.

'Perhaps you should show him these coins,' Dorothy suggested. 'He knows plenty about such things, with being a businessman. Mr Reynolds might be wrong. They look real enough to me. And if someone has had them stolen it's no good just hiding them back where you found them. They need to go back to their owner.'

'Stolen?' Kitty hadn't considered that. It was a worse scenario than them being fakes. She definitely didn't want to be found in possession of stolen property. People were always accusing the Irish – and the rag gatherers in particular – of being dishonest and stealing. She'd have a hard time convincing the police of her innocence if they found the coins in her house and accused her of being a thief. She was beginning to wish that she'd never picked the bag up in the first place. If she'd just left it lying on the ground and walked away, she wouldn't have got herself into this mess.

'Perhaps I should just leave them here?' she suggested.

'No!' Dorothy flapped her hands in horror. 'They aren't anything to do with me. Come back later and show them to Mr Anderton.'

Kitty lingered over her tea as Dorothy talked about how much the town had changed since so many people had moved in from the countryside.

'Times were when everybody knew one another and ye knew whom ye could trust. Ye could leave doors unlocked when ye went out and nothing would be out of place when ye came back. But it's not the same now. Everything has to be locked up.'

Kitty nodded. She was only half listening as she fretted about what to do with the money. She couldn't leave it here. She couldn't hide it again because Dorothy would be watching her. And she didn't want to take it home with her in case a policeman came knocking at her door. She wondered whether to wait for Mr Anderton to come home so she could give the coins to him, but she was anxious about leaving Maria and Peter on their own for too long. She really ought to get back and check that they were all right.

'And I don't want to sound like I'm including thee in this,' went on Dorothy, 'but people do say it's been worse since the Irish started coming over. And they have a point.'

'Do they?' asked Kitty. She knew that Dorothy didn't intend to be unkind, but it upset her to hear the maid speaking about the Irish like that. The people she meant were Kitty's friends, and she knew that most of them were entirely honest and it was only prejudice against strangers that made the local people choose to blame them for every robbery.

'Well, maybe not,' conceded Dorothy as she cleared away the cups and took them to the sink to wash them. 'But those tinkers who were here with the Easter Fair were rogues,' she insisted as she poured the hot water into the bowl. 'I know a woman who lost a silk handkerchief to the pickpockets as she was walking around the crockery stalls.'

Kitty bit back a terse reply. It had taken a long time for Dorothy to accept her as a friend again after the incident when she'd taken Mrs Anderton's baby daughter, Julia, to find some milk for her. It had all been a misunderstanding and Kitty had meant no harm, but folk had accused her of stealing the child – and Kitty knew they wouldn't have been so quick to distrust her if she hadn't been Irish. But it was a burden she had to bear, because it would do her no good to fall out with the few English friends who had helped her in the past.

In the end, she decided that she had no choice but to take the coins back home with her for the time being. Perhaps she could bring them back very early the following morning and put them back where she'd found them. What she would tell Mr Anderton, she had no idea, but she would think of something. She just wanted to be rid of the money.

3

When Kitty arrived home she found Maria and Peter sitting on the back doorstep playing snap with an old set of cards that they'd found. The pack was missing a few numbers so wasn't much use for any other game, but Peter loved snap and Kitty was cheered up by hearing her two younger children laughing together in the sunshine. They didn't get a lot of joy. They had to get out of their beds very early in the morning to accompany her on her rag-gathering round, and some days there was barely enough money to buy food, never mind provide any toys or other amusements.

When Kitty had been young she'd had endless fields to run about in around her parents' smallholding back in Ireland, and she often wished she could bring up her own children in clear country air rather than the smoke and smog of the mill town streets. She tried to take them up on to the hills on a Sunday afternoon after they'd been to church if the weather was fine, but although the views were pretty enough, they weren't home and she missed Ireland desperately. Not that it would be any use going back. There was nothing there for her now. The cottage she'd shared with her husband and the children would probably be completely derelict and their patch of land would be part of a bigger farm, worked by machinery rather than by hand.

She looked around for a safe place to hide the money. In the end she put the bag into the oven beside the fireplace. She must be careful not to forget it and light the fire, she thought. Not that there was any chance of that. The coins were constantly on her mind and she wouldn't rest easy until she was rid of them.

She picked up the kettle to fill it from the bucket of water that she'd fetched from the pump earlier, then she realized that she couldn't make tea without lighting a fire. But it would be a waste of coal on such a hot day anyway, and they could make do with a drink of cold water, or even some of the blue, skimmed milk if it hadn't turned. She'd set the jug on the stone slab in the scullery and wrapped it in a wet cloth to try to keep it cool, but milk didn't stay fresh for long in the summer heat.

As she was slicing bread, she heard her daughter's footsteps coming up the street.

'Have you brought any cheese?' she asked hopefully.

'I have,' said Agnes with a smile, putting a wrapped package down on the table.

'I thought we'd have a cold meal – cheese sandwiches and fruit cake. I saw Dorothy earlier when I was at the back of King Street. She cut some slices for me to bring home.'

'I like a bit of cheese with fruit cake,' agreed Agnes. 'Shall I put the kettle on?'

'No.' Kitty looked towards the closed oven door with a guilty feeling. 'It's so hot I thought we'd do without the fire. You don't mind a cold drink, do you?'

'No,' Agnes said, although Kitty could see that she was surprised. Even though the sun was baking outside, it was still fairly cool inside the little cottage with its stone walls and small windows, and her daughter knew how much she enjoyed a cup of tea.

It wasn't long before Timothy arrived home and they all sat around the table to eat their meal. The children chatted about their day, but Kitty found that she couldn't concentrate on what they were telling her because her thoughts strayed to the coins over and over again. She knew she wouldn't feel comfortable until they were out of the house.

'Is something wrong? You look worried,' said Agnes as she helped her mother clear the table.

'No,' Kitty told her, but then changed her mind. Agnes was familiar with coins and Kitty thought that if she showed them to her she might be able to offer some advice on whether they were real or forgeries. 'It's just that I found some money this morning.'

'Money? How much?'

'Quite a lot,' admitted Kitty. 'But I don't think it's real money.'

She bent to open the oven door and placed the bag on the table before drawing out one of the shillings and giving it to Agnes to look at.

'What do you think of it?' she asked.

Agnes studied the coin, as both Mr Reynolds and Dorothy had, and weighed it in her hand.

'It looks real to me,' she said at last. 'How many more are there in the bag?'

Kitty loosened the string some more and poured the coins out on to the table. They scattered across the oak boards and some spun and fell to the floor. Agnes dived under the table to retrieve them. Then she stared at the silver, twinkling in a beam of sunlight that shone in through the open door where Maria and Peter had gone back to their game.

'There must be five pounds or more!' she exclaimed before beginning to pile the coins into towers of ten to count them. 'Five pounds,' she confirmed after a moment. 'That's a lot of money.'

It was. It was more money than Kitty had ever seen in her life.

'What are you going to do with it? You can't keep it.'

'I've no intention of keeping it. I was going to put it back where I found it after Mr Reynolds said the coins were fake, but Dorothy saw me and she said she would tell Mr Anderton. He'll make me go to the police. I don't want to do that.'

'Perhaps you should,' her daughter advised. 'You can ask to speak to Constable Westwell. He was very kind to me that time I was robbed in the street.'

Kitty remembered the incident well. She'd been terrified when the constable had come knocking on her door. She hadn't known what he wanted and when he'd asked for Agnes, she'd been convinced that her daughter was in some sort of bother.

'Or maybe you could ask Mr Anderton to go with you.'

'But what if they are real and they think I stole them?' asked Kitty, fretfully.

'Why would they think that if you took them to the police station?' Agnes asked.

'I'm so afraid of us being sent back to Ireland,' Kitty confessed. 'We'd starve, or have to go to the workhouse if they sent us back there.'

'They won't send us back,' Agnes reassured her. 'If you don't want to ask Mr Anderton, we could ask Jonas to come with us.'

'I don't know.' Kitty began to pick up the piles of coins and put them back in the bag. She didn't like having them on the table, in view of anyone who might pass the window or come to the door. 'I think I'm just going to put them back.'

'But if they are real and someone has lost them or had them stolen, we should try to return them,' Agnes told her.

'But what if they're not real?'

'Then the police will investigate it because it's a crime,' said Agnes. 'Why did Mr Reynolds think they were fakes?'

'He weighed them. He said they're too light. That they aren't made from silver at all.'

Agnes was nodding. 'Yes,' she agreed. 'I think they make them from spoons – like this,' she went on, picking up a teaspoon that had been left on the table. 'They melt them down and turn them into coins. Jonas told me that I must be careful because it's not easy to tell the difference. But I would have accepted these in the shop without question. If they are fakes, then they're very good ones.'

Kitty put the bag back into the oven. It could stay there until morning, then she would decide what to do.

4

Very early the next morning, Kitty crept down the ginnel that led to the back of the King Street houses. She'd left the children asleep. She didn't want to involve any of them in this. It was her problem and it was up to her to set it right.

On the roof of one of the houses a blackbird was singing in the half light, but everything else was silent. She walked down to the place where she'd found the bag. The water in the gulley had dried up but there were still some rotting leaves and she bent to try to hide the bag amongst them.

She was so absorbed in her task that she didn't hear the man approach her from behind and when he put a hand over her mouth it was an awful shock. She struggled against him, terrified, knowing that she must use all her strength to fight him off. His grasp was fierce. He was taller and much stronger than she was and she had nothing to defend herself except her fingernails.

Kitty tried to break free, but she was helpless and couldn't even cry out. She tried to bite his hand, but he pressed it harder over her mouth and nose. Her heart was racing and she was terrified of what he would do to her.

'What were tha doin' with that bag? Were tha tryin' to steal it? Did Ratcliffe send thee?' His breath was hot in her ear.

She wanted to say that she was putting it back where she'd found it and he was welcome to it if it was his, but she couldn't speak with his palm clamped to her lips.

'Don't scream,' he warned her. 'I have a knife and I'll kill thee if tha screams.'

Kitty could barely get her breath; she felt as if she was going to faint.

'Promise me tha won't scream. Nod thy head.'

Kitty nodded as best she could and the man slowly drew his hand away from her face. She gasped for breath but didn't call out.

'What were tha doing with that bag?' he demanded again.

'Nothing. If it's yours, you can have it. I won't tell a soul,' she promised, wishing that he would let her go.

'How do I know tha'll keep thy promise?' he asked. 'How do I know tha won't go running to the police?'

'I won't,' she gasped. 'I won't say anything. If it's yours, just take it and go.'

She felt his grip on her slacken as he bent to retrieve the bag.

'I'm a rag gatherer,' she told him. 'I find things. But I don't take what's not mine. I wasn't taking it,' she insisted. 'Just let me go.'

She looked towards the houses, wondering if anyone was up. She was tempted to scream for help, but she was afraid that the man would make good his threat to kill her. She must try to stay alive. Her children would never manage without her.

'Let me go,' she pleaded again, hoping that it was

only the bag of money and not her body that he was interested in.

'Did tha look inside it?' he asked her.

Kitty was tempted to lie, but she decided it might be safer to be honest. 'I saw it was money,' she told him. 'But I didn't take any. You can count it.'

Perhaps if she could persuade him to do so, she would be able to break free of him and run. He seemed undecided as he grasped the bag in one hand and her in the other.

'I should make certain tha doesn't talk,' he said, and Kitty feared that he was seriously considering killing her and leaving her body in the alley.

'No,' she whimpered. 'I won't say anything. I promise I won't. Let me go.'

She strained to free herself, wondering if she could outrun him if she did break away. If not, she knew her way around all the back alleys and might be able to hide, although she suspected he knew the backs too, or he wouldn't have hidden the coins here. His grip on her wrist tightened as she fought, and she knew that her predicament was hopeless. After everything she'd been through and struggled for, what a waste it would be to be murdered for a bag of coins that probably weren't even real.

Kitty was praying silently, trying to prepare herself for the end, when she heard a door slam. The man suddenly pushed her away with such force that she was propelled backwards, losing her balance. She fell to the ground, her head smashing against the stone cobbles, and for a moment she lost consciousness. When she sat up and tried to make sense of what was happening, she saw Mr Anderton chasing her assailant down the alley, wearing nothing but his nightshirt.

A few minutes later, he came back, panting heavily and looking defeated. Doors and windows were opening all down the street now as people peered out to try to see what was going on. Dorothy came hurrying out to help her.

'Mrs Cavanah! What happened?'

'She was being attacked,' said Mr Anderton. 'I saw it from the bedroom window, but he's got away from me. I couldn't run fast enough without boots. My feet have grown too soft,' he lamented. 'Here, let's get Mrs Cavanah inside.'

Kitty felt embarrassed to be lifted up in the arms of a man who was wearing next to no clothing, but Mr Anderton didn't seem concerned and she was grateful to be carried inside, out of view of the interested neighbours.

'Put her in the chair,' said Dorothy.

'No,' Mr Anderton said. 'I'll take her upstairs to the parlour. She needs to lie down. She's hit her head, I think.'

Kitty tried to protest, but he ignored her gabbled words and carried her up the back stairs and into the parlour where he put her down on a soft sofa with a cushion under her head.

'I'll send for the doctor,' he said decisively. 'And then I'll send for a constable.'

'No,' protested Kitty, but her faint words went

unheeded and she felt so weak that there was nothing she could do to prevent it.

'What happened?' she heard Mrs Anderton ask. 'I just woke up to see you running out of the bedroom. Is that Mrs Cavanah?'

'It's all right, Bessie,' her husband soothed. 'There's nothing to be afraid of. But Mrs Cavanah needs the doctor. She's hit her head.'

'Did she slip and fall?' asked Mrs Anderton as she came across to the couch. Kitty saw that she too was still in her nightclothes, but she had a dressing gown clutched around her. Her long, dark hair flowed loose over her shoulders and she looked so young and vulnerable that Kitty felt the need to apologize for distressing her.

'I'm so sorry to disturb you, Mrs Anderton,' she said. 'I'll be all right in a minute.'

'No. You must stay there,' Mrs Anderton insisted as Kitty tried to get up, thinking that she must go home before the constable arrived. Mr Anderton had gone and she was afraid that he might be looking for a policeman.

Dorothy entered the room with a steaming basin of water. 'Go and get yourself dressed,' she exclaimed, sounding scandalized to find her mistress in her bedwear. 'I'm sure Julia will be calling for you. No doubt she's been upset as well with all this palaver going on so early in the morning.'

'What happened, Dorothy?' Mrs Anderton asked. 'My husband wouldn't tell me. Was it an intruder? I know you told him about people hanging around in the back alley. He must have heard something. He's a much lighter sleeper than I am.'

'No, it wasn't an intruder. Go and dress yourself and let me bathe Mrs Cavanah's head.'

'I'm all right,' Kitty insisted. 'I must get home to my children.'

'Not until the doctor's seen you. That's what Mr Anderton said.'

'I don't need the doctor. It's only a bump,' said Kitty. She reached to touch the tender lump on the back of her head and winced. There was blood on her fingers when she looked at them.

'Come up like an egg, it has,' remarked Dorothy as she inspected the swelling. 'Here, sit up against another cushion and I'll get it cleaned up at least. Then we'll see what Dr Skaife has to say about it.'

The maid was gentle, but Kitty's head was very tender and she still felt stunned and tearful about what had happened to her.

'I dread to think what that man was going to do to thee,' Dorothy remarked as she worked. 'It was a good job Mr Anderton saw what was happening.'

Kitty agreed. She would have nodded her head if it hadn't been so painful, because she didn't trust herself to speak without breaking into tears. She was desperately trying to be brave and pretend that it had all been nothing, but she had truly feared for her life.

Still, she hoped that was the end of it. The man had his coins, and as long as he didn't come looking for her again she could forget all about them once her head had healed. And in future she would be much more careful what she picked up. It would be rags and bones and nothing more.

5

Constable Sidney Westwell had been on night duty. It was a shift that all the constables hated, although it was less arduous during the summer months when it came light by four or five o'clock in the morning. He'd just returned to the station house on Clayton Street and was looking forward to clocking off and climbing the rickety stairs to the attic room set aside for the policemen to sleep in when the outer door burst open and the chap named Anderton from King Street came rushing in, unshaven and without a cravat.

'Can I help you, sir?' he asked, wondering what he'd been up to. The man considered himself a gentleman, but he always made Sidney feel uneasy. He looked too exotic by far for a mill town like Blackburn.

'There's a woman been attacked in the alley behind my house.'

'I see,' Sidney replied. If only the man had waited another five minutes, Andrew Milne would have come on duty and he would have been in the back kitchen drinking a pint of tea and eating a bacon butty. Reluctantly, he pulled a sheet of paper towards him to take down the details. 'And your name is?' he asked, even though he knew it well enough.

'Joshua Anderton.'

'And who is the woman who was attacked?' he asked. She would be one of the prostitutes who walked the streets after decent folk had gone to bed, he surmised. They hung around the streets nearby, looking for trade, as they called it, all done up to try to look like ladies, but none of them were. He'd come to know a few since he'd taken on this job. At first they'd tried to sell themselves to him, telling him the nights were long and lonely tramping the beat and why didn't he go home with them and rest his feet for a while? He'd soon made it very clear to them that they'd be the ones resting their feet in the lock-up if they bothered him again. They always laughed. Some patted his cheek with their dirty hands and one had even been so forward as to try to kiss him until he'd thrust her away. But they unnerved him because, even though they disgusted him, he'd missed the comfort of a woman's body since Susan had died, and once or twice he'd been tempted.

'I think you may know her,' Mr Anderton replied. 'It's Mrs Cavanah from Mary Ellen Street.'

'Mrs Cavanah?' Sidney looked up, shocked, from the notes he was writing. 'Are you sure?'

'Of course I'm sure. I was the one who sent the man packing and Mrs Cavanah is currently lying on a sofa in my parlour waiting for the doctor to call.'

'Is she badly hurt?' he asked. It wasn't what he'd been expecting. He did remember Mrs Cavanah, although it was her daughter, Agnes, he'd had more dealings with. In fact, if he remembered rightly, it was this chap, Anderton, who'd brought Agnes Cavanah in after she'd been robbed in the street. And now the mother had been attacked and here he was again.

'She was pushed over and banged her head,' Mr Anderton explained. 'I chased after the assailant but I was barefoot and he got away from me.'

'Barefoot, eh?' repeated Sidney, writing it down in his neat copperplate hand. 'How did that occur?'

'I'd just got out of bed. I think the noise had wakened me. I looked out of the window and saw what was going on and I just ran out, as I was. My only concern was to save Mrs Cavanah from harm.'

'I see. And what did he look like, this assailant?'

'Medium height, stocky, maybe in his late thirties. I didn't get a good look at him.'

'What was he wearing?'

'Fustian britches, scuffed leather boots, a patterned waistcoat and a coat over, a cap on his head.'

Sidney wrote it all down. He had to give Mr Anderton credit. He'd been observant, even though it wasn't much to go on.

'Irish?' he asked. They were all Irish, these tinkers.

'I have no idea. I didn't enter into a conversation with the man!' Mr Anderton sounded annoyed.

'No need to raise your voice, sir,' Sidney reminded him. 'Any other distinguishing features?'

'Not that I can recall. But Mrs Cavanah may be able to tell you more.'

'She'll have to come in then,' he replied.

'She can't come in. I've already told you that she's been hurt. You'll have to come back to the house with me and speak to her. The sooner you start to look for this man, the better chance you have of catching him. This,' he gestured towards the pens and paper. 'This writing everything down isn't achieving much, is it?'

Sidney looked up and met the chap's dark eyes with a steady gaze. 'It has to be written down, sir,' he explained, as if the man was an idiot. 'We have to keep records.'

'Well, I think you have it all now,' he replied. 'Shall we go to King Street?'

Sidney was about to tell him that his shift was finished and that if he cared to take a seat for a moment then Constable Milne would be along shortly and he would interview Mrs Cavanah. But he hesitated. He recalled the woman from the day he'd knocked on her door to enquire after Agnes. He remembered how terrified she'd looked at the sight of him and how he'd pitied her – an Irish widow, washed up on these shores with a brood of children and a husband drowned at sea by all accounts. He knew what it was like to lose a partner and he'd felt an affinity with her because of that. And he knew that Andrew Milne could be a bit sharp and overbearing. If Mrs Cavanah had been attacked – and he had no reason to believe it wasn't true – Milne was the last person he would send to speak to her. He sighed and added the report to the pile on the 'in' tray.

'I'll fetch my hat,' he said.

6

Dorothy was clearing up the bloodstained cloth and the basin of water when the doorbell rang.

'That'll be the doctor,' she said, glancing out of the front window to make sure she was right. 'Lie still. I'll go and let him in.'

Kitty felt a flutter of fear in her stomach. The only other time she'd been examined by a doctor had been that dreadful day when they'd reached Liverpool after the *Sirius* had sunk. He'd been kind, but she didn't know what to expect from this one. She'd heard people talk about Dr Skaife and call him eccentric.

'In here,' she heard Dorothy say and a man came in, wrapped in a shabby coat with a pipe clamped between his teeth. He took it in his hand and waved it towards her, wafting the scent of tobacco around the room.

'Is this the patient?' he asked, even though she was the only other person in the room. He looked around for a place to deposit his pipe and as he couldn't see one, he handed it to Dorothy and then drew up a chair to sit down beside the sofa. 'So, what happened to you?' he asked.

'She was attacked!' Dorothy explained.

'Thank you. Thank you.' The doctor waved Dorothy away with his hand. 'Allow me to converse with my patient, please.'

With a snort of indignation, Dorothy withdrew to the other side of the room and Kitty was glad that she wasn't left alone with this man. She was already trembling at the thought of him touching her.

'It's my head,' she explained. 'He pushed me over and I fell backwards and hit it on the cobbles.'

'Let's take a look.' The doctor was unexpectedly tender as he took her head between his palms and drew it towards him. He said nothing more than 'Hm' and 'Hmm' as he examined it, then asked, 'Do you feel dizzy?'

'A little,' Kitty replied.

He held up his hand and raised three fingers. 'How many fingers can you see?'

'Three,' she confirmed.

'Good. Lie back now,' he instructed. 'I think you may have suffered a slight concussion, but there's no major damage. The cut will heal and the swelling will go down in a day or so. But you must rest until then. Bed rest, if possible. Where do you live?'

'On Mary Ellen Street.'

'Do you have any relatives to care for you. A husband?'

'No. I have children.'

'How old?'

'Agnes is eighteen, but she has to go to work. She has the cheese shop on Church Street,' explained Kitty. 'My son Timothy works too, but there's Maria and Peter as well.'

'How old are they?'

'Ten and six.'

'They'll do,' decided the doctor. 'I'll write a prescription for a little something to help with the pain.'

'I really think I ought to go home,' said Kitty after Dorothy had seen the doctor out. Now that he'd confirmed there was nothing seriously wrong with her, she felt awkward about lying on the Andertons' sofa.

'What about your medicine?' asked Dorothy, pointing to the piece of paper that Kitty had clutched between her fingers. Kitty glanced down at it. The doctor had written something down but she had no idea what it said or what the chemist might give her in exchange for it.

'I'll send Maria to get it,' she said, even though she had no intention of doing so. It would cost too many of her precious pennies to buy the medicine and she was sure that she wouldn't even dare to take it. She was deeply suspicious of what might be in it. Her head would improve in a day or so and until then she would bear the pain. She hadn't the time or the money to be lying in bed instead of getting on with her work.

'I think tha'd best stay until Mr Anderton comes back. He might bring the constable with him,' Dorothy said.

'I'm sure the constable has better things to do than bother with me,' said Kitty, sitting up slowly to see if she felt steady enough to try standing. She put her feet to the floor, realizing that someone had removed her boots and that her mended cotton stockings had a hole in the toe. She bent to try to disguise it and looked around for her boots. They were placed neatly side by side at the end of the sofa and she reached for them, trying not to groan as her head throbbed.

As she was lacing them up, Mrs Anderton came back

in with little Julia in her arms, warm and pink from her bed.

'Are you feeling better?' she asked Kitty. 'Has the doctor been?'

'He has, and there's nothing wrong. I'm grateful for your concern, but I'll get on my way now and stop taking up your time,' she replied, sitting rigid for a moment and waiting for a wave of dizziness to pass.

'Dr Skaife said she has a concussion and needs to rest,' interrupted Dorothy, taking the child from Mrs Anderton's arms. 'But she won't listen to me.'

'I can rest in my own home,' insisted Kitty. She heard footsteps outside and hoped that it wasn't Mr Anderton with the policeman, but she knew she'd left her escape too late when, moments later, he came in with Constable Westwell.

The policeman stood near the door whilst Mr Anderton asked if the doctor had been and if she was feeling well enough to talk about what had happened.

'It was nothing,' she told the constable, fearing that her assailant would make good his threat to silence her if she said too much. 'It was just a misunderstanding, and I lost my balance and fell.'

'That's not what Mr Anderton has described,' said Constable Westwell. Kitty wished the man would at least sit down, as the doctor had. It was making her head hurt to keep looking up at him. 'He says he saw you being attacked.'

'It was nothing,' Kitty repeated, wishing that they would all leave her alone so she could go home. Agnes would be up by now and no doubt worried about her. She needed to get back to Mary Ellen Street to reassure her.

'Can you describe the man?' asked the constable, producing a notebook from one of his pockets and a pencil from another.

'He was . . .' Kitty tried to recall what the man had looked like, but it wasn't clear in her head. She could recall the smell of him vividly and the pressure of his grip on her arm and the feel of his waistcoat. She would never forget the sensation of his sour breath on her cheek, but she couldn't be certain about his clothing or what colour his eyes or hair had been.

'He was wearing a waistcoat. I think it had a pattern.'

The constable wrote it down, still standing after he'd shaken his head at the offer of a chair.

'Any distinguishing features? Scars or suchlike?'

'I don't think so. I can't remember.'

'Was he Irish?'

'No,' said Kitty firmly. 'He was a local.'

'The doctor has diagnosed a concussion,' Mrs Anderton explained to the constable. 'Maybe Mrs Cavanah will recall more when she's feeling better.'

'I'm sorry if I've wasted your time,' Kitty told him, still wishing that he would go away.

'No. Don't apologize.' The man's face softened and Kitty remembered his gentle brown eyes from their previous encounter. 'I can see that you've been hurt, and Mr Anderton has given me enough to begin an investigation.' He hesitated. 'What was the disagreement about?' he asked.

'Tell him,' encouraged Mr Anderton.

Kitty looked from one man to the other and realized she had no other option because Mr Anderton clearly understood it was about the coins she had shown Dorothy.

'It was about some money I found and was putting back,' she said. 'At least I thought it was money, but Mr Reynolds at the rag warehouse said the weight of it was wrong and that the coins were probably made from pewter.'

'Fakes?' The information seemed to excite the policeman and he began to write on his notepad again. 'How many coins?' he asked.

'About fifty, perhaps. I'm not certain. They were shillings. Shiny and new, but dated 1850.'

'Did you know about this?' the policeman asked Mr Anderton. 'You never mentioned it at the police station.'

'Miss Dorothy alerted me to some goings-on in the backs. She told me that Mrs Cavanah had found some coins and I suspected it was connected with this morning's attack.'

'Why did you not take these coins to the police?' Constable Westwell asked her.

'I wasn't going to keep them!' she protested, hoping that she wasn't going to get into trouble. 'I was just putting them back when that man came up behind me. He accused me of stealing them, but I wasn't.'

Kitty was beginning to wish that she *had* gone to the police with them instead of trying to sort the matter out herself. She realized that she'd made herself look guilty as well as almost getting murdered – and now she had the added concern that the man might come looking for her if he discovered that she'd talked to the constable.

7

Agnes had rolled over in bed. She always enjoyed having the mattress to herself for a short while after her mother and Maria had got up early to go out gathering. But this morning her foot made contact with another leg and her sister protested.

'Ouch! What are you doing? Your toenails are sharp!' Maria complained as she rubbed her eyes and propped herself on an elbow. 'Where's Mam?'

'She must be downstairs making tea,' said Agnes. She couldn't hear anyone moving about so she guessed her mother had gone out to the privy.

She pushed back the covers and dressed quickly. Now that she was working in her own shop she was a keen riser and looked forward to every day, especially the ones when Jonas came to deliver the cheese. She liked that he lingered a while afterwards, obviously enjoying her company as much as she enjoyed his.

She fastened her stays, pulled on a frock, laced her boots and picked up a hairbrush to tidy her hair. But she still couldn't hear her mother moving about, and she hurried down the steep stairs with her cap and apron in her hands to check that she was all right.

Agnes let herself out into the fresh morning air. It was her favourite time of day, when the smoky air had cleared a little overnight before the fires and mill boilers were lit again. She went to the privy at the end of the street that they shared with their neighbours, but it was empty. Hurriedly, she used it herself and went back to the house wondering where her mother was.

The others had come down and were staring about the kitchen, puzzled.

'Where's Mam?' asked Timothy.

'I don't know.' Agnes was worried. She'd never known their mother to disappear like this before. 'She wouldn't have gone to work without Peter and Maria, and the barrow's still here,' she added. It was completely puzzling and out of character, and Agnes tried desperately to think of a reasonable explanation, but failed. Then she remembered the coins and went across to open the oven door. It was empty. Her mother must have decided to take them back to where she'd found them before the children woke up.

'I think I know where she is. She'll have gone to King Street.'

'What? To the Andertons'? Why?' asked Timothy.

'It was something she found. She decided to put it back before she got into any trouble over it. I'll walk that way with Peter and Maria. You get to work,' she told Timothy. 'I've only myself and customers to answer to if I'm a few minutes late opening, but you don't want to lose your job.'

'All right,' he agreed, soothed by his sister's words. 'I'll take a crust to eat on my way.'

When he'd gone, Agnes quickly cut some bread for her

sister and little brother before helping Maria to get the barrow out of the house. She felt a ripple of anxiety as they set off down Mary Ellen Street. She knew that her mother had been very upset and depressed when they'd first come here, but now that the cheese shop was doing well and there was more money coming in to supplement what she made from the rags, she'd seemed more content and cheerful of late. But still, Agnes had to put aside the niggling worry that her mother might have come to some harm.

She walked quickly towards King Street, looking out for any sign of her mother. By the time they reached the Andertons' house she was very concerned but kept a calm demeanour so as not to alarm the others.

'She'll be round the back,' she said, trying to reassure them, but when they reached the end of the ginnel, the alley was empty and when Agnes saw the bloodstain on the cobbles she almost screamed in alarm. 'Wait here!' she told Maria and Peter before she ran down the steps to the back door and hammered on it with all her strength.

The minutes before it was answered seemed endless. Then Dorothy came, holding Julia in her arms, looking ready to give whoever it was a piece of her mind for making so much noise.

'Have you seen my mother?' asked Agnes before Dorothy could speak.

'It's all right. She's safe upstairs,' the maid said, her face softening at the sight of her. 'Come on inside.'

'I have Peter and Maria with me.'

'Don't fret. I'll call them in and give them some

breakfast. Thy mother's in the parlour. She's bumped her head, but she's fine. There's no need to worry. Mr Anderton's had the doctor to her. Go on up.'

Agnes didn't need encouraging. The back stairs were familiar to her from all her previous visits and she hurried up them. When she reached the top she followed the sound of voices to the parlour door where she hesitated.

She could see the looming figure of a tall police constable, still wearing his hat. He was speaking to her mother who was sitting on the edge of the Andertons' sofa, and both Mr and Mrs Anderton were looking on with anxious faces.

'Counterfeiting coins is a serious offence,' she heard the policeman say.

'My mother didn't counterfeit them! She found them!' Agnes burst out, terrified that the constable was about to take her mother off to the lock-up.

Everyone in the room turned to stare at her and Agnes recognized the policeman as Constable Westwell.

'Miss Cavanah,' he said. 'I'm not accusing your mother of anything.'

'It . . . it sounded as if you were,' replied Agnes, feeling suddenly embarrassed. 'I'm sorry,' she said to the constable, not wanting to antagonize him. 'Dorothy said my mam has hurt her head,' she said to Mrs Anderton. 'Is she all right?'

'I'm perfectly all right,' replied her mother. 'I'm sorry if I gave you a fright by not being at home when you woke up. Where are the others?'

'Timothy's gone to his job. Peter and Maria are

downstairs. Dorothy's feeding them. Are you sure you're all right?' she asked. Her mother looked very pale.

'Dr Skaife came and he's prescribed some medicine and told your mother to rest,' said Mr Anderton. 'I hope you can make her do that because she won't listen to us.'

'I can't lie about on a sofa all day long,' protested her mother. 'I have too much to do.'

'The doctor said she had a mild concussion,' explained Mrs Anderton. 'She's welcome to stay here, but if she does insist on going home I think she should rest today.'

'Yes. You must rest,' agreed Agnes. 'I have to go and open the shop, but Maria will look after you.'

'I think I should let your mother go, then,' the constable said. 'I have enough information for now, but I'd really like to find out who did this and put a stop to their enterprise. There are far too many of these counterfeit coins in circulation. It's a huge problem.'

'I know,' Agnes told him as he put away his notebook and pencil. 'All the shopkeepers are plagued with them, and the banks won't accept your takings if the weight isn't exact. It can just be one bad coin in a pound bag and it's declined, and it's often hard to know which is the false one.'

'You're running the cheesemongers' now, aren't you?' he asked her.

'I am, with Jonas Marsden.'

'It all looks very tasty when I walk past on my beat,' he said with a smile. 'I must pop in and get some one day.'

'Please do,' Agnes replied. 'You'd be very welcome.'

'I hope you feel better soon, Mrs Cavanah,' the

policeman said, turning back to her mother. 'But remember what I said. I'd like you to come to the police station if you remember anything else. I really would like to catch this man and his gang.'

'Thank you for coming,' Mr Anderton said. 'Allow me to show you out.'

When the constable had left the room, Agnes hurried to her mother and sat down beside her.

'What happened?' she asked. It was clear from what had been said that her mother had been attacked and she knew from her own experience how frightening that was.

'It was nothing. There's no need to look so worried.'

'But you were hurt!'

'I fell and bumped my head. It looks worse than it is,' her mother said. 'I'll go home and sit down for a bit. You need to go and open the shop. What time is it?'

'I'll go in a minute. I need to be sure that you're all right first.'

'You're more than welcome to stay here,' Mrs Anderton told Kitty again. 'I'm sure Dorothy won't mind keeping an eye on Maria and Peter.'

'Thank you. It's very generous of you,' she replied. 'But you've done more than enough already.' She paused. 'How much do I owe you for the doctor?'

'Nothing!' said Mrs Anderton firmly. 'I won't hear of it.'

Agnes helped her mother up and they went down to the kitchen to collect Peter and Maria, who were sitting at the kitchen table drinking milk and eating buttered bread.

'You'll have to look after Mam until I get back,' Agnes told her sister. She was torn between staying at home herself and opening the shop, but she couldn't risk losing customers – they would be annoyed enough by her late opening as it was. 'Can you manage?' she asked.

'Yes. Of course I can,' Maria told her.

'Good. Make sure she walks slowly. And go to the chemist for her. Here.' Agnes dug into her own purse and found a sixpence. 'That should be enough,' she said, hoping it would be. It was all the money she had with her.

As Agnes hurried down Church Street towards the cheese shop, she saw that the blinds were raised and the door was open. Her first thought was that she was being burgled, but when she saw a woman coming out with a basket over her arm, she realized that Jonas must have arrived earlier than she expected.

His face took on an expression of relief when he saw her come in through the doorway.

'Are you all right?' he asked, coming from behind the counter and putting his arms around her to give her a hug. 'I was worried when you weren't here. I was going to go up to the post office and ask if Timothy was there and if he knew what had delayed you, but I've been busy serving customers.'

'I'm fine,' she reassured him, although his embrace felt comforting after her unsettling morning. 'But there's been some trouble with my mother. She's been attacked in the alley behind the Andertons' house.'

Agnes told him as much as she knew about what had happened. He looked concerned.

'These coiners are dangerous people,' he said. 'It's bad enough when they try to cheat people out of their hard-earned money, but resorting to violence is a step too far. They need to be stopped.'

'You're right,' Agnes replied. 'But she has very little recall of what the man was like – and she's insistent that she doesn't want to speak to the police again even if she does remember something more.'

'You could go with her. I'll mind the shop as long as it's not a market day.'

'I'll talk to her again when she's feeling better,' said Agnes. 'I know she doesn't like the police in general – I'm not that keen myself – but Constable Westwell seems a decent enough man.'

'He's older than the others,' remarked Jonas. 'Some of them are just rogues themselves, but he seems all right.'

'It would certainly be a relief to see these coiners locked up,' Agnes said thoughtfully. 'I hate having to examine all the coins so carefully when customers pay me. I always feel like I'm accusing them of being dishonest if they try to pay with a bad penny, even though I know they've been duped. I had to give a sixpence back to one woman only last week. It was clearly counterfeit, but the way she responded you would have thought I was the one to blame. She threw her cheese back across the counter at me and stormed out, saying she would never shop here again.'

Jonas frowned. 'I sometimes wonder if it's safe for

you to be here on your own,' he said. 'Maybe it's time we talked seriously about getting an assistant.'

'There's no need,' she told him, tying on a clean white apron. 'It's a busy street. I'm not in any danger here.'

She gave him a smile to reassure him, even though she was putting on a brave face. The attack on her mother had frightened her and she wished that Jonas could be in the shop with her all the time – not just to protect her from any dangers, but because she craved more of his company. They were both so busy that it sometimes seemed they never had time to see one another.

'I hate to think of you being here alone,' he went on. 'I wish I could be here more often.'

'But you have all the markets to go to.'

'I know. But I wish we could be together. I sometimes wonder if we were right when we decided not to get married straight away. I know the shop has been a huge success, thanks to all your hard work, but when we do see each other all we talk about is cheese!'

Agnes laughed. It was true. Cheese seemed to have taken over their lives this past year. But now that the shop was profitable, perhaps it was time to think about the subject of marriage again.

It wasn't that she hadn't wanted to marry him when he'd first asked her. Of course she had. But she'd worked so hard to achieve a shop of her own that she'd wanted to make sure it was established before she handed it over to an assistant, and besides, she hadn't been certain that her mother would agree. She still wasn't. Jonas wasn't a Catholic like them, and her mother was always telling her that she shouldn't have refused Patrick Ryan and that she'd be lucky to find anyone more suitable. Her mother hadn't even been keen on her going into business with Jonas at first, but the cheese shop had done well, despite her dire predictions, and the money that Agnes took home every week was much more than she'd been paid when she was working at the rag warehouse.

But even if her mother could be persuaded to give her permission for a wedding, Agnes was still wary of making such a big change. Marriage would mean going to live at Goosefoot Farm, which meant leaving her mother on her own with the younger children, and she felt she couldn't do that yet – especially not now that her mother had had such a shock.

8

Sidney Westwell stifled a yawn as he walked back towards the police station. Luckily it wasn't far and he would soon be in his bed. But after he'd drunk some tea and sworn under his breath at his colleagues who'd eaten all the bacon, leaving only bread, which he fried in the fat and ate with an egg, he found it impossible to sleep. The events of the morning had unsettled him after a long, tedious night when nothing much had happened. He was angry that Mrs Cavanah had been hurt and determined to catch the man responsible. But it was the prospect of bringing a whole gang of counterfeiters to justice that kept him awake. If he could do that, not only would these criminals be put in prison for a very long time, or even shipped out to New South Wales, but he would also be able to prove to himself that he could make a difference.

If anyone had told him two years ago that he would end up as a member of the police force, he would have laughed. Then, he'd run a beerhouse in Manchester – the Old Elephant on Great Bridgewater Street – with his wife, Susan. It was something he'd always wanted to do, his life's ambition, as it were, and when the tenancy had become vacant he'd persuaded Susan that they should take it on. She'd been a bit unsure at first.

She'd never worked at anything except a loom, but she enjoyed meeting people and she was a good cook into the bargain. So she'd agreed to give it a year to see how it went, with the proviso that if she didn't enjoy it, or they didn't make enough money, she would go back to the mill and he would return to his previous job at the print works.

It had been fun at first. He'd enjoyed polishing the bar and the pewter flagons that hung on the hooks behind it. They'd served beer and ale mostly, with Susan preparing a pot-luck supper in the evening for the workers who didn't want to be bothered going home to cook. They'd had travellers to stay sometimes as well, in the two rooms upstairs that were simple but clean bedchambers, and Susan had always taken care to check that they were respectable folk. She'd always refused the ones who claimed the women they brought with them were their wives, when they clearly weren't.

'We're not having any goings-on here,' she used to say. 'We're a respectable establishment.'

But it was impossible to regulate every customer who came through the doors. He'd always sent the ones who were obviously drunk on their way. Other landlords laughed at him and said that anyone's money was good enough for them, but he'd reply that the trouble the drunks caused cost him more than a couple of lost sales.

Then there were the regulars who came in, the ones he got to know by name. He could set his watch by them and had their preferred drink ready on the bar before they'd fished the right change from their pocket. He'd made some good friends that he'd been reluctant to leave behind. But in the end there'd been no other choice.

It had started insidiously enough.

'We're a flagon short,' he'd said to Susan one night after he'd washed and dried each one and returned them to their hooks.

'It'll be somewhere abouts,' she'd replied. 'Look for it in the morning.'

He'd thought no more about it and gone up to bed. It had been a busy day and he'd been tired. But a week or so later it happened again and they were two flagons short, even though they both searched high and low for them.

'Do you think someone's stealing them?' he'd asked.

'Who would do that?'

'I don't know,' he'd admitted but made a mental note to watch more carefully.

The next time it had happened he'd been certain it was a group of men who came in regularly. They always crowded around a table in the corner furthest from the bar and he'd liked them because they were no trouble – ordered food, never drank too much, spoke quietly and were polite. But when he thought about it he realized he didn't know much about them, even if they did come in at least once a week. None of them made conversation with him or spoke about themselves. He didn't even know their names.

He'd begun to watch them carefully. On the Friday night when the trouble had begun, he'd served their drinks and counted out six flagons. When he went to clear them from the table there'd only been five. Perhaps he shouldn't have made the accusation, shouldn't have pointed out that there was one short and told them to open their coats to prove it wasn't them doing the stealing. It hadn't gone down well. They'd set about him with their fists and when he was lying on the cold, flagged floor with blood pouring from his nose, one of them had kicked him again and told him if he squealed to the law about them, they'd come back and finish him off.

The encounter had terrified Susan. She'd sobbed as she'd helped him to clean his face and begged him to take her away from the place. Looking back, he was sure it was what had made her lose the baby. After that she'd turned her face to the wall and would barely speak to him. In the end he'd agreed to leave. They'd come here to Blackburn to start over, hoping to find friendlier sort of work. But Susan hadn't improved and one morning he'd woken to find her gone from their bed. He'd searched and searched for her, and she'd been found in the canal in the end.

He'd felt so guilty. He still did. He knew that he'd failed her and should have taken more care of her. He should have seen how unhappy she was, even though she kept a smile on her face and insisted nothing was the matter. He should have realized whenever she flinched at sudden noises and refused to be left in the house on her own that she was still afraid of the men who'd threatened them, as well as being devastated at the loss of the baby.

'Coiners,' one of the other landlords had told him when he'd explained why they were leaving Manchester.

'They steal the flagons and melt down the pewter to make counterfeit coins. It shines just like silver. They must have thought you were on to them to give you a hiding like that.'

'I didn't know,' he'd replied as he'd fingered his bruised face.

'Drawback of the pub trade,' the other landlord had said with a shrug. 'Best to say nothing. It does no good to have one of them police constables coming in, interfering with folk's trade.'

Sidney turned over in his narrow bed. He knew that he couldn't bring the gang of coiners in Manchester to justice for what they'd done, but if he could put a stop to this local gang then perhaps it would go some way to atoning for Susan's death.

9

Kitty sat on the chair by the hearth and supervised Peter as he laid some scraps of wood and paper amongst the lumps of coal to start a fire. Even though it was another warm day outside, she couldn't stop shivering now that she'd got home. She knew that it was probably the shock and she hoped she would feel better after a cup of strong sweet tea and the chance to come to terms with what had happened to her.

She got up to strike a flint when the fire was ready. She didn't quite trust Peter to kindle the flame, and Maria had insisted on taking the doctor's paper to the chemist for her. Agnes had given her some money to pay for it, she'd said, and when Kitty thought about how lucky she was to have such good children, she had to wipe away a tear or two before her son saw that she was crying. Even though her life was hard, she was blessed with her family. How proud her husband would have been to see them now. All so grown up. The thought made the tears flow even faster. She missed him so much.

When the sticks had caught light and bluish smoke was rising from the cobs, she sat back down and let Peter fill the kettle with water from the pump. Using up coal in the middle of the day was a luxury she could ill afford, especially as she would earn nothing today, but she felt worse than she had admitted to anyone and she knew that the doctor was right when he'd told her to rest.

Maria came back in time to brew the tea. Kitty was relieved. The kettle was heavy when it was full and she'd worried about Peter scalding himself. Maria put a brown bottle filled with liquid on the table.

'A teaspoonful three times a day, the chemist said,' she told her mother.

'Pass it to me, then,' said Kitty. She popped the cork out of the neck and sniffed at the contents. It didn't smell too bad so she reached for a spoon and swallowed a dose, hoping it would ease the incessant throbbing at her temples.

'Shall Peter and I go out with the barrow?' offered Maria after she'd placed a cup of tea in her mother's hands.

'There'll not be much left by now,' Kitty said.

'We could look.'

'All right,' she agreed. 'But keep an eye on your brother. Don't let him wander off. I think I'll go and lie down when I've drunk this.'

After the children had gone she rose gingerly from the chair and clasped the rail as she hauled herself up the stairs. It was unusual to have the bedroom to herself. In fact, it was unusual to be alone and she felt strangely unsettled by it. Kitty took off her boots, then her frock and hung it over the back of the bentwood chair. She loosened her corset and lay down on the bed with a blanket wrapped around herself. Outside she could hear the sounds of the day – the steady tap of horses' hooves, the groan of cart wheels and distant voices. No one was ever really alone in a town like this. There was always noise from somewhere.

She lay still and wondered if she could have handled the matter of the coins any better. Maybe she would have been better off keeping them, or throwing them into the cut, rather than trying to put them back where she'd found them. The man had been furious and fierce and she was still frightened by the encounter. She hoped he would be satisfied to have got his money back and wouldn't come looking for her.

She also hoped that the constable wouldn't come around either. He'd been quite insistent that she must go to the police station if she remembered any more details, but everything had happened in such a rush that she could barely recall any of it.

Kitty must have drifted off to sleep. It was probably the doctor's concoction, she thought, when she woke and saw Agnes standing anxiously over her.

'What are you doing here? What time is it?' she asked.

'Just after noon. Jonas insisted I come back to see how you are. He says he'll mind the shop for the rest of the day.'

Her daughter must have been worried about her to agree to that, thought Kitty, but she was grateful to Jonas for his consideration.

'Have Peter and Maria come home?'

'They've gone down to the warehouse with the few things they found. It won't be much, but a few pennies won't go amiss.'

'They're good children. You're all good children,' Kitty said, grasping Agnes's hand to reassure her. 'But you're not to worry. I'm all right.'

'I hope Constable Westwell catches the man who did this to you,' Agnes said as she sat down on the edge of the mattress. 'I'd like to see him locked up for a very long time.'

'I wasn't able to give much of a description,' Kitty replied. 'And I don't really want to have to go to the police station to identify him – I could never be certain it was the right man.'

'But surely you want to see him punished?'

'Yes,' Kitty agreed, not sure that she did. She just wanted to forget the events of the last couple of days.

'He was very kind to me, you know, that time I was attacked,' Agnes went on. 'Constable Westwell, I mean. He's a nice man.'

'You know I don't like the police,' Kitty replied, although she knew that Agnes had been treated well by them and she'd always be grateful to Constable Westwell for seeing her daughter safe after the incident on the market.

'He has kind eyes,' persisted Agnes.

'I didn't notice,' Kitty said. It was a lie. She had noticed the constable's brown eyes and they had been compassionate when he spoke to her. She blinked away the image. She didn't want to see him again.

10

Agnes stayed at home with her mother all afternoon, only going back to the shop at closing time to help Jonas move all the cheeses on to the cold slab and wash down the counter.

'How's your mother?' he asked when she came through the door.

'Shaken up,' Agnes told him. 'She's trying to pretend that it's nothing, but she has a huge swelling on her head and she can't stop shaking.'

Jonas closed the door and dropped the latch to lock it before lowering the blinds at the windows.

'Do you think you'll be able to open up tomorrow?' he asked. 'I'd offer to come, but I've got Preston market.'

'I'll manage,' she told him. 'I'll make sure Maria stays at home to look after Mam if she's still unwell.' She followed him into the small back room as he went to put the bucket away. 'I am grateful to you for taking over this afternoon, though.'

'Well, it is my business as well.'

He put the bucket under the stone slab and dried his hands on the towel before rolling down his sleeves. 'I'd best get going,' he said reluctantly. 'I promised Lizzie I'd give her a hand with the evening milking.' He bent to kiss her and she responded eagerly, wishing they could have more of these snatched moments together. But all too soon he reached for his jacket and cap and they went out into the street where Agnes locked the shop door and he strode off towards the livery stable behind the Bull Hotel to fetch the horse and cart.

She walked back home to Mary Ellen Street feeling perturbed by everything that had happened. She let herself into the small cottage. It was cramped with them all living there, she had to admit. Now that Timothy was older it wasn't right for him to be sleeping in the same bedroom as his mother and sisters. Her mother had discussed him having a mattress downstairs, but it wasn't an ideal solution. They really could do with a bigger house with two bedrooms upstairs.

She made a pot of tea and took a cup up to her mother.

'I think I've slept a little,' she said as Agnes helped her prop the bolster behind her so that her sore head wouldn't touch the wall.

'How are you feeling?' she asked.

'A bit better. I'll come down in a while.'

'Stay there,' Agnes advised. 'I'll empty the chamber pot if you need to use it. I don't think you should walk down to the privy tonight.'

'All right,' agreed her mother. 'Help me and I'll use it before Timothy comes in.'

'Would you like something to eat?' asked Agnes when her mother was settled back in bed. 'Bread and butter? A bit of cheese?' She wished she could offer her mother something hot to eat, but the fire had gone out downstairs and it hadn't occurred to her to get some shopping before she came home. She usually relied on her mother to sort out their tea.

'That sounds nice,' replied her mother. 'I don't want to be any trouble.'

'You're not!' Agnes told her. 'I'll bring your medicine and a spoon up as well. It'll help you sleep tonight and you'll feel right as rain in the morning.'

'I thought it might be a good idea if you and Peter slept downstairs – just for tonight,' she suggested to her brother when the tea things had been washed up. 'Maria and I can sleep in your bed and then Mam can have the big bed to herself. I'm worried that we might roll into her in the night and hurt her, with her head being so sore.'

'What? On the floor?' asked Timothy, looking doubtful.

'We can carry blankets down. It's only for one night.'

'All right,' he agreed, even though he sounded unenthusiastic, and Agnes was grateful that he wasn't going to be difficult about it.

They all went to bed early and Agnes lay awake for a while listening to her mother's soft breathing. She was feeling angry now – angry with the man who had attacked her mother. And she was determined that he should be caught and brought to justice, no matter how reluctant her mother was to speak to Constable Westwell again.

11

Kitty was already up and dressed and brewing tea by the time Agnes came downstairs the next morning.

'Surely you're not thinking of going out gathering!' her daughter exclaimed.

'Of course I am. I'm feeling much better today and the swelling has almost gone down.'

'I think you should rest.'

'Stop fussing, Agnes,' Kitty told her. 'I need to work.'

Agnes didn't argue, although Kitty could see that she didn't want her to go. The truth was that she didn't feel entirely well, but she was concerned about having another day with very little money coming in.

Leaving Agnes and Timothy to eat their breakfast, she called to Maria to take the barrow out. She glanced at the bottle of medicine from the doctor and decided not to risk another dose just yet. It had made her sleep soundly last night, but now she needed to keep her wits about her.

They set off, with Maria pushing the barrow and Peter walking beside them. The wheel rumbled over the cobbles.

'Which way?' asked her daughter when they reached the end of the street.

'Up to Richmond Terrace,' instructed Kitty. Surely she would be safe up there? The thought of returning to King Street made her shiver.

Although it was still early, there were a fair few people about, going to their work, and Kitty kept her eyes averted as she passed them by. No one liked the rag gatherers. When they reached Richmond Terrace they began to make their way down the alley, poking at the rubbish with their sticks and adding anything of value to the barrow to be weighed in at the warehouse.

As they worked, Kitty was startled by every unexpected noise, whether it was the clattering of pigeons' wings as they launched themselves from a nearby rooftop or someone slamming a door. She found that she was constantly glancing behind her, careful not to be caught unawares as she had been the previous day. But it was no good giving in to fear, she told herself. She had a job to do and she wasn't going to let that man frighten her into staying at home.

She was worried, though. His voice had sounded so threatening and she kept hearing his words in her head, over and over again. *I should make certain tha doesn't talk.* But she'd been forced to talk, because she couldn't have lied to Mr Anderton after he'd saved her, and when he'd insisted on bringing the constable she'd had to talk to him, too.

'I think we have enough for today,' she said after a while. Maria looked surprised that they were giving up so early with the barrow less than half full, but she took up the handles and pushed it back home.

Later that morning, Kitty heard herself gasp aloud when there was a knock on the door. Her first instinct was to run, except that there was nowhere to run to.

Their small backyard had a high wall all around it and the only way out was through the front door, where she could see a shadow lurking.

'Shh!' She put a finger to her lips to warn the children to be quiet. 'Let's go upstairs and pretend there's no one in,' she suggested. But before they could move, she saw the shadow move to the window and peer in through the sheer curtains.

'Mrs Cavanah! It's only me – Constable Westwell. There's no need to be afraid.'

Kitty was horrified to have a policeman on her step, but she knew that he'd seen her and she had no choice but to go and invite him in: at least that was better than keeping him at the door for all the street to see.

'How are you today?' he asked after he'd removed his tall hat and come inside. He'd still had to duck so as not to bang his head, Kitty noticed. He was an exceptionally tall man, and stockily built with it.

'I'm much better, thank you,' she replied. She wondered if he was just asking out of courtesy, but his eyes were kind and he looked concerned for her. 'Would you like to take a seat?' she invited, and he pulled out one of the wooden chairs from the table and flipped up the tails of his frock coat to sit down on it. He put his hat on her table and it landed with a slight thud.

'I'm back on duty this morning,' he explained, 'and as my beat comes close to the end of your street, I thought I'd just call to check that you were all right.'

'That was very kind. As you can see, I've recovered.'

'And these must be your children?' He smiled at Maria

and Peter who were watching him with apprehension. 'What are your names?' he asked.

Maria glanced at her mother to see if it was all right to answer and Kitty nodded, so she told the constable her name and age.

'Agnes must be busy in her cheese shop. And your other son? He works at the post office, doesn't he?'

'Yes. Timothy,' she confirmed, anxious that the policeman knew so much about her.

'Sit down yourself. Don't let me keep you standing there,' said the constable as Kitty twisted the fringes on the edge of her shawl. She hoped he wasn't going to stay long or ask her any awkward questions.

'Would you like a cup of tea?' she asked. She didn't really want to keep him in her kitchen a moment longer than necessary, but it seemed rude not to offer. Everyone in this town immediately offered tea to anyone who passed through their door – unless it was the rent collector and they were behind with their payments.

'I'll not put you to any trouble,' he replied, and Kitty was glad. 'As I said, I just wanted to check on you. You took a nasty tumble yesterday and I was worried.' He paused. 'Did you recall anything else about the man who attacked you?' he asked.

So that was the crux of it, thought Kitty. He'd really come to see what else she could tell him.

'No,' she replied. She began to shake her head, but it made her feel a bit dizzy so she stopped. 'Like I said, he came up behind me and I didn't really see his face.'

'Well, if anything does occur to you, come to see me at

the station. I'll be there after six o'clock today.' He stood and picked up his hat. 'I'd like to see this man and his accomplices behind bars.'

Kitty showed him out and shut the door behind him with relief. She took a moment to compose herself before she turned to face the children.

'Come on,' she said, as brightly as she could. 'Let's take these things to Mr Reynolds and then we'll go shopping for our dinner.'

12

Sidney walked back up Mary Ellen Street. His beat was some distance away and if the truth was told he was encroaching on Constable Shaw's beat by being in this area at all. But he'd been worried about Mrs Cavanah and wanted to reassure himself that she hadn't come to any permanent harm.

She'd obviously been alarmed by his visit though and he wished that the woman was less afraid of him. He only wanted to help her. That was the trouble with having to wear this uniform every day. People only saw the policeman and not the person he truly was.

He'd had more dealings with her daughter, Agnes. She was a sensible girl who'd done well for herself. She'd stood up to that crooked cheesemonger on the market square, and now that she'd opened a shop she sold to almost everyone in the town. He would have expected her mother to go into the cheese business as well, but Mrs Cavanah clung to her rag gathering, trailing the younger two children around with her when they would have been better off learning a trade or being taught their letters. It was hard to understand the attraction of poking about in the filth for bits and bobs to exchange for a few pennies from the warehouse, and he'd been surprised to see the pile of rags and bones stacked up in her kitchen. It seemed that not even being attacked in broad daylight had put her off.

Sidney was disturbed by the feelings he was experiencing, and it wasn't all related to bringing the coiners to justice. Mrs Cavanah was an attractive woman, although he felt guilty for admitting it. His wife, Susan, had been the only woman he had looked at for many years, despite the temptations from running a public house in the busy streets of Manchester. And since he'd lost her he'd thought that he would never look at another woman in the same way again. The truth was that he'd been determined not to open himself up again to the chance of the overwhelming grief that he'd felt after her death. He'd decided to put all thoughts of another marriage behind him and try something new. That was why he'd been attracted by the advertisement for men to join the newly formed Blackburn Borough Police Force. He'd been just within the age range at twenty-nine years old and knew that if he hesitated the chance would be lost and he would never have it again. So he'd gone into the building on Clayton Street and registered his interest. His height and build had been to his advantage – as they had been on many a rowdy night in Manchester when he'd taken troublemakers by the collar and the seat of their pants and put them out on to the street to sober up. They'd asked him if he could read and write and keep simple accounts, and when he'd proved to them that he was both literate and intelligent, they'd told him that the superintendent, Mr Marshall, considered him acceptable – after warning him that he could have no further interest in the liquor trade without forfeiting his job. It wasn't a problem, he'd told them. His days as a landlord were over.

After he'd had his measurements taken, he'd been issued with his uniform. There was a dark blue woollen tunic with gilt buttons, two pairs each of summer and winter trousers, boots, shirts, gloves and a belt along with a tall stovepipe hat in black, reinforced with bamboo. 'You can keep a sandwich under there,' the superintendent had told him, and Sidney hadn't been sure whether it was a joke. He was also provided with a truncheon, a rattle to call for assistance, a pair of handcuffs and an oil lamp for night-shift duties.

Then he and the other new recruits had been taken before the magistrate to be sworn in. Afterwards, he'd packed up his few belongings, given notice on the little house he'd been renting and moved into the dormitory of the police house. It had been a welcome relief after living alone in his bereavement. His meals were provided, his washing was done and he had no need to fret about cleaning or shopping – tasks that he'd struggled with when he was left alone. At first, he'd looked forward to the camaraderie of the other constables, but he'd soon found that they were all younger than him, being mostly in their early twenties or late teens. The only other constable of his age was Harry Shaw, who'd already worked in the role for a few years. He lived in a rented house with his wife and three small children and thought himself superior to the newcomers, though Sidney found him rather stupid and uncooperative on occasions – more willing to find fault than to help the new recruits learn their job. It was a pity it was his beat he'd had to encroach on to visit Mrs Cavanah, and he hoped the man wouldn't discover his indiscretion.

He made his way to where his own beat began. His role was to walk down Penny Street, up Salford to Eanam and back along Lark Hill looking for any trouble. The prevention of crime was where his efforts were to be concentrated; the superintendent had been emphatic about that. Only the lack of crime on his beat would reflect his effectiveness in his job – too much and he would be accused of a lack of vigilance. The trouble was that much of the crime that took place in this town was unseen. Take the coiners, for example. It would be impossible to see their crimes as he walked the streets. What they did would be tucked away in cellars or attics. Hidden behind closed doors. There was no chance of seeing it unless it was actively investigated, but he'd been told again and again that it was not his concern. He was to watch for robberies and thefts and suchlike petty crimes. He could bring pickpockets to justice and lock up the drunks when they got into fights on the street, but Sidney wanted to do more than that. He wanted to see the coiners brought to justice. It was the only way he could atone for what had happened to Susan. And it was only when he'd paid his debt to her that he would be able to move on and maybe, just maybe, consider being married again.

His thoughts returned to Kitty Cavanah. Agnes had told him that her mother distrusted all policemen. It had been obvious that she'd been reluctant to let him into her house that morning and had wanted him to be gone as quickly as possible. It was why he'd refused her offer of a cup of tea. He'd hated making her feel uncomfortable. Yet the memory of her blue eyes, brimming with tears as she'd recounted her experience to him the day before, and the way she'd fidgeted with her shawl that morning, had made him yearn to take her in his arms and comfort her. She seemed so vulnerable and he longed to protect her.

13

After Kitty had finished her transactions at the warehouse and Mr Reynolds had paid her for her morning's finds, she walked up to the market with Maria and Peter.

'Can we get pies?' asked Peter as they passed the man who was selling them from a tray slung around his neck. They did smell good and for once Kitty decided not to argue that they cost too much.

'All right,' she agreed. 'A butter pie each, but we'll take them home to eat.'

She was waiting in the queue to make the purchase when she looked up, conscious of being watched. Her stomach lurched when she saw him – a scruffy figure lurking outside the door of the Sun public house. Was that not the man who had attacked her? She didn't recognize his face, but the dirty embroidered waistcoat, which looked as if it had once graced the chest of a much richer man, was familiar and the memory of having her cheek pressed up against it flashed into her mind, making her tremble all over again.

'Pay the man for me,' she told Maria, dropping a sixpence into her daughter's hand. She was afraid that she would fumble and drop the coin from her shaking fingers if she tried to give him the money herself.

She glanced back towards the Sun, hoping that her attacker hadn't recognized her – although she feared he had, because he was now staring at her. But in a blink he'd gone and Kitty looked all around her, struck with terror that he might creep up on her again, even though she knew it was unlikely in the middle of the crowded market place.

'What are you looking for?' asked Peter curiously.

'I thought I saw someone I recognized.'

'Who?' he persisted.

'Nobody you know,' she replied as Maria put the pies in the basket she was holding. 'Come on. Let's get home before they go cold.'

Ratcliffe. The name came unbidden to Kitty's mind as she was washing up the plates and cups after their dinner. It was the name her assailant had hissed in her ear. *Did Ratcliffe send thee?* She'd forgotten it until now. She'd been so anxious to save herself that it hadn't meant anything at the time, but it was clearly significant. Maybe it was something that would help the police constable to catch the man.

If it hadn't been for her sighting of him at the market, she would probably have decided that it was best to say nothing. But seeing him again had frightened her and she wondered if he was watching and following her, determined to make good on his threat to make sure she didn't talk. Maybe he already knew that she had spoken to the police. The thought made her uneasy. She didn't want to be afraid every time she went out of the house in case he was lying in wait for her. She wanted him locked up and maybe the best way of ensuring that happened was to tell Constable Westwell what she'd seen and what she'd remembered.

Kitty kept deliberating, but in the end she thought maybe speaking to the constable again would be for the best. He'd been kind when he called earlier, and it had been good of him to spare the time to come and enquire how she was. He'd said he would be at the station after six o'clock, she remembered, so it was no good going before then. He would still be walking his beat and she didn't want to speak to someone she didn't know – or trust. It would have to be Constable Westwell.

Anyway, it was best to wait a while, she thought. Timothy and Agnes would be home soon after six so she could leave them to mind the younger ones whilst she went alone. Or she might ask Agnes to go with her. The thought of going alone made her anxious.

By the time Agnes arrived home Kitty was still undecided.

'I remembered something after he'd gone,' she told her daughter when she'd recounted her visit from Constable Westwell. 'But I'm not sure if it's worth bothering him with.'

'What did you remember?'

'It was just a name. The man asked if Ratcliffe had sent me.'

'Ratcliffe?'

'Yes. I saw him earlier, my attacker,' she confessed. 'He was outside the Sun when we were getting pies for our dinner. I think that's what jogged my memory.'

'It could be important,' Agnes said. 'I think you should go to the police station. You need to tell Constable Westwell where you saw that man.'

'I'm not sure.' Having had all afternoon to ponder on it, Kitty was now leaning towards staying away from the police. Maybe the man hadn't been looking at her at all. He might not have recognized her. She was probably worrying for no reason.

'I'll come with you if you like. Timothy should be home any moment.'

'Do you not mind?'

'Of course not. I want to see this man locked up as much as you do.'

'All right then,' Kitty agreed. 'When Timothy comes, we'll go.'

After her elder son had come home, Kitty wrapped a shawl around her shoulders and walked with Agnes to Clayton Street. Although it was too early for the gas lamps in the streets to be lit, there was lamplight spilling out from the open door of the police station. It seemed bright inside. Too bright. The constable behind the desk looked fierce and Kitty wanted to run away.

'We've come to see Constable Westwell,' explained Agnes.

'He's not on duty. You can speak to me,' snapped the policeman.

'No,' Kitty protested. 'It has to be Constable Westwell. He told me to come. He said he'd be here after six.'

'He's not on duty,' replied the policeman. 'Give me your name and tell me what it's about or stop wasting my time.'

Kitty wanted to leave and she began to turn towards the door, but Agnes grasped her arm.

'Wait,' she implored. 'Please will you ask Constable Westwell if he will speak to my mother?' she asked the policeman behind the desk. 'He invited her to call this evening if she had more information for him.'

The constable looked doubtful. Then he relented, as if he knew it would save him the trouble of writing it all down.

'Wait there,' he told them before disappearing through the inner door.

'We shouldn't have come,' Kitty whispered to her daughter. 'I don't want to make a nuisance of myself.'

'You're not being a nuisance,' Agnes told her. 'Constable Westwell will be glad you've come. I'm sure he will.'

As if to prove her point, the inner door opened again and Constable Westwell came out with a welcoming smile. 'Mrs Cavanah! Miss Cavanah. Please. Come this way.'

He lifted a flap on the desk to allow them through and ushered them into an inner room.

'Please. Sit down. It's private in here,' he explained. 'We can speak freely.'

He wasn't wearing his hat but was still dressed in his policeman's coat and trousers. Kitty wondered if he ever took them off. He must remove them to go to bed, she thought – surely he didn't sleep in them? – but perhaps it was the only clothing he had. If he was off duty, he hadn't changed into anything else.

'How can I help you?' he asked. He was still smiling and looked pleased to see them. It made Kitty feel more at ease.

'I think I saw the man who attacked me today,' she

explained. 'He was hanging about outside the Sun around dinner time – just before twelve.'

Constable Westwell frowned. 'Did he see you?'

'I think so. I thought he was watching me.'

'But he didn't approach you?'

'No. The market was crowded. But I remembered something else as well,' Kitty went on and explained how she'd recalled the name Ratcliffe.

'Well, that certainly is important,' Constable Westwell said. 'Did you remember anything else?'

'No. Just that,' Kitty told him, realizing that it wasn't much after all.

'I'll make some enquiries,' the constable promised. 'But in the meantime you must be careful. Keep your eyes open.'

'Do you think my mother's in danger?' Agnes asked him.

He shook his head. 'No. But I think she should stay away from the back alleys until we catch the man.'

'I can't do that,' Kitty protested. 'It's where I do my work.'

The constable looked troubled. 'If you tell me where you'll be, I'll make sure there's someone there to keep a lookout. In fact, I'm back on duty early tomorrow morning, so if you tell me the streets you're planning to visit, I'll be there. Then, if the man is hanging about and watching you, you can point him out to me.'

14

Kitty wasn't certain that Constable Westwell would keep his word. It seemed a lot of trouble for a policeman to go to for just one person. But as she turned the corner of North Gate with her two younger children, she saw him walking towards her.

'Good morning!' he greeted her. 'How are you today?'

'I'm fine,' she replied as she glanced around. It didn't do to be seen speaking to a police constable on the street. People would think that she'd been caught committing some crime and she wanted to keep her good reputation.

'Where are you planning to start?' he asked.

'We usually go down the backs of Richmond Terrace to begin with.'

'Shall I go ahead and make sure there's nobody about?'

'There may be some other gatherers,' protested Kitty, knowing that they would begin to distrust her if they thought she was bringing a constable on to their patch. 'I don't think I'll be in any danger if there are others about.'

'Well, I'll be here, walking up and down this street,' he told her. 'I'll wait until you're finished and then maybe we can move on together?'

'All right,' she agreed reluctantly. She really didn't want to have her footsteps dogged by him, but she was at a loss to know how to refuse his protection.

'Call out if there's any trouble. It's what I'm here for,' he told her.

She nodded and then went down the ginnel to the back of the houses. Sure enough, there were some other gatherers there. Kitty was cross with herself for not being here sooner. All the best finds would be gone. Normally, she would have turned back and gone to get ahead of the others on the next street, but she hesitated. She knew that Constable Westwell would be watching out for her. When she'd agreed to his protection, she'd thought that he would be watching her from a distance. She'd never considered that he would be following her around as if he needed to guard her closely.

She began to poke her stick into anything that looked promising, but as she feared, everything of value had already been picked up.

'Do you think we should move on?' asked Maria. She was obviously puzzled by her mother's reluctance.

'Yes,' Kitty agreed. 'There's nothing left here. Come on.'

Maria followed her back down the ginnel with the barrow. Kitty thought about sending Peter ahead and asking him if he could see the constable, but she decided against it. She wanted to make the morning as normal as possible for the children. It would do no good to alarm them with her own fears.

Thankfully, Constable Westwell gave her only the briefest of nods as they passed him and although he did follow them, he kept his distance, for which Kitty was grateful. Around the back of Tacketts she found a pan that had been left to burn. It was no good for cooking but the metal was valuable. She added it to the barrow and they continued on their way, finding a rag or two and a few nails in the gutter and one or two bones from the backs of the houses on James Street.

As the mill hooters broke the silence and the streets filled with the sound of clogs and carts, Kitty decided that they'd gathered enough for the day and she turned for home. She'd lost sight of Constable Westwell now, but there had been no sign of her assailant either and she suspected that he was probably still abed. The most likely place she would see him again was outside the Sun with a pint in his hand. Whatever it was he was mixed up in, it was providing him with the money for both leisure time and alcohol.

Sure enough, when the rags had been sorted and they were on their way to the warehouse, Kitty saw him. He was coming out of the Dun Horse on Market Street Lane this time, with an expression that reminded her of a cat that had stolen a titbit from the table. He didn't look guilty so much as pleased with himself, and he hurried down the street as if he wanted to put a distance between himself and the public house. He'd probably picked a pocket, thought Kitty. She knew it was imperative to take good care of your money in a town like this. The pickpockets were clever and used tricks like asking a gentleman the time so that he would draw out his pocket watch to consult it whilst an accomplice dipped into his purse or stole his silk handkerchief.

At least he hadn't noticed her this time, but she would tell Constable Westwell what she'd seen. Even if he was locked up for a different crime, it would get him off the streets and she would be able to sleep more easily in her bed.

15

Sidney had returned to the police house after he'd seen Kitty safely home. He'd known that she would go down to the warehouse later, but the streets were busy now and he doubted she was in much danger. It was the early morning that had concerned him.

He wanted to have a drink of tea and some breakfast before his official shift began. He took off his hat and went through to the kitchen. There was a fire kept burning here all the time, which provided a welcome place to warm up on cold winter's nights, and there was always a kettle singing on the hob beside it ready to make tea. It seemed that the police constables were fuelled by an endless amount of hot, sweet tea.

Constable Shaw was already there with a cup in his hand and a pipe clenched between his teeth. He greeted Sidney with a grunt, then removed the pipe to speak.

'What were tha doin' up Tacketts earlier on?' he asked. His tone wasn't friendly.

'Just taking a breath of air,' replied Sidney as he poured himself a drink.

'Tha knows that's my beat?'

'Aye, of course I know.'

'Tha can't go walking other constables' beats, tha knows. Tha's to stick to thine own streets.'

'I wasn't walking your beat. It was in my own time and it was my own business,' Sidney replied, irritated by the man and his petty attitude.

'Own business?' Shaw replied. 'Hast got a woman up there, then? I bet if I goes upstairs I'll find thy bed's not been slept in.'

Sidney was about to snap back that it was nothing to do with Shaw what he did in his own time, but he was wary that the man might decide to report him to Sergeant Watkins. He hadn't appreciated when he first enrolled that the job would govern every aspect of his life. Any hint that he might not be obeying every rule of his employment might see him dismissed, and he knew that drinking on duty or carrying on with women were offences that would see him out on the street with no home and no income.

Instead, he drank his tea in a surly silence, hoping that Shaw would soon go out so that he could fry himself some bacon and eggs in peace. He hadn't slept well and, combined with his early morning and several hours already spent on his feet, he was tired and in need of some comfort.

'I'll be watchin' thee,' Shaw told him, as he buttoned up his jacket.

Sidney didn't reply, but once he was alone he let out a sigh. It was bad enough fighting the criminals without having to fight his colleagues as well.

16

Kitty wondered if she should go to the police station to tell Constable Westwell that she'd seen her attacker outside the Dun Horse. She'd never have thought that she would attend twice in as many days, but she was keen to do everything she could to get the man locked up so that she could have some peace of mind. It was frightening to keep seeing him, and she feared it was only a matter of time before he recognized her and made good on his threats.

After tea, when she was sure that it was six o'clock, she walked down to Clayton Street again, hoping that Constable Westwell would be on duty at the desk so that she wouldn't have to ask for him, but her spirits flagged when she saw a different constable. She hoped he would be more amenable than the one the previous day.

'Can I help you?' asked the man. He barely looked up at her.

'I'm looking for Constable Westwell. Is he here, please?'

The man gave her a closer inspection and a smirk twisted the edges of his lips.

'And who would thee be?' he asked, using the familiar form of address that Kitty had learned was sometimes spoken as a mild insult.

'My name's Mrs Cavanah. I'm assisting Constable Westwell with an investigation.'

'I see,' he replied. Then he opened the door behind him and shouted, 'Westwell! Thy fancy woman's at the desk asking for thee!'

'I'm not . . .' began Kitty indignantly, but the man wasn't interested. He ignored her and went back to the newspaper he was reading, and she was left to wait until Constable Westwell appeared at the door and invited her through.

She took the chair that was offered.

'I must apologize for my colleague,' he said, looking embarrassed. 'He thinks he's being humorous. Don't take any notice of him.'

It was easy to say so, thought Kitty, but she'd found the man rude and it hadn't improved her poor opinion and distrust of these blue-clad officers. She would have liked to show her disdain by walking out, but she needed help and Constable Westwell wasn't like the rest of them.

'So, have you remembered something else?' he asked eagerly.

Kitty explained that she'd seen her assailant again. 'He looked shifty, as if he might have stolen something,' she said. 'I'm willing to point him out to you,' she offered. 'I'm sure it was him. I remember his waistcoat. You could lock him up.'

'I could,' agreed Constable Westwell. 'But if I'm to lock him up I'd much rather it was for coining. That demands a much stiffer sentence. He'd most probably be sent out of the country for good and you'd never need to be concerned about him again.'

The thought of the man being gone for good was appealing to Kitty, but she couldn't understand why the constable was reluctant to arrest him for his attack on her.

'Can you not just lock him up for attacking me?' she asked. 'I'd feel much safer.' The constable didn't seem to share her enthusiasm. He was biting his lip and looked pensive.

'The trouble is, Mrs Cavanah, that he might not even be sent to prison for what he did to you. He might claim it was an accident. The magistrate might just issue a fine and let him go. I'd like to see him receive a much harsher sentence. If I could catch him using counterfeits to pay for something, it would be a start. That's a serious crime.'

Kitty knew this was true. Agnes had spoken to her about it and she knew her daughter was terrified of being caught with counterfeits in her shop, because if she passed them on to customers in their change, she could be accused of uttering – the crime of deliberately passing off false money as real.

'Would that be enough to see him sent to prison?' she asked.

'Possibly. The trouble is he might plead that he'd been duped himself, and sometimes the magistrate is cautious. He doesn't want to send innocent men to the prison when it's already filled to overflowing. Ideally, I'd like to catch this coiner in the act of manufacturing the counterfeits,' he explained. 'He would be certain to be transported for that.

He must be doing it somewhere locally and he won't be doing it alone. There will be a whole gang of them hidden away somewhere, and the challenge is to find out where.'

'Couldn't you just follow him home?' Kitty asked.

'I'm a bit conspicuous in this uniform, and I'm required to wear it all the time,' Constable Westwell explained, fiddling with the buttons on his tunic. 'If he sees a policeman following him along the street it's doubtful that he'll go home at all. He'll lead me on a merry dance all around the streets of the town until he reaches some public house and sits there laughing at me. It would need to be more subtle.'

Kitty felt disappointed. She'd been hoping that Constable Westwell would arrest the man straight away so that she wouldn't have to worry about him any more, but although she'd listened to his explanation, she couldn't see how it was going to benefit her. All she knew was, the policeman intended to leave her assailant free to wander the streets, and she felt completely let down by the man she'd been sure was going to help her.

Wishing that she hadn't bothered coming, Kitty stood up to leave.

'Let me walk you home,' offered Constable Westwell. 'The least I can do is see you safely to your door.'

'There's no need,' she told him.

'Please. It would make me feel better to know you're safe.'

Kitty thought privately that she would be a lot safer with her assailant off the streets, but she allowed Constable Westwell to open the door for her.

The constable on duty at the desk grinned again as they passed him.

'You should be more discreet, Westwell,' he said. 'You could lose your job over that.' He nodded his head towards Kitty and she knew that he wasn't making a joke. There was spite in his tone.

Constable Westwell didn't respond. He held the outer door for her and they walked towards Mary Ellen Street in silence. Kitty was angry. No wonder people didn't like the policemen. They were supposed to be there to help, but she hadn't received much help tonight.

At last Constable Westwell broke the awkward silence. 'I understand that you're afraid,' he said. 'But I'll make sure that you don't come to any harm.'

'You can't protect me all the time,' she told him, even though she was grateful that he was walking alongside her down the dark streets, especially when they left the gas lamps behind and turned into the gloom of Mary Ellen Street.

'I'll be about when you go gathering in the morning,' he promised.

Kitty felt irritated. 'There'd be no need to keep such a close watch on me if the man was locked up,' she told him.

'I'm sorry. I know I've upset you,' he told her, 'but it's important to me to bring this man to justice for coining, so I don't want to rush in and arrest him before I have enough evidence to make sure he's found guilty of that.'

They reached Kitty's door and she put her hand to the latch. 'Thank you for seeing me home,' she said, opening the door. The constable nodded his head and walked back down the street. He was soon enveloped by the darkness and Kitty shivered as she closed and locked the door from the inside. Her trust in the policeman had diminished and the hope that she could soon put the attack behind her had been snatched away by his determination to follow his own investigations.

17

Sidney Westwell knew he'd let Mrs Cavanah down. She'd been angry with him, that had been plain to see. Of course she wanted her assailant to be locked up so that she could feel safe again. He didn't blame her. How could she possibly understand that he was determined to bring the man to justice for a much more serious crime?

Shaw and his stupid remarks hadn't helped, either. Sidney itched to take a swing at him and knock him to the ground. He knew that he could. He also knew that if he did, it would be the end of his job with the police and he would lose the chance to bring the coiners to justice. So he would have to try to keep his own temper under control and not give Shaw the satisfaction of seeing that he had rattled him.

His colleague was still sitting behind the desk reading his paper when Sidney arrived back at the police station. He decided to ignore him and went up the stairs to his bed, thankful that at least he wasn't forced to share a dormitory with his enemy.

He undressed and hung up his uniform. Tonight he was glad to take it off. It would be so much easier to trace the coiners' den if he could go out in ordinary clothes and blend in with the crowd. He knew that the reason police had to wear their uniform all the time was to reassure the populace, but it didn't aid any investigation that wasn't a straightforward enquiry. If anything, it helped the criminals, but the superintendent said those were the rules and wouldn't even discuss it.

Sidney lay down and thought about his own clothes which were folded in the trunk that was stored under his bed. The only time he could envisage wearing them again was if he left this job — and he'd kept them for that very reason. He always liked to see a way out of a difficult situation. The streets of Manchester had taught him that, if nothing else.

He was tired, but sleep evaded him. There were too many things going around and around in his head. Not least, the knowledge that Mrs Cavanah might never trust him. It was important to him that she did; he wanted her to think well of him. He wanted to help her, but her expression tonight had betrayed disappointment, which made him feel sad. Maybe he should have explained himself fully to her and told her that he wanted to bring the coiners to justice to atone for the death of his late wife. Maybe she would have understood that, but he didn't like to talk much about Susan. He found it too hard; the grief was still raw.

He slept fitfully, waking almost every hour with unsettling dreams that he couldn't quite remember. When it grew light he gave up trying to rest and got up quietly so as not to disturb his companions. He dressed himself and went downstairs to the privy, and then washed his face and had a shave, which he hated. He'd had a beard once — a dark, luxurious one — but he'd had to shave it off when he joined the police. He kept his whiskers long – almost down to his chin – but he still resented having to set to with a razor every morning.

He wiped the suds away with a towel and hung it up to dry. The kettle he'd put on the hob was boiling so he made tea and ate a thick slice of bread with plenty of butter and a smear of treacle. At least there was no shortage of food here, but it made him feel guilty when he walked his beat and saw the starvation in the worst-off parts of the town. He could understand why some people stole, and although it was his job to stop them, he sometimes turned a blind eye if he saw a child taking a loaf. He couldn't bring himself to put them in the lock-up for simply trying to survive, even though he always felt guilty afterwards about the baker who'd been robbed, because that man was trying to feed his family as well.

Sidney unlocked the main door and let himself out on to the quiet streets. He had an hour or two before his shift began and he walked towards Mary Ellen Street. He wanted to show Mrs Cavanah that he hadn't abandoned her and that he would do his best to keep her safe. Still, it was true what she'd said. He couldn't watch over her all the time, and he asked himself how he would feel if some harm came to her that he hadn't been able to prevent. The question troubled him, and he wondered if he ought to find the man with the waistcoat and question him. Maybe he should do that and forget the pact he'd made with the soul of his dead wife to avenge her. Perhaps he should take care to protect the living instead.

*

When Kitty came out of the door she saw Constable Westwell at the end of the street and she wondered if he'd been there all night. But as she approached him she saw that he was freshly shaved with a trickle of dried blood on his chin where he'd been careless and cut himself. She was partly relieved to see him and partly irritated that he thought this was a solution to her problem.

She returned his greeting with a half-hearted 'Good morning' but didn't pause to make conversation. She was keen to be on the streets before the other gatherers today as she needed to make some good finds so she could earn a decent payment from Mr Reynolds. With Maria pushing the barrow, they made their way down North Gate, around the back of Cockcrofts and then down Astley Gate to where the fish stones had once stood before the new market house was built. The barrow was gradually filled and Peter had a sack for the greasy bones that they found. But all the time, Kitty was aware of being watched. She hoped it was Constable Westwell and not her assailant.

Coming down Church Street as the shops were beginning to open, she passed Timothy who was walking briskly to his job. She always felt so proud when she saw him in the jacket and hat he wore to deliver letters, but every time his resemblance to his father filled her with sadness for what they'd lost. Kitty often thought of her husband and sometimes couldn't help imagining what life would have been like if he'd still been with them. It was pointless, she knew. That life had been snatched from her and would never return, but sometimes it comforted her to think of him as still living. The remote possibility of it being true haunted her, because his body had never been found.

At the cheese shop, Agnes was carrying the wheels of cheese from her cold room and placing them on the marble counter. She smiled as they went by, looking immaculate in her clean apron and cap. Kitty was thankful that her children were doing well despite the loss of their father.

As they turned to go down Clayton Street, Kitty saw Constable Westwell following them at a distance. The sight reassured her even though she wasn't certain how long he would keep up his protection of her. His talk of finding the coiners' den and bringing them all to justice seemed impossible to Kitty. He appeared to have no clear plan to achieve it, and sooner or later he would lose interest and then she would have to take her chances. The best she could hope for was that her attacker would eventually forget about her.

It was after she'd finished at the warehouse and was on her way home that she saw the man again, coming out of the Golden Lion this time.

'Come on! Don't dawdle!' she urged the children, terrified that he might see them and threaten her again, even though it was busy on the street.

Once they'd reached a safe distance she risked looking back. The man was definitely watching her, although she couldn't be certain that he had recognized her. Then he turned and went on his way and she tried to steady herself so as not to alarm Maria and Peter. But the encounter had shaken her and her legs trembled as she walked home.

Sidney was pensive as he walked his regular beat. He kept asking himself whether he was doing the right thing.

When he reached the Spread Eagle he ducked in under the low lintel to speak to the landlord. The man, Billy Yates, looked up as he came in and Sidney saw the flicker of resentment that was so familiar to him. He was well aware that many people were suspicious of the police and thought that the formation of the force was part of a government plot to control them. He always tried to reassure them that his intentions were good, although it wasn't easy when other constables took advantage of their status by putting their own desires first. The bad apples were thrown out, of course, like those who were found drunk when on duty, but not before the harm was done. And when there was unrest in the town, Sidney knew that it could easily spill over into violence against him and his fellow constables.

'What would you like?' asked Billy, reaching for a pewter mug.

'I'm on duty,' replied Sidney, although he would have enjoyed sitting down with a pint of ale and taking the weight off his feet for a while. 'I just wanted to make some enquiries. There's a man with a patterned waistcoat been hanging about the town. I'm after him for some petty thefts and I wondered if you'd seen him in here.'

'Most of my customers wear waistcoats,' replied the landlord uncertainly.

'This particular man wears one that looks as if it was once expensive – not your run-of-the-mill workwear,' Sidney explained. He suspected that Billy Yates knew very well who he meant. The landlord hesitated and then decided to talk.

'Aye. I know who you mean,' he said slowly. 'He comes in here sometimes, although I don't encourage him. I always find myself a few spoons short after he's gone.'

'You think he's stealing them?'

'I know he's stealing them, but I've never caught him in the act and it's difficult to go accusing folk without any evidence.' Sidney knew how true that was. 'And you know why he wants them?' Billy went on.

'To melt down,' Sidney replied.

'Aye. That's the top and bottom of it. He's well known for it all over town. Some places have banned him altogether. I considered doing the same, but it's more trouble than it's worth.'

'But if he's making fake coins and using them to buy beer from you, then it would be worth your trouble,' Sidney suggested. 'I know not being paid in real money is a problem. I used to run a pub myself, in Manchester,' he confided, hoping to get the man on side.

'So you know what hard work is,' Billy replied, as if he thought being a police constable was walking an easy street.

'Aye. And I know what a problem the counterfeits are. I'm determined to stamp it out in Blackburn. That's why I'm asking about this man with the waistcoat. Do you know where he lives?'

'No. I've no idea. He keeps himself to himself.'

'Does he come in alone? Or have you seen him with anyone else?'

'He comes in with a woman sometimes. Or he meets her here, to be more specific. They come in separately, but they sit together and talk. They may pass stuff to one another; I don't look too closely.'

Sidney nodded. He understood that sometimes it was easier to turn a blind eye to illegal goings-on rather than challenge folk.

'He doesn't meet with other men?'

'Not that I've seen.'

Sidney was content that the landlord was telling the truth. Not that it helped much. He knew that tracking the coiners down to their den wouldn't be easy. Once more, he wondered if he was doing the right thing, when he could simply have the man up before the magistrate for the attack. It would ease Mrs Cavanah's worries and she would be grateful to him. He liked the idea of that.

18

Agnes noticed the woman come into the shop as she was serving another customer. She looked uneasy and kept fidgeting with her purse as she glanced towards the door, as if she was unsure whether to stay and wait to be served or go back out.

'A quarter of that cheese, please,' she said when it was her turn. She pointed to the wheel of creamy Lancashire that stood on the counter.

'A quarter?' asked Agnes, thinking that she must have misheard her because she'd spoken so quietly. It was rare for anyone to ask for less than half a pound, even if they were poor, and this woman didn't look poor. Her frock and shawl seemed good quality.

'Aye. Is it a problem?' the woman asked her anxiously.

'No. Not a problem at all,' said Agnes with a smile as she reached for the wire and cut a sliver of the cheese. She knew it would be difficult to get a slice without it crumbling, but she managed and lifted it on to the weighing scales. 'It's just over, but you can have it for a penny ha'penny.'

She wrapped the cheese and passed it to the woman, expecting her to have scraped together a few coppers to pay for it, so she was surprised when she produced a shiny shilling and proffered it.

'That'll be tenpence ha'penny change,' her customer whispered.

'Yes. I know.' Agnes hesitated before accepting the shilling. It looked new and reminded her of the ones her mother had shown her. She turned it over on her palm and sure enough it was dated 1850.

'Is there something wrong?' asked the woman, looking worried.

Agnes was suspicious. It seemed obvious to her that the woman had asked for the smallest amount of cheese possible so that she could get rid of the counterfeit coin and receive real money in change.

'I think it might be a bad coin,' she said, wishing that Jonas was in the shop with her.

The woman looked as if she might burst into tears. 'Well, give it back to me then,' she said and snatched the coin from Agnes's hand before hurrying out with the cheese still clutched in her other hand.

For a moment, Agnes considered running after her. But that would mean leaving the shop unattended. It was only a quarter, she told herself, even though any loss was a bad thing. But she'd have been much worse off if she'd been tricked, she reminded herself. She'd have been nearly a shilling worse off as well as giving the cheese away.

She was still fretting about the incident later that afternoon when Jonas came in on his way back from Bolton market.

'Do you remember me telling you about those coins my mother found?' she asked him. 'I've just had a woman in here trying to buy cheese with one.'

'Perhaps we should speak to Constable Westwell,' he suggested when he'd heard her out. 'He might be able to find this woman.'

'I don't know,' said Agnes, beginning to wipe down the counter in preparation for locking up for the day. 'I don't want to have to go and give evidence in front of the magistrate.'

'If this woman's connected to the man who attacked your mother, the constable might be able to track her down and get them all in court,' said Jonas. 'They need locking up.'

'I know,' said Agnes. She knew that her mother was afraid to go about her work with her assailant still on the loose.

'I'll come with you,' Jonas offered.

'No. You need to get off home,' she told him, although she hated saying goodbye to him at the end of each day.

'Well, promise me you'll be careful,' Jonas said. 'I'm on the market at Preston all day tomorrow.'

'I know. I'll be all right. Don't worry. I won't let anyone take advantage of me.'

'I wish you'd let me take advantage of you,' he said with a grin as he came around the back of the counter.

Agnes threatened him with her wet cloth. 'Don't! People might see!' she reprimanded him as he tried to kiss her.

'When will you agree to marry me, Agnes?' he asked. 'I'm getting tired of waiting.'

'Soon,' she promised. It was what she always said, but she knew that it wouldn't satisfy him for ever. Before long she would have to face up to the difficulties that accepting his proposal would bring.

After he'd gone, Agnes turned her thoughts to the more pressing matter of the fake coins and considered calling at the police station. She thought that it might be better to go now, on her way home, rather than have to explain things to her mother who might worry even more if she knew what had happened that afternoon.

She made her way along Clayton Street and went in to the station.

'Is Constable Westwell here?' she asked the constable who was behind the heavy oak desk.

The man raked her up and down with his eyes, making her feel uncomfortable. Then he opened the door behind him.

'Westwell! I've got another of thy fancy women out here!'

Anger rose rapidly in Agnes. 'How dare you speak about me like that?' she demanded. 'You have no idea who I am, and I'd advise you to be civil unless you want me to make a complaint about you!'

'Calm down, missy,' replied the man. 'I'm only having a joke.'

'It isn't funny,' she told him. 'It was disrespectful to me and to Constable Westwell.'

She was still glaring at the man when Constable Westwell came through the door and saw her.

'Miss Cavanah. Would you like to come through?'

'Not until this man has apologized to me.'

'I don't think there's any need to make such a fuss,' said the constable at the desk. 'Like I said, it was just a bit of well-meant humour.' He tried to make it sound as if she was the one at fault.

'I can see that Miss Cavanah is upset, Constable Shaw,' said Constable Westwell. 'What did you say to her?'

Agnes watched as the two policemen glared at one another. She saw the dislike and was surprised. There was clearly more going on here than she'd realized. But after a moment Constable Shaw shrugged and laughed.

'I'm sorry if I offended thee, miss,' he said and raised the flap on the desk for her to go through into the back room.

'I must apologize for my colleague,' said Constable Westwell. 'He . . .'

'He's a difficult man. I can see that,' Agnes told him.

'Yes. But he's been here much longer than me so I have to . . .'

'You have to be careful?'

'Yes.' Constable Westwell nodded. He looked uncomfortable and Agnes felt sorry for him. 'Well,' he went on. 'What brings you here again?'

Agnes described the woman who had come into her shop.

'It does sound as if she was trying to pass on one of the shillings,' he agreed. 'I wouldn't be surprised if there's a whole gang of them doing it. I'd like to bring them to justice. All of them.' He bit his lip. 'I know your mother would feel better if the man who attacked her was locked up straight away, but I'd like to get him locked up for good. Will you talk to her? Explain it to her?' he asked. 'I worry she thinks that I'm refusing to do anything about it.'

Agnes saw that the constable was truly concerned about what her mother thought of him. It surprised her, because at first she'd only seen the uniform and hadn't considered the man underneath it.

As she walked home, after promising that she would talk to her mother, Agnes pondered on the encounter some more. She'd never considered that another man might show an interest in her mother, and her mother had never spoken of any man except her father. Agnes had always believed that her mother was still clinging to some hope that he might come, one day, to find them. But she did wonder if Constable Westwell found her mother attractive.

She hoped it wasn't going to make things difficult, because the only important issue she could see was getting this coiner taken off the streets so that her mother didn't need to be afraid.

19

Kitty felt relieved when Agnes came in. Her daughter was later than usual and she'd been growing anxious about where she was and if any harm had befallen her. She didn't say anything, though. She didn't want Agnes to think she was fussing. Her daughter was a grown woman now, but Kitty still worried until she knew that she was safely home, especially with that man still walking free about the town.

'Come to the table. Your tea's ready,' she told her as she stirred the pot where she'd made a stew. The aroma rose on the steam and the smell sparked a memory of her home in Ireland. She wiped her eyes with the back of her hand, hoping the children would think it was the heat that was making them tear up.

She began to dish out the food and passed the plates around the table.

'Take some bread with it,' she urged the children. She knew that it would help to fill them up.

Kitty wanted to ask Agnes why she was late, but she tried to quell her curiosity.

'Have you had a busy day?' she asked instead when she'd said grace and they'd begun to eat.

'Quite busy.' Agnes hesitated as if she was keeping something back, and as Kitty watched her daughter blow on a hot spoonful of stew to avoid burning her tongue, she wondered what might have happened. She knew her daughter well enough to see that something was bothering her. She hoped it wasn't anything to do with Jonas Marsden. It wasn't that she didn't like him – she did. He was a nice lad, but she worried that Agnes had grown too close to him and that one day she might have her heart broken if Jonas announced that he was to be married to some other girl – someone from his own church.

'Something odd happened at the post office,' Timothy told them.

'Did it? What was that?' asked Kitty. She liked to hear her son talk about his work and was glad that he enjoyed it.

'This woman came in,' he recounted, 'and said she wanted to buy a penny stamp. Then she pulled a shilling out of her purse and wanted the eleven pence change. Mr Sharples was out, so Mrs Sharples had to deal with her and she was most put out about having to find that much in change for so small a sale.'

'What was odd about that?' Kitty asked him.

'Her manner was a bit suspicious,' Timothy explained. 'She seemed on edge.'

'What did she look like?' Agnes asked. Kitty was surprised at her keen interest.

'Well . . .' Timothy screwed up his face as if he was trying to picture the woman in his head. 'She was ordinary, really. She had a shawl – a paisley patterned one – but she didn't have gloves on, and all the well-to-do ladies wear their gloves.'

'A green frock, battered boots, dark hair parted down the middle and pinned up at the back?' enquired Agnes.

'Yes. That was her,' Timothy agreed.

'She came in the cheese shop as well, trying to get change for her shilling. Did Mrs Sharples give her the money?'

'Yes, of course she did.'

Kitty met her daughter's troubled look and knew what she was thinking.

'It was one of the counterfeit shillings,' she said.

Agnes nodded. 'I think so.' She turned to her brother. 'You'll have to tell Mr and Mrs Sharples first thing tomorrow,' she instructed him. 'Tell them that the shilling might be a bad coin and they must report it to Constable Westwell at the police station.'

'Is that where you've been?' Kitty asked Agnes, relieved that there hadn't been any trouble with Jonas.

'Yes. I went to tell him about this woman. I didn't say anything because I didn't want to worry you. But I ought to have realized that if she didn't get it changed in my shop she would try someone else.'

'Mrs Sharples won't be pleased to have been caught out,' Kitty remarked. 'She always likes to think she knows best. Don't tell her I said that,' she added with a warning glance at Timothy. Heaven knows it had taken the woman long enough to accept them as family after they'd arrived from Ireland, penniless and seeking help from their cousin, and she didn't want to provoke any ill feeling.

'It must be their plan,' Agnes went on. 'The coiners, I mean. They make these false coins and then buy something as cheaply as possible to get the change, which is proper money. And us shopkeepers end up out of pocket. Constable Westwell is right,' she told her mother. 'There must be a whole gang of them and they need to be stopped.'

Kitty agreed. It made her angry to think of her daughter and the Sharples being cheated.

'If the constable were to arrest that man, he might tell him who the rest of the gang are,' Timothy suggested.

'That's not very likely,' Agnes replied. 'It's not the Middle Ages. He can't torture him on the rack or use thumb screws.' She turned to Kitty. 'Constable Westwell thought that you were angry with him for not arresting the man straight away.'

'I was,' Kitty admitted. 'I still am. I won't feel safe until he's off the streets.'

'He asked me to explain to you that he wants to get the man locked up too, but he wants to be certain it will be for good. He can only do that if he's found guilty of the counterfeiting. He's trying to find out where the man lives, because he thinks that's where the coins are being made. He doesn't want you to think he's doing nothing or that he doesn't care.' Kitty nodded. 'He's a nice man,' Agnes persisted. 'I think he genuinely cares about you.'

'He's a policeman,' Kitty replied. 'He's just doing his job. Don't let your imagination run away with you,' she warned her daughter.

20

As soon as Agnes Cavanah had mentioned the woman, Sidney had suspected that she was the one who met with the coiner in the Spread Eagle. It wasn't a lot to go on, but the situation was becoming clearer. And then there was the name, Ratcliffe. He wasn't sure where that fitted in, but he'd find out. Sidney was determined to get to the bottom of it. That was if he managed to keep his job.

He had mixed feelings about the confrontation between Agnes and Constable Shaw. He'd admired the way the lass had stood up to the man, but it had annoyed Shaw and Sidney suspected that he would take it out on him. He'd already made a comment about Sidney being unable to keep his women in order. It wasn't that he cared what Shaw thought of him, but the man was his superior as he'd been here longer, and he had the ear of the superintendent, Mr Marshall. If he criticized Sidney's work or put it about that he was carrying on with women instead of doing his job, then he might find that he was shown the door.

Sidney knew that Shaw had been watching him and that he would be watching even more closely now. As he washed and shaved himself the next morning, he wondered whether it was a sensible thing to go out early and follow Mrs Cavanah on her rounds. The trouble was that he didn't want to let her down. He'd never forgive himself if she was attacked again. It was a pity he had to wear this conspicuous uniform, he thought as he buttoned up the tunic and fastened the wide leather belt. For a moment he considered getting changed, but he knew that if Shaw saw him on the street out of his uniform, he would report him and he would be sacked for certain.

Sidney let himself out of the police house. After he was sure Mrs Cavanah was safe, he'd go back to the Spread Eagle and see what else he could find out from Billy Yates. He wanted to know more about the woman who met with the coiner and whether she answered the description that Miss Cavanah had given him.

When he reached the corner of Mary Ellen Street, he saw that Mrs Cavanah was waiting for him and he was thankful that he'd decided to come.

'Good morning!' he greeted her. 'Which way are you heading today?'

'North Gate,' she replied. 'But I wanted a word with you first.'

'What is it?' he asked, wishing that he dared to clasp hold of her hand to give her some comfort. She looked so afraid that it pained him.

'Agnes told you about a woman trying to get change for one of the shillings I found?' He nodded. 'Well, the woman went into the post office and Mrs Sharples gave her change. Timothy was there.'

Sidney wasn't surprised. It was typical of coiners. Although they often had shopkeepers who were in league with them and would pass on the counterfeits for a cut of the profits, they also tried to pass off coins to unsuspecting ones. He wanted to promise that he would go to speak to the Sharples as Mrs Cavanah was asking, but it wasn't on his beat and he feared further trouble if he was to stand on any more toes.

'I'll have to ask Constable Milne,' he told her. 'It's on his patch. But he'll tell me what he finds out.'

Sidney hoped that he would, anyway. Some of the constables were very protective of their patches and didn't like to talk about what they knew unless it was to boast. It would be just like Milne to begin his own investigation and then take all the credit for it when Sidney was hoping that some successful arrests would raise his standing with the superintendent as well as avenging his late wife.

'Can you not go yourself?' Mrs Cavanah asked him.

'I'm afraid it doesn't work like that,' he replied. It was a daft way of doing things, he agreed. But as the superintendent was always telling them, 'rules is rules'.

Kitty made her way down North Gate. The people who lived there weren't as wealthy as those on King Street and Richmond Terrace, but they still threw away clothing and other items that had plenty of life left in them. She didn't see Constable Westwell again, but she was sure he wasn't far away, looking out for her. Although it was Agnes she was worried about today. It concerned her that her daughter had become mixed up in this coining business as well. Kitty knew that Jonas would be standing on the market at Preston and Agnes would be alone in the shop. She'd never considered it to be dangerous before, not like the time when Agnes was robbed as she was selling door to door. But the story about the woman yesterday had bothered her. She'd hate to see Agnes robbed or cheated again when she'd worked so hard to make her business a success.

Once she'd decided that they'd found enough, Kitty took Maria and Peter down Church Street so that she could check on her daughter before they went to the warehouse. She paused outside the post office, but there was no sign of Timothy and she was about to move on when John Sharples came to the door and called to her. She told the children to wait with the barrow and went to speak to him.

'Timothy's been telling me about these counterfeit shillings. I had no idea tha'd been attacked.'

'It was nothing,' she told him. 'I just got a fright.'

'I bet tha did. The man needs catching and locking up. What are the police doing about it?' he demanded.

Kitty told him that she'd spoken to Constable Westwell and that he'd promised to send one of the other constables round. 'I didn't know if you'd want to go to the police station yourself,' she explained.

'They're worse than useless,' John complained. 'All they do is parade up and down and they never see what's right under their noses. We're eleven pence down because of it. And I've just had to sort through all the shillings in the drawer to find the right one.'

'They're shiny. Dated 1850.'

'Aye. I've got it now. But it's a clever job. Peggy's blaming herself for accepting it, but I think I would have done, too. It looks real enough. It's only the weight that gives it away. Anyway, we'll be looking very carefully at any shillings that cross our counter from now on.' He paused. 'You must be worried about being out in the early morning whilst this man's still on the loose.'

'I have my work to do,' Kitty explained.

'Aye.' He nodded. 'Well, take care,' he told her.

Kitty moved on and was pleased to see Agnes in her shop looking happy. She waved to her and went on to the warehouse. She hoped that John Sharples was wrong when he claimed the police were useless. She wanted these criminals caught quickly so she could get on with her life without this constant worry.

21

Sidney Westwell began his beat with a clear intention. He walked briskly down Penny Street and pushed open the door of the Spread Eagle. He saw Billy Yates's face crease into a frown. The landlord didn't look overly pleased to see him again, but after Sidney had waited for him to serve a couple of early customers who looked as if they'd come straight from the stone quarry, Billy came to speak to him with a tea towel draped over one shoulder and wiping his hands on his apron.

'I take it you're still lookin' for t' chap with the fancy waistcoat?' he asked.

'I am,' replied Sidney. 'Have you seen him?'

'Aye,' replied Billy. 'The woman an' all.'

'Can you describe her?'

'Aye.' Billy nodded. 'Paisley shawl around her head and wearing a green frock.'

That was her, thought Sidney as the landlord glanced around and continued to speak in a low voice.

'She came in late yesterday afternoon,' he told him. 'Didn't order owt. Just sat by the door over there. Looked as if she were waitin' for someone. She were here a while and I was minded to tell her to make a purchase or go, but I remembered what you'd said and I thought I'd keep watch.'

'Thank you. I'm grateful,' Sidney said.

'I wouldn't do it for just anyone,' Billy replied and Sidney understood that he meant he wouldn't cooperate with any other constable. 'It's just that with you tellin' me you used to be a landlord yourself, I know you'll appreciate how difficult these things can be.'

'I do understand,' Sidney replied. 'I know you don't want any trouble in your establishment.' He could sympathize with the man. There wasn't a day went past when he didn't wish he'd turned a blind eye to the coiners in Manchester. He might still have been there, with Susan and a child. What had happened hadn't been worth it for a few lost flagons.

'The woman seemed afraid,' whispered Billy, leaning towards him over the bar. 'And when the waistcoated man came in, she seemed to flinch. He came to the bar and ordered a pint of beer, but he didn't buy her a drink. I tried to speak to him, civilly enough, but he didn't say much, so I just watched as much as I could without it being obvious. There were other customers in by then, so I couldn't give them my full attention, but I did see the woman give him some money.'

'How much?' asked Sidney.

Billy shrugged. 'Hard to say. She emptied a purse into his hand. It seemed a lot, but it might have been mostly coppers. Then the man with the waistcoat drained his pint and went out. She sat for a while longer, as if she'd been told to stay. She kept her head down and after about five minutes she went out herself.'

'You've been very helpful,' Sidney told him.

The landlord's face brightened. 'It doesn't seem much,' he said as he began to wipe the countertop.

'No. But you've given me an idea,' replied Sidney.

He left the Spread Eagle with a plan beginning to form in his mind. It was when Billy Yates had told him that the woman seemed afraid that he'd begun to wonder if it could be used to his advantage. If the woman wasn't a willing member of the coining gang, she might be more amenable to being approached. And who better to befriend a woman in need than another woman?

Of course it might not be easy to persuade Kitty Cavanah to help him, but if he could get her to agree, it might be the break he needed to find out who these coiners were and where they were operating from.

Kitty listened to what Constable Westwell was asking her to do with a growing feeling of fear. She was shaking her head before he'd even stopped speaking.

'I can't do that,' she told him emphatically. 'What if the man sees me with her and recognizes me?'

'I know it sounds dangerous, but it isn't,' Constable Westwell told her. 'I would never ask you to do anything dangerous. All I'm asking is that you try to get talking to this woman, gain her confidence and hope that she confides in you.'

'You make it sound easy,' she told him. 'But I don't even know who she is. How am I supposed to find her?'

'She goes in the Spread Eagle.'

'I hope you don't expect me to go into a public house

on my own,' Kitty said. 'I don't want to be mistaken for the sort of woman who hangs about in those places!'

She wished that Constable Westwell would go. She was worried about what the neighbours were thinking, but he'd accepted her offer of a cup of tea and was sitting in the chair opposite her looking for all the world as if he was settled for the afternoon with his hat on the floor at his feet and the cup resting on his knee.

'It's a very respectable establishment,' he reassured her. 'I would introduce you to the landlord, Billy Yates, and he would keep a close eye on you. You're not being left to do this alone, Mrs Cavanah. There would always be someone nearby watching out for you. And as things stand, I know you won't feel safe until this man is locked up.'

'I'd rather not get involved,' she told him.

'But it could be the best chance we have to bring the man who attacked you to justice,' he persisted.

Kitty had to admire his determination, although she was beginning to suspect that Constable Westwell wanted to arrest these coiners for his own benefit rather than hers. He seemed very keen to prove himself as a policeman. She could see that he was ambitious and he probably had his eye on a promotion.

'I wish you'd just go to the Spread Eagle and arrest him for stealing the spoons,' she said. 'Would the landlord not give evidence against him?'

'But I want him for the coining,' he reminded her. 'I want them all – him, the man called Ratcliffe and everyone else who's involved. And you can help me catch them. Get them out of the town – out of the country.

Isn't that what you want? For your sake? And for Agnes's as well? You wouldn't want her to be in trouble for handling false coins, would you? And it would be so easy for her to accept one at her shop.' Kitty wondered if the constable was making a threat, but his face seemed genial enough. 'I'm trying to help you,' he added, reaching out to put his cup and saucer on the table. 'I want you to be able to walk the streets without fear.'

It was what Kitty wanted too. But she was afraid that getting herself wrapped up in the affair would only make matters worse. The waistcoated man wasn't somebody who would take kindly to an informant in his midst. And if she did as the constable asked, she would be putting this other woman in danger as well as herself.

'At least think about it. Please?' he asked her.

'All right, I'll think about it,' Kitty agreed reluctantly. She had no intention of agreeing, but she was wary of antagonizing him. Besides, she'd become glad of his reassuring presence as she did her rounds in the mornings and she didn't want him to decide against watching over her.

He reached for his hat and she was so relieved that she jumped up to show him to the door.

'May I call again this evening? After my shift?' he asked her.

Kitty looked up and met his dark eyes. They looked hopeful and she didn't know how to say no.

'All right,' she agreed reluctantly. She hoped that Agnes and Timothy would be home by the time he came and that Agnes would help her to refuse his request.

*

'The woman didn't strike me as being a felon,' said Agnes later when Kitty had told her about Constable Westwell's visit. 'She seemed unsure of herself – as if it was the first time she'd done something like that. To tell the truth, I felt a bit sorry for her. I thought she was going to cry when I refused to give her change for the shilling.'

'I can understand her being afraid of that man,' Kitty agreed. 'I would like to see him sent away for good, but I think it's too much of a risk to do what Constable Westwell is asking. He's the policeman. It's up to him to find these criminals, not me.'

'He's trying his best,' Agnes reminded her. 'He's not like the others. A lot of them do as little as they can get away with – and some of them are very rude. At least Constable Westwell is trying to bring criminals to justice.'

As she was pondering on the matter, there was a knock on the front door and Kitty sent Agnes to answer it. Moments later their small kitchen was filled with the aroma of roasted meat and Constable Westwell was standing there with a steaming package in his hands.

'I've brought pies,' he told her.

He placed his package on the table and reached up to take off his tall hat, looking around for somewhere to put it.

'I hope you don't mind me bringing something,' he explained as he propped the hat against the corner of the hearth and ran a hand through his thick dark hair. 'I often get a pie for my tea and I haven't had time to eat yet.'

'I'll get a plate for you,' said Kitty. 'Please, sit down.' She offered the chair by the hearth where she'd been sitting a moment before.

'Thank you.'

Constable Westwell lowered himself into it, although he still seemed to overpower the room with his size and his presence.

Kitty went to brew some tea and Agnes unwrapped the paper on the parcel the constable had brought. There were six pies inside and Kitty wondered if the constable intended to eat them all himself. She had considered offering him some of their stew as well, but now she was unsure.

'There's one for everyone,' he said as he saw her hesitation. 'You didn't think I was going to eat them all, did you?'

'No.' Kitty felt herself blush and was thankful the room was gloomy. 'I'll pay you for ours,' she said, taking her purse down from the mantelpiece.

'You will not! They're a gift,' he told her firmly.

'Then you must share our stew as well,' Kitty insisted.

'I'd be glad to. It smells good.'

She busied herself with plates and dishes whilst Agnes poured the tea and then they gathered around the table. There were only four chairs, but Agnes and Maria shared one, shuffling against one another and giggling, whilst Peter stood up so that their visitor could have a seat.

The pies were made from mutton with plenty of onions and seasoning and, along with the stew that had been simmering on the hearth, it was more food than Kitty and the children had eaten for one meal in a long time.

'Thank you. That was delicious. You're very generous,'

Kitty told the constable as she set her spoon down, relishing the unaccustomed feeling of a full stomach. She hoped that the pies hadn't been a bribe to persuade her to agree to his scheme. She knew it would be harder to say no after accepting them.

'It feels good to be sitting at a table again,' Constable Westwell replied. 'We do have a table at the police house,' he explained, 'but because we're all on different shifts, I often have to eat alone. And even if others are there, it's not the same as a family gathering. I've missed that.'

'Do you not have any family hereabouts?' Kitty asked him curiously as he loosened the belt around his tunic.

'No. My parents live in Todmorden. We're Yorkshire folk,' he explained. 'My wife and I had a beerhouse in Manchester for a while, but it didn't work out.' He looked sad and Kitty could see that there was a sorrow that surrounded him. She suspected that he had suffered some loss. She recognized the signs.

'My wife died last year,' he told her.

'I'm sorry. That must have been hard for you.'

'It was. I joined the police force afterwards. I want to make a difference,' he said. 'And I understand you had a loss of your own.'

Kitty nodded. She found it a little easier to talk to someone about Peter when she knew they understood how difficult it was.

'That must have been hard – to not be able to bury him,' Constable Westwell sympathized. 'My Susan is buried at the parish church. I go to visit her every week.'

'That must give you some comfort.'

'It does. If only a little,' he agreed.

There was a silence which Kitty broke by telling Agnes and Maria to clear the table. 'And it's time you were in bed,' she said to Peter. 'He needs his sleep. We get up very early,' she explained to the constable.

'Aye. Get the little lad to his cot. I'll just sit here and wait.'

Kitty shooed her youngest up the stairs. He was reluctant to go and was obviously fascinated by the policeman. It was almost unheard of for them to have a visitor and the last man he'd sat at a table with must have been his father. Kitty wasn't sure if he even remembered him. She tried to talk about her husband often. She wanted to keep his memory alive so the children wouldn't forget him, but for the younger ones especially, she knew that their memories were few and would easily fade.

She got Peter undressed and into bed, though she doubted he would sleep. He was excited and kept asking questions about the constable that Kitty had little patience to answer.

'Will he come again?' asked Peter for the umpteenth time.

'Maybe,' she repeated.

'I hope he does. I like him,' Peter said as she drew the blanket over him and he flung it off yet again.

At last, she kissed her son on the forehead and went back down, albeit reluctantly. She knew the conversation she was about to have wouldn't be easy.

'So,' Constable Westwell said when she was settled on her chair with a cup of fresh tea in her hand. 'About this woman.'

'Yes.' Kitty sipped her tea. Agnes had her hands plunged into a bowl of hot water and was washing up the pots whilst chatting to Maria who was drying them. Only Timothy seemed to be taking notice of the conversation, and she suspected that he would find the idea of being a spy exciting.

'She could be key to bringing these coiners to justice,' said the constable. 'She might know where the man lives and who else is involved. All I need to discover is their names and an address. Once I have that, then I can catch them at their work and that will provide plenty of evidence to see them sent away for a very long time.'

'You make it sound easy,' observed Kitty. She looked at Timothy. She didn't want to admit her worries in front of him. She was trying her best to shield her children from the worst of what had happened. Only Agnes knew how badly she'd been hurt, and she'd tried to make light of that, even though she still had the bruises to prove otherwise.

'I think I know where she lives,' Timothy told them unexpectedly. 'I thought she looked a bit familiar that day she came into the post office, but I couldn't think where I'd seen her before. It's been puzzling me, but I think she's from Moore Street. I think she lives with her mother, and there's another woman there who's not . . . well . . . she's a bit odd,' he said, as if he didn't know how else to describe her. 'I once delivered a letter to them and they were very excited. I don't think they'd ever had a letter before. I doubt it was good news, though. You get a feeling for these things.'

'That's an interesting development. Well done, lad!'

said Constable Westwell. He turned to Kitty. 'Now that we know where she lives, it will make it much easier for you to make a friend of her.'

'How am I supposed to do that?' asked Kitty, thinking that he was over-simplifying things. 'I can't just go and knock on the door.'

'It's a pity your Agnes isn't still going door to door with her cheese,' he replied. 'I don't suppose you could go round as if you were selling it?'

'No.' Kitty's answer was emphatic. 'It would just raise suspicion and that's the last thing I want.'

She didn't want to have to do as the constable asked at all, but it was becoming difficult to refuse him after he'd sat at her table and shared his food with them. It did seem like a bribe, even though he'd probably never intended it that way.

'I'm sorry,' he said, although he looked deflated. 'I was getting too excited at the prospect of finding these coiners. I don't want to force you into something that makes you uncomfortable. I just thought . . .'

'It's all right,' Kitty told him.

'No, it isn't,' he replied. 'I'm asking too much. I can see that now. It's just . . .' He hesitated and Kitty saw that there was more he wanted to tell her, but not in front of the children.

'Perhaps it's time you and Maria were going up,' she said to Timothy. 'You look tired and we need to be up early.'

She could see that her son was reluctant to leave, but he didn't argue even though Maria said she wasn't tired and could she stay up another half an hour. Kitty gave her a warning frown not to make a fuss whilst they had a visitor and reluctantly both children said goodnight and climbed the stairs.

Agnes sat down on one of the chairs at the table and Kitty allowed her to stay. She was old enough to hear whatever the constable wanted to say, and besides, it was better not to be alone with him. He seemed a decent sort, but you never knew with men and it wasn't as if she really knew him well.

'I have my own reason for wanting to catch these coiners,' Constable Westwell confessed, and bit by bit he told them the story of the coiners in his beerhouse in Manchester and what had happened there and how he believed it had led to the tragic death of his wife.

'I'm so sorry,' Kitty told him after he'd finished speaking. 'No wonder you want to do something to make amends.'

'Will you keep it to yourself?' he asked, looking up from where he'd kept his gaze fixed on the hearth whilst he was telling his story. Kitty saw that there were tears in his eyes and she put a hand on his arm by way of comfort.

'Of course I will. Agnes too,' she added as her daughter nodded. 'We're not the sort to spread gossip.'

'I know. I wouldn't have told you otherwise,' he said. 'Of course my colleagues know that I'm a widower, but none know the circumstances. People judge,' he added, 'but it wasn't Susan's fault. Her mind was disturbed by what had happened.'

Kitty withdrew her hand from the rough serge of his

uniform and wondered if he ever wished he could wear something more comfortable. It wasn't the sort of clothing to help him relax.

'It's late,' he said. 'I'd best go. They'll be wondering where I've been all this time.'

'It isn't any of their business,' Kitty said.

'It is, though,' he said sadly. 'I never realized when I joined how much it would rule my life. Sometimes it feels like a sentence and I begin to resent it. I wanted to do some good, but I never considered how much it would bind me, having to live every day in this uniform whether I'm on shift or not. I sometimes feel like I'm losing myself,' he added as he picked up his hat and put it on. 'People only see the constable.' Kitty knew that she was guilty of doing the same. It was only now that she saw the kind and vulnerable man beneath the blue clothing, and in that moment she knew that she was bound to help him because she doubted that anyone else would.

22

Next morning, as Kitty gathered her rags, she wondered how she could safely approach the woman from Moore Street. That's if she could even find her. All she had to go on was a description, and it wouldn't help anyone if she befriended the wrong person.

By the time she'd weighed in her finds at the warehouse, Constable Westwell had gone to walk his beat, but the streets were busy now and she didn't think there was much danger in walking down to Moore Street to see what she could find out.

She considered the idea of taking some cheese to sell after all, but decided against it. Instead, she took the barrow but went alone, leaving Maria and Peter in the house. They would be all right for an hour or so, and she thought that it would draw less attention if she was by herself.

Moore Street was set on the far edge of town and had probably, at one time, been on the edge of the moors it was named for that rolled beyond, still wild and covered in heather that was just beginning to show its first delicate pink flowers. The street seemed poor and neglected – even worse than Mary Ellen Street. There were no cobbles here, just ground-down earth that was baked hard in the summer heat yet still held small puddles where flies gathered and buzzed. The houses were ramshackle – each one different as if they'd been built piecemeal rather than the rows of modern terraces where each one looked identical.

The putrid smell coming from the two privies at the top of the street wafted towards Kitty, making her feel slightly nauseous. There were even more flies gathered there and it seemed they hadn't been cleaned out or emptied for quite some time. She felt conspicuous standing there with her barrow. It was obvious there was nothing to find of any value, and short of going to every door, she had no idea which one was the home of the woman she was seeking.

It seemed that she wasn't going to be able to do anything useful after all. Just as she started to walk away, back towards Penny Street, she heard the sound of loud laughter coming from a nearby house and turned to look, wondering who on earth could find any pleasure on a street like this.

A front door suddenly burst open and a figure dressed in nothing more than a soiled petticoat ran out into the street. Her hair was wild about her shoulders and her feet were bare as she danced on the spot, looking back towards the door as if she was expecting someone to chase her. She laughed again as she tugged at her hair, pulling it with such force that Kitty thought she must surely be hurting herself.

'Nancy!' cried a voice and out came another woman, properly dressed in a green frock with a hairbrush in her hand. 'Nancy! Come inside at once! I'll not come after you,' she warned as the first woman hopped from foot to foot in delight as if she were a small child.

The second woman's eyes met Kitty's. She looked uncomfortable, but also worried.

'Can you help me stop her?' she pleaded. 'Please don't let her get out of the street. She's quick and I can't have her running through the town like that.' She sounded desperate and Kitty felt sorry for her. The woman she was caring for obviously had the mind of a child even though her body was that of a woman, and Kitty quickly appreciated her concern and how dangerous it would be to allow Nancy to be out alone. Heaven knows there were plenty of drunken men outside the pubs who wouldn't think twice about taking advantage of such an opportunity.

Kitty put the barrow down and slowly approached Nancy.

'Hello,' she said.

'She'll not answer. She doesn't speak,' explained the woman as she cautiously approached. 'She's my sister,' she added. She managed to grasp Nancy firmly by the wrist, but she resisted and was strong.

'You must go inside, Nancy,' said Kitty gently as she took her other arm and helped her sister to guide her. 'You can't be seen outside in your underclothes.'

Nancy giggled but became more amenable, and between them they managed to get her into the house. The woman guided her to an old wooden box that was placed in front of an empty hearth and persuaded her to sit down. Nancy became calm and rocked herself to and fro whilst twisting strands of her dark hair around her fingers.

Kitty was shocked by what she saw. The only other

furniture in the room was a chair and it was occupied by a tiny lady who was bent double so that her head was resting on her lap. She appeared to be asleep. There was nothing else as far as she could see. Not a table nor pan nor a scrap of food. Just empty shelves and a filthy curtain moving in the slight breeze that was coming in through a broken window.

'Thank you for your help,' said the woman. 'I was terrified I was going to lose her. I was brushing her hair and for no reason she just jumped up and ran. I usually keep the door locked to prevent her getting out, but I must have forgotten to turn the key. It was a good job you were there. Heaven sent,' she added.

Kitty felt guilty. She knew that she hadn't been sent by heaven at all. The only reason she was in Moore Street was to trick this woman into a friendship, because there was no doubt that this was the woman who had been described to her. And looking at her circumstances, Kitty saw why she had been reduced to doing what she had.

'I'm Grace Dewhurst,' said the woman. 'And this is my mother. I'd offer you some tea, but our fire's gone out.'

'I'm Kitty Cavanah. And please, don't trouble yourself. I can see that you have your hands full.'

'Well, thank you for your help. I'm grateful. A lot of folk would have walked away,' she added. 'They're afraid of Nancy, but there's no harm in her.'

Kitty was unsure what to do. She could see that Grace was anxious for her to go and there was no reason for her to stay. She supposed that now she knew where she lived and had spoken to her it was progress of a sort, but she was at a loss to know how to gain the woman's confidence. Because now she felt she genuinely wanted to befriend her. Not just to help Constable Westwell bring the coiners to justice, but because this woman looked in need of a friend. The anger she'd felt previously had been softened by Grace's appalling plight. It was clear that she was as much a victim as any of them in this conspiracy.

23

Kitty walked home thoughtfully. She'd been cursing the woman as a thief and a trickster, but now that she'd seen how Grace was living, she felt nothing but sorrow that the woman had fallen on such hard times. It made her wonder what she would have done herself to feed her family when they'd come to Blackburn penniless if she hadn't received the help she had from the Andertons and her cousin John. She shivered at the thought, wondering if she would ever have been brave enough to do something that risked such a harsh sentence. It was bad enough to think of being sent back to Ireland, but being shipped to New South Wales as a convict was even more terrifying.

She wondered what she could do to help Grace. It was clear that the woman was struggling to care for her mother and her sister, and she feared that the only advice she would receive from someone in authority was that the woman must find herself a job. But Kitty could see that Grace would be unable to leave her sister alone all day. It would be like abandoning a small child, except that she was big and strong enough to do real harm. Kitty supposed that her mother had looked after her in the past, but the frail old lady she'd seen today wasn't capable of caring for herself now, let alone a daughter like Nancy.

'You'll have to tell Constable Westwell what you've found out,' said Agnes when she described what she'd seen to her daughter. 'Tell him that you can't do as he's asked. It would be unfair to make a sham friendship if the woman is as desperate as you say.'

Kitty was inclined to agree, but she felt she couldn't simply walk away and do nothing.

'Part of me wishes I hadn't found her,' she admitted. 'Then I wouldn't be faced with this dilemma.'

'You have to speak to Constable Westwell. I'm sure he'll understand.'

'I know. Not tonight, though,' Kitty added. 'I need to think about it. Besides, I'm reluctant to keep going to the police station. People will talk about me.'

'Perhaps you could speak to him tomorrow,' Agnes suggested. 'You said that he's still keeping an eye out for you in the mornings.'

'He is,' agreed Kitty, although she knew that she must be careful. One or two of the gatherers had commented on the constable who kept hanging around. They weren't happy because they thought he was watching them and trying to find a reason to accuse them of some theft. If they saw her speaking to him, they might think she was an informer, and Kitty knew she couldn't afford to make any more enemies.

The following day was Sunday and Kitty took the younger children to church with her. After the service her friend Aileen Walsh, who had taken her in when she first arrived in Blackburn, came to speak to her.

'Kitty,' she greeted her. 'Have you got a moment?'

'Of course. What's the matter?'

'Do you know what's going on with that constable who's been hanging around?' she asked.

'It's Constable Westwell,' Kitty told her. 'He's the one who helped Agnes that time she was robbed in the street.'

'I thought I recognized him,' Aileen said. 'But do you know what he wants? People have seen him most mornings for a week or so now and there's talk that the gatherers are going to be cleared off the streets. Folk are worried about their livings. Michael was just saying yesterday that he doesn't know what we'll do for money if we're stopped.'

'There's no need to worry,' Kitty reassured her. 'He's just keeping an eye on me,' she confessed. 'He's worried that the coiner who attacked me might come back.'

'I don't think he needs to do that,' said Aileen. 'There are enough of us about to keep a lookout for you ourselves.'

Kitty nodded. She didn't point out to Aileen that there had been nobody there to save her except Mr Anderton on the morning she was attacked.

'I know,' she said. 'But I am afraid. It was a horrible experience and I shan't feel safe until the man is locked up.'

'Well, the constable would be better off doing that rather than traipsing about behind you every day.' She paused and fixed Kitty with an enquiring look. 'You don't suppose he has other reasons, do you?' she asked.

'What other reasons?'

'Well, I hear he's a widower. Do you think he might be interested in you?'

'Of course not!' Kitty gave a forced laugh. 'A police constable wouldn't be wanting to involve himself with me. Besides, I'm not sure they're even allowed to be married.'

'Some of them are married. That Constable Shaw is. He has a house of his own provided for him where he lives with his family.'

'Does he?'

Aileen nodded. 'In a nice part of the town as well,' she went on. 'I've heard people talking about it, saying it's more than he deserves.'

'Constable Westwell isn't like him,' Kitty told her friend. 'He's honest and it's real crime he's trying to put a stop to.'

'You talk about him as if you like him,' teased Aileen, and Kitty felt herself blush.

'What rubbish,' she said, pulling at her shawl to cover her embarrassment. 'I wouldn't get involved with a policeman.'

The next morning she saw Constable Westwell waiting for her near the end of the street and as there was no one else about, she beckoned to him and explained what she'd discovered on Moore Street.

'What number house was it?'

'I'm sorry. I forgot to look. It was about halfway up. I'd know which one it was if I went again, but I don't want to do anything that will get her into trouble,' Kitty told him. 'The woman has a lot of problems and it isn't any wonder she's been tempted to get some extra money any way she can. I feel I ought to be helping her.'

Constable Westwell frowned. 'If she's passing off counterfeit coins then she's breaking the law,' he reminded her.

'I know, but I don't think she has much choice.'

'She could go to the parish if she's as desperate as you say. There is help,' he said. 'She doesn't have to turn to crime.'

'I wondered whether to take her some food. Her shelves were empty. She had nothing.'

The constable frowned again. 'It's not as if you have that much yourself,' he reminded Kitty. 'Here,' he rummaged in his trouser pocket and pulled out a sixpence. 'Buy some bread and potatoes with that if you must. It'll at least give you an excuse to go back and see what else you can find out. Try to get her to confide in you,' he advised. 'Try to find out who this man in the waistcoat is and where he lives.'

Kitty took the money reluctantly. It meant she didn't have to dip into her own meagre funds, but she felt guilty. Like the gift of the pies, the money came with conditions, and the last thing she wanted to do was bring down the law on Grace. Still, she thought, as she went on her way with the barrow, the money would buy the food that Grace desperately needed and she'd made no promises to the constable.

That afternoon, she left the children at home sorting out some finds and she bought a loaf and several pounds of potatoes, along with a pint of milk, and went to see Grace.

She knocked on the door, noting that it was number six.

It was a moment or two before her knock was answered. She could hear Nancy inside and Grace telling her to be quiet and sit down. Then the door was opened a crack and Grace's worried face peered out.

'Hello. It's only me, Kitty. May I come in?'

Grace opened the door just wide enough for her to pass through and closed it behind her, remembering to turn the key in the lock.

'What do you want?' she asked anxiously.

'I brought these.' Kitty offered the food. 'I thought you might find it difficult to get out to the shop.' She'd been wondering what to say and decided this was a way of making it seem less like charity.

'Thanks. But I don't need anything,' said Grace irritably, pushing the food away. 'I don't know why you came. I don't even know you.'

Kitty could see that she wasn't welcome and that helping Grace was going to be harder than she'd anticipated.

'Please take it. It's a gift,' she confessed. 'I saw your shelves were empty and I was worried about you.'

Grace glanced towards her sister and mother, seeming undecided what to do. 'All right,' she said after a moment. 'Thank you. But I don't want charity. I'll pay you back as soon as I can.'

Kitty was glad when she accepted. Looking around the sparse room, she wished that she'd had more money so that she could have provided some coal for the fire and some tea for the pot – if Grace even had a pot.

There was an awkward silence as Kitty stood, uncertain what to do next. There was nowhere to sit, even if she had been invited to stay, and she sensed that Grace was keen for her to go.

'Could you get some help from the parish?' she asked at last. She knew there was help to be had – as long as you weren't Irish, because the Irish were seen as a burden and sent back to Ireland. But this woman wasn't from Ireland. She was a local.

'I don't want charity,' Grace repeated.

'But for your sister, and your mother?'

'No. I'll not risk them being put in the workhouse. They're my flesh and blood and I'll care for them no matter what it takes. I have a bit of a job as a charwoman. It pays something. I'm not destitute.'

Kitty saw that Grace was proud and determined. They were qualities she admired and she warmed to her.

'How is your sister today?' she asked. Nancy seemed subdued compared with the day before. She was dressed in a simple pink frock and her hair was neatly tied with a scrap of string. Sitting on the box, she ignored everyone and rocked and sang to a bundle of cloth that might once have been a doll. Opposite her, Grace's mother was still bent double and a quiet snoring betrayed that she was sleeping. Her clothes were patched but looked as if they had once been good quality, and Kitty wondered what had happened to the family that they should have fallen into such despair.

'She's well enough,' replied Grace. 'I was grateful for your help yesterday.'

'I was glad to help.'

After a minute or so of silence, Kitty realized that she

would have to leave. It was clear that Grace wasn't going to say anything more. She seemed wary and defensive, and making a friend of her looked like it might be an impossible task.

'May I come again?' she asked.

'Why would you want to do that?' asked Grace, obviously suspicious.

'I just thought you could use a friend,' Kitty replied, feeling guilty that her offer of friendship was not as innocent as she would have liked it to be.

Grace was shaking her head. 'I don't need any interference – or any do-gooders.'

'I'm not a do-gooder,' Kitty protested. 'I've little enough myself. I just wanted to offer you friendship.'

Grace snorted. 'You've money enough to make gifts,' she told Kitty, pointing to the food she'd put on her shelf. 'It's not that I'm not grateful – I am – but gifts come with consequences in my experience. I've been caught out before and I won't make the same mistake again.'

Kitty wondered if she was talking about the coiner, but she knew she couldn't ask outright, and Grace had moved to unlock the door. It was a clear request for her to go. So, with no other choice, she said goodbye and stepped out into the street. Grace closed and locked the door behind her and Kitty turned to walk away. At least they had some food, she thought. Though there was little more she could report back to Constable Westwell.

24

When Sidney got back to the police house after his shift that evening, Superintendent Marshall called to him.

'Can I have a word, Constable Westwell?' He led him into the kitchen, which was empty. 'Shut the door,' he said.

Sidney stood stiffly, wondering what was coming. He suspected that it wasn't going to be anything good, although he was sure that he couldn't be accused of not doing his job. He'd been careful not to put a foot wrong.

'It's come to my attention that you've been walking another man's beat,' said the superintendent with a look of disappointment.

'No, sir!' Sidney replied, with a sense of incredulity at the accusation. 'I've walked my own beat every day.'

'Yes. When it's your shift,' agreed Mr Marshall. 'But this other matter has been happening early in the morning, apparently. Constable Bleasedale has seen you on his patch and he's not happy about it. He thought you might have been sent out to watch him. What's going on, Westwell?'

'I enjoy an early morning stroll, sir,' Sidney told him.

'Really? Most constables walk far enough in a day without doing more. They like to put their feet up when they're not on duty, or have a lie-in. It's unusual for a man to be sleeping late and rising early. It's suspicious, constable.'

'I can assure you there's no cause for worry,' Sidney told him. 'If Constable Bleasedale has seen me on his beat then it's entirely coincidental.'

'Every morning this week?' the superintendent queried. 'I'm not a stupid man, Constable Westwell. What's going on?' he asked again.

'Nothing,' Sidney replied. 'It was in my own time, sir,' he added.

Mr Marshall paused to brush a few flecks of lint from the shoulder of his jacket. 'Constable Shaw tells me you're carrying on with a woman.'

'No, sir!'

'In fact, Constable Shaw's of the opinion you have two on the go – a mother and daughter. It's all a bit sordid, constable. I expected better from you. You seemed a decent sort when you put in your application – a widower, more mature in years. I thought you'd be an asset.'

'It isn't true, sir,' Sidney protested.

'Shaw tells me these women have been here, looking for you.'

'They have been here, sir. Yes,' Sidney admitted. 'But it's in connection with a case I'm investigating.'

'Investigating?' replied the superintendent with a look of scepticism. 'I don't hold with that sort of thing here. Leave it to the likes of the Detective Branches and their new ideas about having men in plain clothes. Your job is to walk your beat and be seen and prevent crime. If crime has been committed then you're not doing your job properly. Is that clear?'

'Yes, sir,' Sidney agreed reluctantly. He was irritated by the man and his old-fashioned attitude, but he knew it would do him no good to argue. If the man was convinced he had even one woman, he could decide to dismiss him for that alone, and then he would never be able to bring the coiners to justice.

'Well, I've decided to change your shifts and your beat,' the superintendent told him. 'Bring you to heel, as it were. Think of it as a second chance – and in future you don't interfere with other constables' patches. All right?'

'Yes, sir.'

'Good. I feel let down, to tell the truth, Constable Westwell. I'm usually a good judge of character, but my instincts were wrong with you. Still, as you're so keen on early rising, I'm putting you on the first shift from tomorrow and you'll be walking Blackburn south.'

Sidney went upstairs and sat on the end of his bed. He was furious and convinced that Constable Shaw was behind it all. The man seemed set on making trouble for him.

The change in his shifts meant that he would be walking the streets on the far side of the parish church and out towards Eanam the next morning, and he wouldn't be able to guard Kitty. It worried him. He wondered if he should go to explain to her, but it was late and he knew that Sergeant Watkins was at the front desk. There was no way to get out of the building without passing him, and he was reluctant to reinforce the belief that he was carrying on with a woman. If the sergeant decided to follow him or send one of the other constables after him to see where he went, he would find it difficult to explain why he was visiting Kitty Cavanah. A swift dismissal would most likely follow and he couldn't risk that.

With a sigh he reached down and pulled off his boots. The many hours of walking had made his feet sore. He longed to fill a basin with hot water and plunge them in to soak, but he had to make do with wiping them with a soapy rag before donning his nightshirt and getting into bed. He would try to see Kitty after his shift tomorrow and explain what had happened. He just hoped that no harm would come to her in the meantime.

The next morning, when Kitty came out of the house she glanced about for Constable Westwell and was surprised when there was no sign of him. Maybe he'd decided that she wasn't in much danger because if her attacker was going to return, he would have done so by now. But Kitty felt vulnerable and afraid as they walked along. She felt the need to keep looking behind her to ensure they weren't being followed, and every time they turned down a back alley her heart beat a little faster.

As they came out on to Church Street she thought she saw Constable Westwell. She almost called out to him, but when the man walking towards them drew closer she saw that it was another constable. He gave her a warning look as if he thought she was up to something.

'What are you doing about so early?' he asked as they drew level.

'Rag gathering,' replied Kitty, although it was obvious to the man what her job was.

'Let me take a look at what you've got,' he insisted and drew his truncheon to move aside the rags in the barrow to check there was nothing of value beneath them. Kitty felt irritated. The man had no business interfering, and she was cross that he'd stopped her outside the post office of all places.

'It's just rags,' she told him.

He nodded. 'You can go,' he said at last and Kitty took the handles of the barrow herself so that they could hurry away before he changed his mind. She worried that word had got around about the coins and that even some of the policemen thought that she was involved. She wished Constable Westwell had been there to explain. She hoped everything was all right with him and wondered if she should go to the police station and ask for him, but she hated going to that place. It would be better to look out for him on the street and speak to him there.

It wasn't until after she'd been to weigh in her rags at the warehouse that she saw him. He was coming briskly up Darwen Street. His expression turned to a smile when he saw her.

'Mrs Cavanah! I'm glad I ran into you. I wanted to explain about this morning.' He drew her aside under the shade of a verandah, looking about to ensure nobody was watching them.

'It's all right,' she told him. 'I can't expect you to be there every day.'

'I would if I could,' he replied. 'But the superintendent

changed my shift.' He gave her a brief explanation, although Kitty thought there was more to it than he told her. She hoped that she hadn't done anything to get him into trouble. It was clear that he was concerned about being seen speaking to her.

'The superintendent doesn't believe in investigations,' he told her, 'but that doesn't mean I'm giving up. It's just that we'll need to be more prudent. I hope you understand.'

'I think I do,' Kitty said. 'But I don't want you to get into any trouble because of me. Perhaps you should just arrest the man and leave it at that.'

Constable Westwell shook his head. 'No,' he said. 'I'll not be satisfied until that man and his fellow thieves are either locked up for good or are on a ship to the other side of the world where they can do no more harm. Will you go to see Grace again?' he asked. His tone was almost pleading. 'She can lead us to these men, I'm sure of it.'

'I'll try,' Kitty promised, knowing that she couldn't count on a warm welcome. But if it would help him, she would do it. She wanted the men caught too.

So, later that afternoon, she knocked once again on the door of number six Moore Street, still uncertain what excuse she would make for her visit.

When Grace saw her she seemed to freeze, and for a moment Kitty thought she was going to close the door in her face, but then she asked her to come in.

'Who's sent you?' she demanded as soon as she'd locked the door to keep Nancy inside. 'Was it David Harper?'

Kitty felt her stomach flip over. Was this the name of the man in the waistcoat?

'I'm sorry. I don't know who you're talking about,' she said.

'I'm not stupid!' Grace told her fiercely. 'It's Harper, isn't it? Was it him who sent the food yesterday? I shouldn't have accepted it,' she said, although Kitty saw that the bread had been half-eaten. 'I told him I wasn't doing it any more. He promised he'd write off the debt after last time, but I suppose he's still not satisfied. I should have known better than to believe him when he promised.'

'Is he the man who wears a patterned waistcoat?' Kitty ventured.

'That's him. I knew it would be him,' sighed Grace. Her legs seemed to buckle under her and she clutched at the arm of the chair where her mother was sleeping. 'Tell him I can't pay him,' she pleaded as tears streaked the dirt on her face. 'Look at us. You can see how we live. And tell him I'll not do the coins any more. It's too risky. I don't want to be transported.'

Kitty could see that she was desperate. 'It's all right,' she told Grace. 'I haven't come from him. I promise.'

'Then was it Ratcliffe? I'll not help him either. I'll not rat on Harper. I may hate him, but I'll not tell where he got his die from.'

'I wasn't sent by him either, although I've heard his name,' Kitty said. Grace looked as though she thought she was being tricked, and Kitty decided that honesty was her best option.

'I'm helping Constable Westwell,' she confessed. 'He's determined to bring these coiners to justice. He thought that you could help us.'

'What's it got to do with you?' asked Grace. 'Why are you helping a policeman?'

Kitty explained that she'd found the bag of coins and then been attacked by Harper.

'I was supposed to collect that bag,' Grace admitted. 'I told Harper that it was too risky giving the coins to me in the Spread Eagle where people were watching, and he agreed to hide the coins for me to pick up. But Nancy was in a state and I couldn't calm her enough to take her with me or leave her alone with our mother. So I decided not to bother. I decided that I wanted nothing more to do with David Harper. I thought if I kept out of his way then somehow everything would be all right.' She paused. 'I can't help this policeman,' she said firmly. 'I want nothing more to do with it.'

'You've already helped,' Kitty told her. 'You've told me the name of the coiner. Do you know where he lives?'

Grace's face turned stony. 'No,' she replied, although Kitty wasn't sure if she believed her. The strained atmosphere had clearly upset Nancy and she suddenly threw her doll to the floor and let out a long, piercing wail of anguish.

'Hush, hush.' Grace moved to soothe her sister, rubbing her back as she curled herself into a ball and whimpered. 'Please go,' she said to Kitty. 'You're distressing her.'

'I wish I could help you,' Kitty told her.

'I don't need help from you. We can manage. Just go.'

Reluctantly, Kitty turned the key in the front door and let herself out. It was obvious that Grace was in debt to this David Harper, but that she was too afraid of him to give Kitty the information she needed. Still, she had his name and that was a start. And she knew that he and the man called Ratcliffe were rivals. It wasn't much to go on, but she supposed it was better than nothing.

25

'You did well,' Constable Westwell told her later that day. He'd come to call, bringing pies from the market as he had the time before, and Kitty knew that people had begun to talk.

'That constable's been at your door three times this week,' her neighbour Edna had observed when she'd seen her that morning. 'I hope there's nowt wrong?'

'No. Nothing's wrong,' Kitty had assured her.

'Social call then?' she'd asked with a gleam in her eye. 'Tha wants to be careful,' she'd warned before dipping her scrubbing brush in her bucket of water and going back to cleaning her step. 'A lot of folk don't hold with them policemen.'

'Grace couldn't tell me where this David Harper lives, though,' Kitty told the constable. 'She seemed afraid. I think she owes him money. She kept talking about being in debt.'

'It wouldn't surprise me,' he said. 'He's probably lent her money and now wants it back with interest. It's a common enough ploy. It gives him power over her so that he can use her.'

'I feel so sorry for her,' Kitty told him. 'I'd hate to see her taken before the magistrate. I know what she did was wrong, but I don't think she had any choice.'

'The best thing for her would be to see this man locked up. You need to convince her of that,' the constable told her. 'He'll not let her off the hook; you need to make her understand that. The sooner she tells you everything she knows, the better it will be for her.'

Kitty longed to ask Constable Westwell if she could reassure the woman that she wouldn't get into any trouble if she helped them, but she didn't think that it was in his power to make such a promise. She wasn't exactly sure how things worked, but she knew that Constable Westwell had other men who were senior to him. He'd complained earlier about the superintendent changing his shifts, and Kitty thought it might be the superintendent who would decide whether or not Grace was brought to trial. Part of her wished that she'd never got involved at all. If she could turn back time, she would leave that bag of shillings where she'd first seen it and walk away. Although that wouldn't have stopped Grace going into Agnes's shop and then the post office to try to exchange a coin for real money. And if Agnes had been found with a counterfeit, *she* might have been the one answering to the magistrate. It was all very complex.

'That was a heartfelt sigh,' observed Constable Westwell.

'I'm sorry,' she apologized. 'It wasn't aimed at you. I was just thinking about how many people are affected by this coining.'

'I know,' the constable agreed, looking bereft, and Kitty knew he was thinking of his wife. She reached out and put a hand on his in sympathy.

'I will help you,' she promised. 'But we must try to protect Grace if we can – she doesn't deserve to go to prison over this. And I don't know what will become of her sister and her mother if she's sent away.'

'I'll try to make some discreet enquiries about David Harper,' he promised. 'Maybe we can find out more about him elsewhere now that we have his name. If we can find where he's making these coins then maybe we won't need to mention Grace at all.'

Kitty was thankful that he understood her dilemma. He was a good man, she thought as she watched him tuck into the pies and the jug of gravy that he'd brought.

After he'd gone, saying that he must be early to bed for his shift the next morning, and Peter and Timothy had gone up to their bed, Kitty stood and dried the pots as Agnes put them to drain on the wooden board beside the sink.

'Constable Westwell is becoming quite a regular visitor,' her daughter observed.

'He's keen to catch the coiners.'

'I know he is. But do you think that's the only reason he keeps coming round?'

'Why else would he come?' Kitty bristled, suspecting her daughter was going to say the same thing that Aileen had.

'Perhaps he's lonely,' Agnes replied. 'It can't be much fun living in that police house without even a chair or a fireside to call your own.'

'Perhaps,' Kitty echoed. What Agnes said was true. The unmarried constables had all their needs provided for, but it wasn't the same as having a proper home. She supposed it was all right for the younger ones, but for Constable Westwell, who had once had a wife and a house to live in, it must be difficult. 'He must miss his wife,' she said.

'Maybe he's looking for another one,' Agnes said as she wrung out the dishcloth and draped it over the edge of the sink to dry.

Kitty laughed. 'He'll not find one here,' she joked.

'Are you sure?'

'What nonsense you're talking,' Kitty told her daughter, turning away so that Agnes wouldn't see her face.

'Would you ever think of marrying again?' Agnes asked.

'Of course not!' Kitty sat down on the chair by the fire. It still held a vestige of the warmth of the constable's body and this perturbed her more than she expected. 'How can I?' she went on. 'What if your father were to come back?'

'I don't think he will. I thought you'd accepted that.'

'I can't be certain,' Kitty told her daughter. 'Some nights I dream of him,' she confessed. 'And he's so real. It's like he's here, living with us, and we're a family again.'

'But it isn't real,' Agnes said gently. 'And I wouldn't mind,' she added. 'I wouldn't be upset if you were to marry again. You mustn't be lonely for my sake or the others'. We all loved Da. We'll never forget him. But I worry about you being on your own, especially in the future when we're not living here with you.'

'I hope that's not why you turned down Patrick Ryan,'

Kitty told her sharply. 'Good Catholic boys are few and far between in this town. It's not like it was back home.'

'Of course not. But I will marry someone eventually,' Agnes replied. 'And Timothy will meet a lass and set up a home with her. Maria will grow up. And Peter too. What will become of you then?'

Kitty shook her head. It was a thought that often worried her, although she'd never said anything. She hadn't realized that her daughter had thought about it too.

'You don't need to worry about me,' she told Agnes.

'But I do. And I don't want you to lose a chance of happiness for yourself.'

'Constable Westwell is only interested in catching the coiners,' Kitty replied firmly. 'As soon as he's done that, we'll not see him any more.'

'I wouldn't be so sure,' Agnes told her. 'He always looks so pleased to see you, and when you're putting the pots on the table he never takes his eyes off you. He watches you – and he has this look in his eyes. He likes you.'

'Get yourself off to bed and stop your silly talk!' said Kitty, more harshly than she intended.

Agnes said nothing more, but seemed satisfied that she'd spoken up. The trouble was, Kitty had to admit to herself as she changed into a nightgown and unpinned her long hair, that Agnes was perceptive and she often saw the truth in things. Whether she was right this time, Kitty didn't know, but she lay awake for a long time thinking about what her daughter had said. She wondered if she ought to discourage the constable from coming more often than was necessary. She knew that, as a single woman, she had to be careful to guard her reputation. It didn't take much for gossip to take hold and the last thing she needed was more of her neighbours speculating on why the police constable was making so many visits to her door.

26

Kitty had managed to keep back one of the pies. She'd slipped it into the oven when she thought no one was looking and now she put it in her basket and covered it with a clean cloth.

'I won't be long,' she told Maria and Peter. 'I just have to go out on a quick errand.'

She walked briskly to Moore Street, hoping that Grace would let her in. If she wouldn't then Kitty thought that she would leave the pie on the doorstep. She hoped that it might be seen as a peace offering and convince Grace that she did have her welfare at heart.

All seemed quiet after she'd knocked on the door of number six and Kitty wondered if anyone was at home. Then she saw the flimsy curtain at the window move and she called out.

'Grace? It's only me. Kitty Cavanah.'

A moment later the door was inched open and Kitty stared in horror at Grace's bruised and battered face. One eye was so swollen that it was almost closed. There was a gash on Grace's temple and her top lip was split. She didn't say anything but moved aside and motioned Kitty to go in.

'What happened?' asked Kitty, fearing the worst. She found she was trembling as she recalled the threatening voice of the man she assumed was David Harper in her own ear. 'Who did this? Was it the coiner?'

Grace nodded miserably. 'I bumped into him outside the Spread Eagle,' she whispered. It seemed painful for her to speak. 'He took me in and offered to buy me a drink and I told him what I told you – that I wasn't going to help him pass the shillings any more. He told me in that case I must pay him the money I owed him, and when I said I couldn't, he started to get nasty.'

'He hit you?' asked Kitty, not able to take her gaze off Grace's poor face.

She shook her head. 'He followed me out. He grabbed me from behind.' Kitty knew exactly how that felt. 'I tried to fight him off and as we struggled I banged my face against a wall. Or maybe he pushed me, I'm not certain. I'm so frightened.'

'Then help us bring him to justice,' Kitty urged.

'I'm afraid he'll kill me if I try,' Grace told her. 'He threatened me. He said he knows where I live, and I'm scared for Nancy and my mother more than for myself.'

Kitty looked at the old woman in the chair. She was awake today and watching them, but her eyes seemed blank as if she didn't understand what she was seeing. Nancy was subdued too. She seemed sleepy, and Kitty followed Grace's guilty look towards the bottle on the windowsill.

'It's her medicine,' she said. 'It calms her down. I get it from the dispensary. I don't like to use it too often, but it keeps her quiet when I have to go to do my work.'

Grace looked defeated and Kitty stepped forward to hug her, but she pulled away.

'Don't touch me,' she said. 'Everything hurts.'

'I've brought some food,' Kitty told her, reaching down to the basket that she'd put on the floor. 'It isn't much,' she added as she took out the pie and offered it to Grace, who didn't refuse it.

'Thank you,' she said. 'I'll share it between my mother and Nancy. I don't think I can eat anything, my mouth's that sore.'

'Perhaps you should go to the dispensary yourself,' Kitty suggested. 'Dr Skaife came out to see me when I was hurt and he was quite kind.'

'I can't afford it,' Grace said with a shrug. 'I work so I have to pay and it costs me sixpence for Nancy's bottle.'

Kitty took out her purse to see if she could spare anything herself, but Grace was already shaking her head.

'I'm in enough debt already.'

'I'll not press you to pay me back,' Kitty told her, holding out a coin, but Grace refused to take it.

'I'll heal in a day or two,' she said. 'It's probably not as bad as it looks.'

'How did you come to owe money to this David Harper?' Kitty asked her, reluctantly dropping the sixpence back into her purse. She wondered if she should go to the chemist herself and buy something to help Grace. She might accept medicine if it was already paid for.

'I was short,' she admitted, pulling a couple of boxes from the side of the room for them to sit down. 'I had a job in the mill and we were managing all right because Mam looked after Nancy whilst I was out. But that was before she worsened. I didn't realize at first how bad she was getting. Nancy used to be so hungry when I came home, but I thought it was just greed until I realized that Mam was forgetting to give her any dinner. I used to try to come home in my break, but I worked at Eanam Mill and it's on the other side of town, and once or twice I was late back and lost an afternoon's work and wages because of it. I explained my circumstances to the overlooker, but he didn't have much compassion, and in the end I had to sell some of our furnishings to make ends meet.'

'Is that when you got involved with David Harper?' Kitty asked.

'Yes. I met him outside the pawnshop on Shorrock Fold. He asked what I'd been selling and I told him it was a tea set and teapot. He asked what I'd got for it and when I told him a shilling, he said he would have given me two. He said that the pawnbroker was a thief to give me so little and that if I was in need of money in the future, I should see him and he'd deal fairly. I asked if he had a shop and he said no, because the cost of the rent and such was too much. He said he preferred to deal directly with his customers but that if I needed to find him he was usually in the Spread Eagle on Penny Street around dinner time.

'He seemed so kind,' Grace said, tears brimming in her eyes. 'I explained about my mam and our Nancy and he seemed to have nothing but sympathy, and he said he felt so sorry for me but not to worry, he would see me right. So the next time I was desperate I went to the Spread Eagle, and sure enough, there he was, sitting with a pint of ale in front of him, looking for all the world like a respectable gentleman. He even remembered me. Recalled my name and everything, and he bought me a half-pint of beer and let me tell him my sorry tale, that I'd been let go at the mill and that I had nothing coming in and that I didn't dare go to the parish in case they put Mam and Nancy in the workhouse.'

Grace pulled a rag from her sleeve and blew her nose. 'I'm sorry,' she said.

'So he loaned you money?' asked Kitty.

Grace nodded. 'I was so thankful at first. I promised I'd pay him back as soon as I had work again and he told me not to worry about it, that he could wait and that he'd not see me and my family starve. He was so kind,' she repeated. 'I would never have believed how much someone could change.'

'How much did you borrow?' Kitty asked.

'Just a shilling or two at first. It didn't seem much, but when I got work as a char and I asked him what I owed, he told me it was nearly two pounds – and I couldn't understand why, because I knew he hadn't given me anything like that much. Then he explained it was interest, and he laughed when I said I'd never agreed to that and said surely I wasn't so foolish as to think I could borrow for nowt.'

'What do you owe him now?'

Grace wiped her eyes on the heels of her hands. 'Five pounds,' she admitted in a whisper. 'I don't want Mam to know. I don't think she'd understand, but some days she seems more aware than others. I can't pay it,' she told Kitty. 'I think he knew that right from the start. I think he built up the debt deliberately so he could have a hold over me, because when I was crying and pleading with him to give me more time to pay, he said that he would write it all off if I helped him with some little jobs.'

'And that's how you became involved with the counterfeit coins,' said Kitty.

'I've been so stupid,' Grace said.

'No! No, you haven't.' Kitty put a hand on her arm and she flinched. 'Don't blame yourself,' she told Grace. 'You did what you had to do for the sake of your family. It wasn't stupid.'

'But I don't know what to do now,' Grace admitted as she twisted the rag between her fingers. 'I can't risk getting arrested because they'll send me away to prison for a long time, or even to New South Wales. And who'll care for Nancy and Mam then?'

'But if you help to get David Harper arrested, you'll not need to pay him a penny,' Kitty reasoned with her. 'And the magistrate might look kindly on you if you'd helped to bring him to justice.'

'I couldn't go before the magistrate and admit my own guilt,' Grace said. 'It would be too risky.'

'Could you just help us to find out where he lives?' asked Kitty. 'We can leave the rest to Constable Westwell.'

Grace looked sad. 'I don't know where he lives,' she said. 'I always met him at the Spread Eagle.'

27

After Sidney had finished his shift, he peeled off the armband that showed he was on duty and stuffed it into his pocket. Then he walked to the Spread Eagle. He was hungry and thirsty, and although there would be a meal at the police house, it was the last place he wanted to go, with Sergeant Watkins watching his every move and Constable Shaw determined to make his life difficult.

He opened the door of the pub and was met with the familiar smell of ale and smoke and hot food. It made him feel homesick for the house he'd shared with Susan in Manchester, where they'd converted the front parlour into a cosy place to serve beer and good, honest home cooking. It had been successful, too, until those coiners had begun to use it for their meetings. Sidney felt himself filled with hatred for the men who had ruined his life and he was gloomy as he ordered a pint of beer and a potato pie.

Billy Yates seemed to sense his mood and served him in silence before he cleared his throat.

'That chap you were asking after was in again yesterday, and the woman I told you about was with him. They looked as if they were having a disagreement,' he told Sidney. 'I was keeping an eye out because I didn't want any bother, but then she left and he went after her.' He hesitated. 'I couldn't follow them. I had too many customers, but I was a bit concerned about the woman's safety. He had a nasty look about him, like he was out for trouble.'

The news made Sidney feel even more miserable. He hated to think of anyone else getting hurt — especially a woman — because he hadn't simply arrested the man over his attack on Kitty Cavanah.

'There was talk of a fight,' the landlord went on, 'although I saw nowt myself. But I thought you'd like to know.'

'Thanks,' Sidney replied and Billy moved on to pull his next pint. Sidney took a long drink, but his appetite had suddenly deserted him. He was beginning to doubt that he was doing the right thing.

His misgivings were proved correct when he went round to Mary Ellen Street later that afternoon.

'I'm sorry. I haven't brought anything,' he apologized to Kitty, realizing that he'd walked through the market so lost in thought that he'd forgotten to stop at any of the stalls.

'I don't expect you to bring food every time you visit,' she reassured him. 'And if you have anything to spare then Grace deserves it more than me.' She went on to tell him about her visit and Sidney was horrified as she described Grace's injuries. 'But she says she doesn't know where David Harper lives. And I think she'd tell me if she did. So it's not that helpful,' she said as she added the carrots and potatoes she'd prepared to the bubbling cauldron on her hearth.

Sidney supposed it would have been too easy for the woman to give them an address and for him to organize a police raid that would catch the coiners in the act. He felt himself frowning as he wondered what to do next and whether he should pursue these men or simply arrest David Harper and leave the rest to the magistrate. He knew it was what he was expected to do as a constable, and it would mean that both Grace and Kitty would be safe from the man – for the meantime, at least. But it wasn't the solution he wanted. He wanted to bring all the coiners to justice and have them sent away for good.

Kitty poured a cup of tea and put it down on the table in front of Constable Westwell. She wished that she'd been able to give him an address. It would have helped bring the matter to a close and prevented both her and Grace from living in fear of another attack.

'Someone must know where he lives,' she said.

'No one who's willing to help us,' he replied gloomily.

'I'm worried about Grace,' she told him. 'She's very frightened, and Harper isn't going to leave her alone. Might it not be for the best if you arrest him?'

She'd been worrying about it ever since she came home. Grace had locked the door as she'd left. She'd waited to hear the key turn in the lock, but she doubted that the flimsy door would keep her friend safe from the coiner. And unless she could find the five pounds she owed him, Kitty suspected that Grace would be left with no choice but to agree to pass the counterfeit shillings again, which would put her in even more danger.

Constable Westwell took a drink of his tea and put the cup down thoughtfully. 'I've been wondering the same myself,' he admitted. 'Though I hate to think of him getting away with the coining. He must be making them somewhere. I know I can't follow him, but maybe we can find someone who wouldn't look so conspicuous.'

Kitty heard the outer door open and Timothy came in wearing his postboy's uniform. He pulled off his cap when he saw the constable and looked at Kitty to reassure himself that all was well.

'Constable Westwell has just called to talk about his investigation,' she said, hoping that the sight of the policeman with his feet under her table wasn't going to make her son suspicious about the real reason for his frequent visits. Kitty had been thinking about what Agnes had said and she'd begun to realize that the constable was coming around more often than could be explained away by his job. And despite her best intentions, she hadn't discouraged him. She was beginning to enjoy having his company. It had felt good to have a man in the house. It made her feel safer, too.

'Timothy wouldn't draw attention on the street,' remarked the constable thoughtfully.

'No!' Kitty answered sharply.

'Do you think Harper knows that he's your son?' continued the constable.

'I don't want him involved,' Kitty told him firmly.

'Involved in what? What are you talking about?' asked Timothy curiously as he unbuttoned his jacket.

'The constable is trying to discover where the coiner lives and where he's making the coins.'

'I can't follow him myself,' explained Constable Westwell. 'I'd stick out like a sore thumb in this uniform.'

'Do you want me to follow him?' asked Timothy. Kitty saw that the idea excited him and she was quick to make it clear that no such thing was going to happen.

'He's a dangerous man. I won't let you do it,' she told her son.

Timothy looked disappointed. 'No one takes any notice of me,' he said. 'And I might even know where he lives already. I knew where Grace lived,' he reminded his mother. 'What does he look like?' he asked the constable.

'He wears a patterned waistcoat. Not new, but it looks quality. Fustian britches. Leather boots, fairly worn. He's smaller than me but taller than your mother. Dark hair. Wears it long, over his collar. Looks none too clean.'

'He's a local man,' Kitty said. 'And he has bad breath,' she added, remembering his face so close to hers. 'Not that you'll ever be so close to him to smell it.'

'I don't think I know him,' Timothy said.

'I doubt he's the sort who receives letters,' Kitty said.

'I could point him out to you,' suggested Constable Westwell.

'I'll not let him do it!' Kitty repeated. She was determined not to involve Timothy, but her son had his own idea.

'If I know what he looks like I could keep an eye out for him. Not follow him as such,' he said to Kitty in an attempt to pacify her. 'But if I happened to see him turning into a street or court, I could let you know.'

Kitty saw that there was little she could do short of keeping Timothy home from his job.

'Well, as long as you don't actually follow him, I suppose there's no harm in just watching out for him,' she conceded.

'It'll be like being a police constable myself,' Timothy said, and Kitty saw that the idea pleased him. 'I'd like that,' he went on and his mother sighed. The future she'd envisaged for him at the post office faded as she saw that he craved more excitement than delivering letters.

28

Timothy rose eagerly the next morning. His mother looked surprised when he clattered down the stairs before Agnes had been sent up to pull him from his bed. She said nothing as she set down a bowl of oatmeal in front of him, but Timothy knew that she didn't want him to be involved with the search for the coiners.

His mother sometimes forgot that he was almost a man now. She often treated him as if he were still a child, like Peter. But he would be sixteen next birthday. He had a job and brought home his wages on a Friday evening and put them on the table to help pay for food and fuel. He felt proud to be contributing to the household, but he also felt that his mother should give him a little more freedom. True, he went to his class on a Sunday afternoon and the teachers there praised the progress he had made in reading and writing and arithmetic. And he'd had a lot of catching up to do because he'd had no education at all until he began work for Mr and Mrs Sharples at the post office. But the rest of his free time was spent going to church or fetching and carrying water and slops and helping look after the younger children.

Mind you, he supposed he was luckier than some that were stuck inside a mill all day, amidst the noise and the fluff. He loved his job and the freedom it gave him to walk around the town with the letters in his satchel, knocking on doors or walking into the town's offices without the need for an invitation. Most people knew him now and greeted him by name. There were even a couple of places where he could be pretty sure he would be offered a cup of tea and sometimes a slice of cake if he was lucky. He knew he would always be invited in for cake if he had to deliver to Mr and Mrs Anderton on King Street – and their maid Dorothy made the most delicious sponges with plenty of jam in the middle. His mouth watered at the thought, although his tastebuds were disappointed by another spoonful of porridge.

When he was finished he put his bowl in the sink and took his hat from the peg by the door.

'Are you going so soon?' asked his mother.

'I mustn't be late,' he told her. He swung out of the door into the warmth of the early morning. It looked like being another hot day, he thought as he walked towards King Street, all the while keeping a lookout for the man in the patterned waistcoat. Harper, the constable had said his name was. It wasn't a name he'd seen on any letters, and he had a good memory for them. He knew the regular ones, and most mornings he had them sorted out in no time so that he could plan a route around the town without having to double back on himself. Mr Sharples had told him that he had a very efficient system and he wished he'd done the same when he was delivering the letters himself. It had made him feel good.

The door of the post office was still locked when he arrived, and he had to knock. Even his sister Agnes's shop was still locked up. It looked strange because she was usually out before him, but he'd been so restless today. He'd wanted to get started because he felt that he could be the one to find this man Harper. And it would make such a difference when he was locked up and taken away. His mother had looked miserable ever since her encounter with him. She hadn't talked about what had happened, but Timothy wasn't stupid and he knew she was afraid of the man. It made him angry. His father was no longer here to protect her and so it fell to him to do his best to keep her safe, and even though she'd pleaded with him not to get involved, he wasn't going to stand by and see her attacked again if there was anything he could do to prevent it.

He heard the rattle of the key in the lock and Mrs Sharples opened the door.

'Timothy!' She looked surprised. 'You're early today!'

He nodded briefly and went to the shelf behind the counter to collect the letters that were to be put on the early morning train. He knew that he had plenty of time – unlike the mornings when he had to run all the way to the railway station for fear of seeing the engine puffing and steaming out without the post.

He packed the letters and two small packages into his satchel and slung it over his shoulder as he went out again. There would be some letters for delivery left at the station to be collected, and once he had these he would add them to the local post and begin his round. It surprised him sometimes where the letters came from. There were always some from Manchester and London and other cities, but he was always excited when he picked up a letter that had come over the sea from America or New South Wales. Sometimes he just held them and tried to imagine all the places they'd been – not just the trains and the ships and the carts, but homes that he could scarcely imagine that people had built for themselves in places like Wisconsin where Mrs Anderton's father lived. Or from the penal colonies in New South Wales – letters sent by men who would most probably never see their homes again. It was where they'd send Harper, if he could find him. And Timothy was determined to find him.

He gave the bundles of letters to the stationmaster. One for the train to London. One for Preston. One for Manchester and one that was to be sent in the other direction to a place in Scotland. He'd had to ask Mr Sharples about that. He'd never heard of Edinburgh before and Mr Sharples had chuckled at his attempts to say the name and had taught him to pronounce it correctly. He'd try to catch out the other boys with it when he went to the school on Sunday.

He heard the whistle of the train as it approached and braced himself for the noise as it came in under the glass verandah that covered the platforms. As the engine squealed to a stop, the driver released a great rush of steam from the chimney, almost making Timothy want to cover his ears at the din of it. Then the train seemed to settle and breathe more easily as the doors were flung open and businessmen in tall hats came rushing down the platform, eager to tend to their business. Others stepped up into the carriages, seeking a seat, and Timothy saw Mr

Anderton in the distance, boarding the train along with some others.

The porters hurried forward to the doors of the goods truck and began to unload churns of milk, boxes and baskets of produce, a small flock of reluctant sheep for the market and a couple of trunks with labels on that seemed to belong to no one but were carried off to a room marked with the sign 'left luggage'. He moved forward as he saw the sack of post handed down. It was passed directly to him and he grasped hold of the rope that tied it closed and walked back down the slope to the square outside and up past the parish church to the post office.

It was when he was passing the Sun that he saw him. He was sure it was Harper. He looked just as the constable had said. The man paused for a moment and glanced up and down the street as if to check he was in no danger of being followed, then he struck out in the direction of Blakeley Moor as if he had urgent business there.

Timothy knew he should go back to his work, but the temptation was too great and he began to walk in the same direction as Harper, keeping his distance but being sure not to let him out of his sight.

At the end of North Gate, Harper took a path which led out beyond the town on to the moors. Timothy knew that it would be more difficult to follow him there as he would be more obvious, but he decided to go anyway and pretend that he was on his way to deliver to one of the outlying farms.

Luckily, Harper never glanced back. He walked with

a confident swagger, as if no one could touch him, and when he took a sharp right off Nab Lane on to a track that led down to a row of handloom weavers' cottages known as Old Dadds, Timothy ducked down behind a patch of yellow gorse. This must be where the coiner lived, he thought. He could tell Constable Westwell where to find him!

29

Sidney pulled the metal trunk that held his belongings out from under his bed. He hadn't opened it since he'd arrived at the police house. The contents held too many painful memories.

When he'd packed up his home there had been so many things that he hadn't been able to part with. Not just his clothing and his prayer book and bible, but things that had belonged to Susan. He hadn't kept her clothes, even though it had almost broken him to part with them, but he had kept her jewellery – her wedding ring, a pair of gold earrings and a necklace that he had bought for her one Christmas in Manchester. He'd also kept a pair of her summer gloves, a lace handkerchief and a bottle of the cologne that she used to dab behind her ears on Sundays and holidays. He twisted the top off it now and sniffed the contents. He had to take a breath to steady himself. He wiped his nose on the back of his hand, then recalled how she would tell him off for doing it and insist on him keeping a pocket handkerchief. He pulled one out and mopped at his face, thankful that he'd waited until there was no one else around. It wouldn't have done for a colleague to walk in and find him weeping over his dead wife's belongings.

Sidney stoppered the bottle and put it back into the

trunk. What he wanted was his clothes – his ordinary clothes. Thankful that it was summer and that he didn't need much, he got out a cotton checked shirt and his moleskin trousers. He'd need his shoes too, he realized. Police boots would be a giveaway. He added a neckerchief and a waistcoat and put the items on the bed before closing and locking the trunk again and pushing it away.

He had intended to get changed here, but it struck him that he couldn't. It would be difficult for him to stroll out of the police station wearing anything but his uniform.

He pondered on the alternatives. He needed somewhere where he could safely leave his uniform. There was really only one place that he could go.

Sidney folded up the clothing as tightly as he could and looked about for something to carry it in. There was nothing in the dormitory. It had to be kept clean and tidy with nothing unnecessary on show, but he knew that there were some sheets of brown paper in the kitchen, so he ran down the stairs to fetch one and a length of string. If he was challenged, he would say that the parcel was some old shirts he was taking to the parish office to help clothe the poor and destitute.

With the package tucked under his arm, he went down the steps and out of the front door. Constable Milne was on duty at the front desk and Sergeant Watkins was in his office with the door ajar, but neither paid him any attention. Even so, it wasn't until he'd turned the corner and was making his way up King Street that Sidney allowed himself a sigh of relief.

When Mrs Cavanah came to the door of her house she looked at his parcel suspiciously, and Sidney wondered if she thought he'd brought her another gift.

'I've come to ask a favour,' he explained after she'd invited him inside. 'I need somewhere to change my clothes.'

'What? Change out of your uniform? I thought it wasn't allowed?'

'Hence my need to beg the favour,' he explained.

'Are you going after the coiners?' she asked.

'I'm only going to look for the place I think Harper might live. I've had some information,' he added.

'You'd best go upstairs, then,' she said, opening a door that concealed the steep flight of steps.

He climbed them and found himself in a bedroom. There were two beds crowded into it, leaving hardly any room for him to stand and pull off his boots and trousers – he didn't want to sit on the edge of a bed. It seemed too intimate. He heard the floorboards creaking beneath his feet as he shifted his weight and got out of the blue serge and into his moleskin. The comfort of them was a relief on such a hot afternoon. Once changed, he folded his uniform and seeing that there was nowhere else to leave it, he put it on one of the beds and tucked his boots under as best he could. He felt uneasy being in Mrs Cavanah's private space – not that she had much privacy. All the family slept in this room. The upstairs of the cottage was just as cramped as the downstairs.

'Are you going alone?' she asked when he went back down. She sounded concerned and he was quick to allay her fears.

'He'll not recognize me,' he said.

'Who told you where to find him?' she asked.

Sidney hesitated. He was unsure whether to reveal Timothy's part in it, but he decided that it was best to be honest. He respected Mrs Cavanah and he didn't want there to be any secrets between them. He needed her to trust him.

'Timothy saw him,' he said, registering the look of dismay that flickered across her face. 'It was whilst he was out on his rounds,' he added. 'He saw Harper going up Nab Lane in the direction of Old Dadds. There's a small hamlet of handloom weavers' cottages up there. I think it must be where he lives. But I need to be sure.'

'What will you do if you find him?' she asked.

'I'll not approach him. Not on my own. Once I'm sure he does live there, then I'll speak to my sergeant about arranging a raid so we can try to catch him with the coining equipment, or even making the coins if we're lucky.'

Mrs Cavanah nodded and he wished that his words could be as reassuring to himself as they were to her. The truth was that he wasn't sure how the sergeant would respond when he told him what he wanted to do. But surely the man couldn't turn a blind eye to such a serious crime? He must agree to let him take some colleagues and arrest the man.

Sidney left Mary Ellen Street, promising that he would return before long to change back into his uniform. Mrs Cavanah didn't linger at the door and he had the impression that she was worried about his frequent visits to her house. He hoped he wasn't making things difficult for her. He knew that people talked and that they judged as well, and the last thing he wanted was to damage her reputation. Yet the thought of not coming any more saddened him. He enjoyed her company.

He strode along with a feeling of freedom that he hadn't experienced for a long time. It was good to be rid of the cumbersome uniform and the clumsy boots. Good to be free from the hostile glances that were all too often cast his way as well. He'd forgotten what it was like to be an ordinary man, walking the sun-baked streets on a hot afternoon. Life seemed to go more slowly on hot days and the women didn't have their heads bent and their shawls pulled up high under their chins. They strolled with baskets over their arms and took more time to look around them. He exchanged a brief smile with one or two people as they passed him and it lifted his spirits. He'd always enjoyed company. It was one of the reasons he'd liked running the beerhouse so much, and it struck him how lonely and isolated he'd become since joining the police force.

Had it been a bad idea? he wondered as he walked. It had seemed the right thing to do at the time, and even now he didn't want to give up the opportunity of bringing these coiners to justice. He was determined to have vengeance for Susan. And not just Susan. He wanted to see Harper summarily punished for what he'd done to Kitty Cavanah and Grace Dewhurst.

He reached the edge of the town and paused to look across the barren wasteland that they called Blakeley Moor. It was where the cattle fairs were held. Where the fairground set up when it came to the town on Easter Monday, and where there had been horse racing and cock fights until such sports had been either moved or banned. Beyond it was mostly open countryside, though there wasn't much of it to be made out today, obscured as it was by the low-lying smog that lingered in the valley.

Sidney was so used to the smoke of the mills and the filth on the streets that he rarely thought about the alternative. Yet he knew that if he walked on for a mile or so, the air would clear and the sun would beat down even more intensely. The noise would dissipate and it would be like stepping back in time to the days before the cotton came, when men and women lived in small villages and hamlets, farming, spinning and weaving wool from their sheep and growing their own food rather than buying it from shops or eating in public houses.

Life had once been like that in Old Dadds. A few of the older generation still lived in such places, eking out a poor living, but most of the young people had moved into the towns to toil in the mills. They had expected to be better off, but from what Sidney had seen of life in Blackburn and Manchester, he doubted that it was the improvement they had anticipated.

He walked on, pondering that there was no way back to life as it had been for most people. Their lives were ruled by the mill owners now, and their day began with the knocker-up tapping on their window with her pole rather than the crowing of the cock in the farmyard. Part of him could understand the temptation of finding an easier way to make a living, but he couldn't condone what amounted to stealing from those who were worse off than you. Every person who had a counterfeit coin put in their hand had been robbed of the coin's real worth, and it had to stop.

There was smoke rising from one of the cottages in the hamlet. It wasn't so remarkable. Even in a heatwave the fire had to burn to bake bread and cook food. But a fire was also necessary to heat and melt the metal of stolen spoons so that they could be moulded into counterfeits.

Sidney walked slowly; the sun was beating down and he wished that he'd brought a hat to shield his head. There was no one else about and as the sounds of the town receded behind him he could hear a skylark singing in the sky, keeping watch over her nest. He must take care where he put his feet, he thought. The eggs were well camouflaged and he would hate to step on them.

He listened hard for other sounds that might give the counterfeiters away, but he heard none and the doors of the cottages seemed closed and the places deserted. If it hadn't been for the smoke he would never have believed that the place was inhabited. Sidney knew that he would draw suspicion on himself if he lingered, so he walked on, deciding to go back by a circular route that would take him up on to the turnpike road that led to Preston.

It was only when he was past the cottages that he heard a sound and looked back. One of the cottage doors was open and a man was watching him. Although he was at a distance, Sidney was sure that it was David Harper. It wasn't much to go on, but he hoped it was enough to persuade the sergeant to allow a raid on the property.

30

Sergeant Watkins stared at Sidney with incredulity. 'A raid?' he repeated.

'Yes, sir,' replied Sidney. 'If we can take him by surprise and catch him in the act, then there will be more than enough evidence to bring him before the magistrate.'

'I don't know,' the sergeant said. 'Our job is to prevent crime. I'm not sure we should be going out looking for it.'

'I'm sure the townsfolk would be glad to be rid of the man. These coins are causing such a problem for every shopkeeper in the town. It might help people to view us more sympathetically.'

The sergeant still looked doubtful, but Sidney could see that he might be persuaded.

'I would have to ask for volunteers,' he said. 'I wouldn't order any constables to take part.'

'Then may I have your permission to speak to one or two of the men?' asked Sidney. He knew it would be a struggle and that the likes of Constable Shaw would never agree to take part, but he hoped that some of the others might be more amenable – if only to add some excitement to their day. If there was one thing he had discovered about being a police constable, it was that it was tedious, walking the same streets over and over again, looking for crimes that he knew were there but were cunningly hidden from his eyes.

The sergeant seemed undecided, but when he appeared to nod and say that he would consider the matter, Sidney took it as permission to forge ahead with his plan. He went to the kitchen to see who was about. If he could persuade just two or three of the others to help him, then surely it would be enough? Having seen the cottages at Old Dadds, he doubted that there was a huge gang of coiners involved.

He was disappointed when he found Constable Shaw sitting at the table with a cup of tea. 'What did the sergeant want with thee?' asked Shaw, barely disguising his pleasure that Sidney might be in some more bother. 'I was told that tha were seen coming out of that Cavanah house again.'

Sidney lifted the teapot and was disappointed to find it contained only dregs.

'Who told you that?' he asked, trying to keep his tone steady but wondering if he had been seen and followed, and by whom. He'd thought that he'd been vigilant, and he was worried more for Kitty's reputation than his own.

'I have my spies,' replied Shaw with a nauseating grin. It was a pity he didn't use them to catch criminals rather than his fellow constables, mused Sidney, but he kept his opinion to himself.

'What's tha up to?' Shaw wanted to know.

'I'm following a line of enquiry regarding the counterfeiters who are flooding the town with their bogus coins,' Sidney told him. 'In fact, I'm determined to bring them to justice and I'm hoping there might be a promotion in it!'

As soon as the words were out, Sidney knew they were a mistake. The worst thing he could do was to antagonize Shaw and that's what he'd just done – especially by mentioning a promotion. The best he could probably hope for was to hold on to his job and not be dismissed.

Shaw laughed. Then he drained his cup and banged it down on the table. 'Wash that up,' he instructed. 'And remember that I'm watching thee.'

When he'd gone, Sidney ignored the cup. It could sit there until Judgement Day as far as he was concerned. He wasn't the man's lackey. And if Shaw had actually known that he'd been out without his uniform, he would surely have reported it. It was a serious offence. But the man had got wind of something, and he must remember to tread with the utmost caution.

In the end Constable Milne and Constable Bleasedale were persuaded to go with Sidney, and the sergeant reluctantly agreed to them being away from their beats for an hour or so the next morning.

'What we're going to be looking for is evidence of his trade,' Sidney explained to them in the police house kitchen. It was still very early. The sun had not long risen in a sky glorious with gold and crimson.

'Shepherd's warning,' Bleasedale had commented when he drew back the blind at the window.

'We'll be looking for things like a crucible that's been used to melt down metal,' explained Sidney. 'But most important of all we'll be looking for the dies that these coiners are using to make their counterfeit coins. Once we have those then the evidence will be incontrovertible. The magistrate will send them to Preston or up to Lancaster and we'll have rid the town of an undeniable menace.'

Milne and Bleasedale looked far from convinced. Sidney knew that they'd only agreed to go with him because it would make a change from their regular beats. He just hoped that they would play their part when the time came and not let Harper escape. He would never be able to face Kitty Cavanah if he had to tell her that the man had got away. Heaven knows, she'd been patient with him so far, although he knew she would have much preferred to see her attacker locked up long before now.

The morning was cooler than of late as they walked across town, their boots making far more noise than Sidney would have liked in the almost deserted streets. A knocker-up, doing his rounds to waken the mill workers, crossed the street when he saw them coming and a few of the nightwatchmen who were making their way home to their beds did the same, all watching them with distrust.

'We must be circumspect,' advised Sidney as they struck out across Blakeley Moor. 'Hopefully, Harper will still be abed, but we mustn't warn him of our approach. I think we should split up. I'll go up to knock on his door and you, Milne, stay at the end of the lane until I've gained admission then follow me in swiftly. And you, Bleasedale, station yourself around the back of the house in case he tries to make a run for it. Once Milne and myself are inside, then join us in case there's more men and we need help restraining them.'

'Who do you think you are, ordering us about?' grumbled Bleasedale.

'It's my investigation so I'm in charge,' Sidney told him, although he saw the man wasn't happy and he wasn't entirely sure of his cooperation. Still, it was his best chance and he knew that he should be grateful that Sergeant Watkins had agreed in the first place – even if he suspected that the sergeant was hoping he would make a fool of himself.

'I thought these cottages were deserted,' said Milne as they drew nearer to Old Dadds. 'There's no sign of life.'

'Wild goose chase,' Bleasedale said.

Sidney hoped they were wrong. There was no smoke from any of the chimneys, but it was early yet, and if Harper was still asleep they could surprise him before he had the chance to hide or destroy any of his equipment.

He sent a reluctant Bleasedale around the back of the row of buildings and left Milne chewing on a piece of grass and leaning on what had been the gatepost belonging to the farm. Alone, he quickened his pace, but tried to step softly as he came close to the doorway where he'd last seen David Harper.

He drew his truncheon from its pocket and used it to rap loudly on the door. 'David Harper!' he shouted. 'Open up in the name of the law!'

Moments later an upstairs casement window was thrust open and a tousled head peered out.

'Police!' bellowed Sidney. 'Open the door!'

The head retreated as quickly as it had appeared and Sidney heard raised voices inside. One was a woman's, but how many people there were he couldn't be certain. He banged on the door again, but it was clear it wasn't going to be opened to him willingly, and guessing that the occupants of the cottage were hurrying to hide any incriminating evidence, he decided that brute force was called for. He took a run at the door and barged into it with his shoulder. It shuddered on its hinges but stood fast.

'Mind out the way and let me have a try.' Sidney turned at the sound of Milne's voice. He hadn't heard him come up behind him. He stood aside, rubbing his sore shoulder, and watched as Milne raised a leg and kicked the door. Whether he'd done it before or whether it was good luck, Sidney couldn't tell, but he struck it on a weak spot and it splintered and broke. Grinning, Milne kicked it again and was able to reach inside to turn the key and lift the latch.

'Lucky they left it in the door,' he said as the battered wood swung open to reveal the residents in their nightclothes with various tools and implements clutched in their hands.

The woman threw a pan at his head, but Sidney ducked and it flew past him, narrowly missing Bleasedale who had followed them in, his bored face animated at the unexpected excitement.

Harper tried to make a run for it, but as the three police constables closed in on him, Sidney saw him throw an object across the room in an attempt to hide it. As Milne held him fast, Sidney retrieved the small, round die from under the table. When he examined it, he saw it was the reverse imprint of the face of a shilling.

'This is all the evidence I need to take you before the magistrate,' he announced.

'Where did you get that from?' demanded Harper, feigning a look of surprise and indignation. 'I've never seen that in my life before!'

31

'He's in the lock-up!' announced Constable Westwell before Kitty even had the chance to invite him inside. He took off his hat and beamed at her. 'He'll be up before the magistrate tomorrow morning and then he'll be on his way to Preston for trial and a sentence of transportation for certain.'

Kitty felt all the worry and tension of the past few weeks flow from her. Her shoulders relaxed and she smiled back at the constable. She was momentarily tempted to kiss him but managed to think better of it. Even a peck on the cheek as he stood on her doorstep would give the neighbours far too much to gossip about.

'Thank you,' she told him. 'I'm so relieved.'

'That's why I came straight round to tell you. We went up to Old Dadds early this morning and caught him still in bed. He didn't stand a chance!'

Constable Westwell was still grinning after Kitty had invited him inside and offered him a cup of tea.

'I shouldn't really. I'm supposed to be walking my beat,' he admitted, but he sat down and watched as she spooned tea into the pot and waited for the kettle to boil.

'Was he alone?' asked Kitty curiously.

'There was a woman there. His wife, I think. She made

a run for it when we got hold of him, but I didn't go after her.'

'She must be guilty as well. She must have known what he was doing.'

'Aye. She'll not get far, though. One of the other constables will probably soon find her. The main thing is we got David Harper.'

Kitty poured his tea and sliced some bread, offering butter and treacle. It meant she would have to go and buy more later, but Constable Westwell had been so generous, bringing pies for them to eat, that she was glad to return some hospitality.

He took a drink of his tea and sighed with pleasure. 'That's welcome,' he told her. 'It's been a busy morning.'

'Is it all right if I go to tell Grace?' asked Kitty. 'She's been just as frightened as me – and probably with more reason. She'll be relieved to know Harper can't bother her any more.'

'Aye. It would be better if you go,' he agreed. 'I doubt she'll open the door to me.'

After Constable Westwell had gone to walk his beat, Kitty tidied the pots and then walked up to Moore Street to visit Grace. She was sorry that she had no food to take for her today, but she hoped that what she had to tell her would make up for it.

She heard Nancy laughing and shouting before she knocked on the door and she had to knock twice to make herself heard. She realized it was a bad time to call, but she was keen to give Grace the good news.

'What is it?' asked Grace when she'd opened the door

just an inch. The swelling on her face had almost gone down, but the bruising appeared to have spread and was a rainbow of green and yellow and purple.

'I know it's not a good time,' Kitty told her. 'But I wanted to let you know that Constable Westwell has arrested David Harper. He'll be going before the magistrate on Monday. He can't harm you again and you won't have to pay him any money.'

Kitty expected to see relief on Grace's face, but the woman still seemed concerned at the news. 'Come in,' she said. 'Be quick! Don't let Nancy slip past you.'

Grace closed and locked the door behind them and put the key into her pocket. 'She's learned how to turn it in the lock,' Grace explained as she urged her sister to sit down. But Nancy was full of energy today and wanted to dance about the kitchen, throwing her arms wide and only just missing striking her mother in the face.

'I'm sorry. I'll give her something,' said Grace, reaching for the medicine bottle. Kitty saw it was almost empty. Grace poured some on to a spoon and managed to get it between her sister's lips. 'She'll quieten in a moment,' she said as she pushed the cork back into the bottle. 'There's a wind getting up and it always seems to overexcite her. I've no idea why.'

Kitty saw that Grace was struggling. Caring for her sister and her mother was hard for her on her own. Much harder even than bringing up children as a single mother had been for her, because although Nancy had the mind of a child, she was big and strong. If she was taken to the workhouse they would chain her up, and

Kitty admired Grace's determination not to allow that to happen.

'Constable Westwell and a couple of his colleagues went out to Old Dadds on the other side of Blakeley Moor early this morning,' Kitty told her. 'My son Timothy works as a postal delivery boy and he'd seen David Harper going that way. They found the die he's been using to strike the counterfeits, so there's evidence to see him sent away.'

'Thank you for coming to tell me,' said Grace.

'It must be a weight off your mind,' Kitty persisted, still wondering why Grace didn't seem as relieved as she'd expected. 'I know I feel less worried. He'd threatened me as well, and I can barely believe it's safe to walk out without worrying that he's going to attack me again.'

'So you think I won't need to pay him what I owe?' asked Grace.

'I don't see that he can do much about it if he's in prison,' Kitty said. 'I wouldn't worry. I'm sure Constable Westwell will be able to explain it to you, but I think you can probably forget all about your debt.'

'And I won't have to go before the court myself?' Kitty could see that Grace was still anxious. 'They won't call me to give any testimony against him?'

'I hope that won't be necessary,' said Kitty in an attempt to reassure her. 'He was found with the counterfeiting equipment and that should be enough to convict him.'

'Thank goodness,' breathed Grace as she allowed herself to relax at last. 'I'm so grateful to you.'

'Well, it's Constable Westwell who deserves your thanks. He was determined to bring the man to justice.'

'Will you tell him I'm grateful?'

'I will,' Kitty promised.

Grace hugged her and Kitty held her close for a few moments. The woman was stick-thin and Kitty could feel all her bones.

'I'm sorry I couldn't bring any food today,' she said. 'I'm sure the parish would help you out if you asked. There's no shame in it. Just until you get back on your feet.'

'No!' Grace was adamant. 'I'll not risk it,' she said, reaching to stroke her sister's hair as Nancy sat calmly and rocked herself.

Kitty knew better than to press the matter, but she wondered if it was worth mentioning Grace's situation to Mr and Mrs Anderton. She knew she couldn't expect them to help everyone in the town who had fallen on hard times, but they'd helped her and they were kind, generous people – and they might know whether Grace's fears about the workhouse were justified.

She walked home via Church Street, calling first at her daughter's cheese shop. She waited until Agnes had finished serving a customer before she shared the news.

'They got him!' she said. 'They have him in the lock-up!'

Agnes came around the counter and hugged her. 'I'm so glad,' she said. 'I've hated seeing how worried you've been. I knew Constable Westwell was a good policeman. He is, isn't he?'

'He is,' agreed Kitty. She could see a knowing look in her daughter's eyes.

'And you like him, don't you?' Agnes pressed her.

'Yes. He is nice. But I think he did this mostly to avenge his late wife. From the way he talks, it's clear that he thought the world of her.'

'It doesn't stop him moving on, though,' Agnes argued. 'I think you should encourage him. You deserve to be happy after all the troubles we've had.'

'I don't know,' Kitty replied. 'I still think about your father.'

'I'm sure he would want you to find happiness again,' Agnes persisted.

Kitty smiled at her daughter's eager face. She wished she could find a suitable boy to marry and give up her infatuation with Jonas Marsden. She worried that it would end in Agnes being disappointed and, not for the first time, she wished that Peter was still here to help her guide their children.

Kitty left her daughter to her cheese selling and pushed open the door of the post office. She always worried about going in there because her relationship with Mrs Sharples was difficult – she felt the woman disapproved of her and considered her a poor relation – but there was no sign of her this morning and Mr Sharples was alone behind the counter.

'The police have arrested David Harper,' she told him.

'That is good news!' he replied.

'And Timothy had a hand in it,' she told him. 'I didn't want him to, but he followed the man home and discovered where he lived.'

'He's growing up,' John Sharples told her. 'And he has

a sensible head on his shoulders. Even Mrs Sharples was saying she's glad we took him on.'

'Really?' That was the second piece of good news Kitty had had that morning. It did look like things were improving for her and her family.

32

'Constable Westwell, you can assist Constable Bleasedale in taking Harper before the magistrate,' Sergeant Watkins told Sidney early on Monday. 'You may have to give evidence.' He'd been faint in his praise so far, but even he could not deny that a good job had been done and one serious crime removed from the streets of Blackburn. 'Don't lose him,' he added as Sidney went out of the door.

With his handcuffs in his hand, Sidney went down to the cellar where the prisoners were held in cells. Harper looked up when he saw him and gave a cocky grin. The man didn't seem to have accepted that his fate was sealed and still thought that he could weasel his way out of this trouble.

Harper stood up and buttoned his waistcoat. 'Who's the magistrate today?' he asked.

'Mr Thompson,' Sidney told him.

'Oh, him! He'll let me off. No question.'

'I wouldn't count on it,' Sidney replied as he secured the man's hands behind his back. He knew the evidence against him was overwhelming. 'If I was a betting man, I'd put a pound on you being on the coach to Preston prison before the end of the day.'

Harper laughed again. 'Or in the snug in the Sun. Or the bar in the Spread Eagle. That's where I'll be,' he predicted.

Sidney took no notice of the man's boasting. It was all a bluff. Surely he knew his final destination would be a convict ship to New South Wales? There could be no other outcome.

He settled his hat firmly on his head and he and Constable Bleasedale escorted the prisoner up from the cells and across King Street to the assembly rooms where the magistrates' court was held. Even with his hands secured behind his back, Harper walked with an arrogant gait, nodding his head and exchanging a greeting with one or two acquaintances along the way as if he were simply out for a morning stroll.

Sidney and Constable Bleasedale walked on either side of him, each holding on to an arm, although Harper showed no inclination to make a run for it. They hurried him up the stone steps outside the main door and into the hallway beyond with its mosaic tiled floor and lofty vaulted ceiling. The courtroom was at the far side and they settled their prisoner on one of the oak benches that served as a waiting room until an usher opened the tall doors and called Harper's name.

Sidney hustled him inside and into the dock. Mr Thompson was sitting up on a dais in an elaborately carved chair, his abundant whiskers almost quivering in anticipation.

'So, you're the coiner who's been causing us so much trouble!' he said, leaning forward with his hands braced on the carved arms of his chair.

'No, sir! Not me, sir!' replied Harper, as if hurt and affronted by the accusation.

Mr Thompson looked hesitant and glanced at Sidney. 'What's the evidence?' he asked.

Bleasedale indicated that Sidney should step forward to the witness stand to describe how they had raided Harper's cottage and discovered the die that he was using to prepare the counterfeit coins.

'It sounds cut and dried to me,' Mr Thompson told the prisoner. 'How do you plead?'

'Not guilty, sir. Not guilty at all, sir,' he insisted.

'Was this object found in your house?' he asked, picking up the die that had been placed on the table in front of him as evidence.

'So these constables say, sir. They came very early yesterday morning whilst my wife and I were still sleeping. They made such a terrible commotion and my wife was much upset by it all. She ran off, sir, in her nightclothes, and I don't rightly know whether she's safe or not. These constables refuse to offer me any assistance in that respect. One constable did have that object in his hand, sir, it's true. He said that he'd found it in my house and accused me of coining counterfeit shillings. But it doesn't belong to me. I've never seen it in my life before until he showed it to me yesterday. I think he must have brought it in with him.'

A look of doubt crossed the magistrate's face. Sidney felt a fury boiling up inside him. Harper should have been on the stage, he thought, such was his talent for play-acting. He stood in the dock, a picture of innocence, with tears brimming in his eyes at the supposed injustice of it all.

The magistrate turned to Constable Bleasedale and beckoned him forward. 'Were you present when this die was found?' he asked.

'I was, sir.'

'And where was it found?' asked the magistrate.

Sidney's hopes fell as Bleasedale hesitated.

'I didn't rightly see,' he admitted. 'It was Constable Westwell that found it. He said he found it on the floor.'

'Did you see it on the floor?'

'No, sir.'

'So is it possible it was brought into this man's house by your colleague?'

Sidney met Bleasedale's eyes briefly, willing him to back him up even if he hadn't witnessed him retrieve the die from under the table.

'I suppose so,' he mumbled, making Sidney want to shake him in frustration.

'So, in fact, the evidence against this man is very tenuous,' said the magistrate. 'It seems a very poor effort on the part of the police.'

'There was another officer,' Sidney interrupted, hoping that Andrew Milne might tell a better version of events.

'Is he here?' asked the magistrate.

'No, sir. He's walking his beat.'

The magistrate frowned, obviously unsure what to do, and turned his attention back to Harper who clearly saw he had an advantage.

'If it's a coiner you're after, it should be Elijah Ratcliffe you have here in the dock, not me,' he suddenly announced. 'He's the one who should be standing here by rights.'

'Do you know about this man Ratcliffe?' the magistrate asked Sidney.

'I believe he is also a coiner, sir. But the prisoner here is the man we found in possession of this particular die.'

'These constables only know how to walk the streets,' Harper told the magistrate. 'They don't see what goes on. It was easy for them to arrest me and make this false accusation against me. But you'll not stop the counterfeits in this town until you stop Ratcliffe. Believe me.'

'And where can this Ratcliffe be found?' asked Mr Thompson.

'Ah, well, that would be telling, wouldn't it, sir.'

'Then tell!' replied the magistrate, losing patience.

'Not with my hands tied like a common prisoner,' Harper said. 'I'm perfectly willing to help these gentlemen with their investigations, but not whilst I'm held accused of a crime I did not commit.'

Mr Thompson leaned back in his chair and studied Harper. Then he addressed Sidney.

'Did you catch him actually making false shillings?' he asked.

'No, sir,' Sidney admitted. 'But he was in possession of this die. That in itself is evidence enough to find him guilty, I think.'

The magistrate looked unconvinced. David Harper had planted a seed of doubt in his mind and Sidney realized that it was just his word against the coiner's.

'We need to get to the bottom of this,' the magistrate said as he stroked his whiskers thoughtfully. 'I'm determined to rid the town of this menace and if what this prisoner says is true, maybe we should heed his words. Perhaps you should go and find this man Ratcliffe.'

'I'm certain the accused has been producing counterfeit coins,' insisted Sidney, becoming increasingly concerned that the magistrate was going to be swayed by Harper's charm and not send him to be convicted after all.

'You need to bring me more evidence,' the magistrate told him. 'Has anyone witnessed him handling the false shillings?'

'Well . . .' Sidney hesitated. He knew that if Grace were here she could give damning evidence against him. But that would mean damning herself as well, and he'd promised Kitty that he wouldn't involve her.

Out of the corner of his eye, he could see Harper smirking now. He was tempted to plead with the magistrate not to let him go. How was he going to face Kitty if he had to admit that the man had been set free?

'At least allow us to keep the prisoner in custody until we can come back with the evidence you require,' he asked.

Mr Thompson considered the matter. 'Very well,' he said at last. 'I'll let you keep him for another twenty-four hours. But if all you can present me with is a die of dubious ownership then I'll have no choice but to release him.

'And you,' he went on, turning back to Harper. 'If you are telling the truth and you assist the constables in this matter, then I will look favourably on you when you are returned here tomorrow.'

'Yes, sir. Thank you, sir,' Harper grovelled, keeping his eyes downcast so as not to give himself away. He sensed his freedom, thought Sidney, and also his revenge on Elijah Ratcliffe, and it made Sidney even more determined to find evidence against both of them.

33

Back at the police station, Sidney was forced to explain himself to Sergeant Watkins.

'So he's not being sent for trial after all,' concluded the sergeant angrily. 'You said you had the evidence, but it seems you're not so clever as you think. You've wasted your time and Milne's and Bleasedale's and achieved nothing!'

Sidney squirmed under the sergeant's onslaught.

'The magistrate has allowed us to keep him under lock and key until tomorrow,' he replied, hoping that the extra time would give him the chance to redeem himself. 'And Harper says he can tell us where to find this man Ratcliffe. So maybe it's not as bad as it might seem. Hopefully we can bring at least one of the coiners to justice.'

'But it seems the magistrate is set on allowing Harper to go free,' the sergeant said with a shake of his head.

'It looks that way, sir,' Sidney admitted. 'Unless I can find something else that will condemn him.' He felt so foolish after he'd told the sergeant that he was sure he could take Harper off the street. He knew the man would hold it against him and use it as an example of why police officers should be content to remain visual deterrents and leave any investigating well alone.

'And do you think you can do that?' the sergeant asked doubtfully.

'I'll try, sir,' Sidney told him, although he had no idea how he might come by the evidence the magistrate required. There was no chance of catching Harper coining whilst he was in a cell, and any other equipment there had been at his house would have been disposed of by his wife by now. There was only Grace and Kitty who could testify against him, and Sidney was still afraid of involving either of them.

'You'd better go,' the sergeant sighed with a wave of his hand.

Sidney knew he'd let everyone down. Himself included. He went down to the cells, determined to get as much information from Harper as he could. He hoped he would be more cooperative now that he'd seen a way of getting rid of his rival, Ratcliffe.

As he made his way down, he met Constable Shaw coming up the stairs.

'What's tha up to now?' he demanded.

'I'm on my way to talk to Harper about who else is involved in the counterfeiting. I'll not be happy until I've caught them all,' Sidney told him irritably.

Shaw laughed. 'Tha's still wet behind the ears,' he said. 'He'll tell thee nowt.'

Sidney feared that the man was right, but didn't admit it. Instead he went down the dark stone steps and found Harper lying on a mattress and enjoying a cup of tea. He wondered whether it was Shaw who had provided the comforts. It wouldn't have surprised him.

'So,' he greeted Harper. 'You said you'd tell us where we could find Elijah Ratcliffe.'

Harper took another drink of his tea and studied Sidney for a while. 'Aye. I did,' he conceded at last, seeming more amenable than he had earlier.

'So?' Sidney repeated impatiently.

'Up at Sunny Bower,' said Harper at last. 'He makes florins up there and half-crowns.'

'Not shillings, then?' asked Sidney.

Harper shrugged. 'Not unless that die you planted on me was his.'

'Whereabouts at Sunny Bower?' Sidney asked.

'The old manor house.'

'Aye. I know it,' Sidney replied, wondering whether to believe anything he was being told. He suspected that David Harper would find it amusing to send him on some fool's errand into the middle of nowhere.

'I'm telling thee the honest truth,' Harper said, swinging his legs to the floor and meeting Sidney's gaze with a sincere expression. 'I'd like nothing better than to see him locked up.'

'And to gain your own freedom,' said Sidney. Harper grinned. With Ratcliffe out of the way, he would have a monopoly on the counterfeited coins in the town.

Harper leaned back again. 'I've said as much as I'm willing to say,' he replied. 'I said I'd tell thee where to find him and I have, so I'm expecting to be a free man again afore dinner time tomorrow. I'm tired of this "hotel". I much prefer the Spread Eagle. The food's better.'

'Have they fed you?' asked Sidney.

'Someone brought me a pie, but they expected me to pay them for it.'

'I hope you gave them an honest coin!'

Harper laughed. 'A constable with a sense of humour,' he remarked. 'I never thought I'd see the day.'

Realizing that he wouldn't get any more information from Harper, Sidney went up to the police house and found Bleasedale and Milne.

'Sunny Bower?' said Milne. 'That's quite a stretch.'

'Do we all have to go?' Bleasedale moaned. 'What does the sergeant say?'

Sidney didn't like to admit that he hadn't asked him. He suspected that Watkins would refuse permission for another raid, as being yet more time-wasting.

'It is voluntary,' he conceded.

'Count me out, then,' replied Bleasedale.

'Andrew?' asked Sidney, turning to Constable Milne. 'Will you come with me?' He could hear the pleading tone in his voice and hated himself for it. He shouldn't be the one trying to persuade his colleagues. If the superintendent and the sergeant had anything about them, they would realize that investigative policing was the way forward and would give this enterprise their blessing.

'All right,' his friend replied, even if he didn't sound particularly enthusiastic. 'Shall we go now?'

'Let's wait until tonight,' Sidney said. 'There's more chance we'll catch them at home then.'

Sidney knew he couldn't put off telling Kitty what had happened any longer. He walked reluctantly up to Mary Ellen Street and knocked on the door. She opened it eagerly, obviously expecting to hear good news, and

Sidney felt a failure when her face fell in response to his expression.

'I can scarcely believe what you're telling me,' she said after he'd explained how David Harper had hoodwinked the magistrate and convinced him that he wasn't the one responsible for the counterfeit shillings.

'He intimated that we'd planted the die on him,' Sidney explained. 'And he was so plausible I wasn't entirely surprised when the magistrate tended to believe him. I was so sure that I had the evidence we needed. I was stupid not to realize what a cunning devil Harper is. He wouldn't have got away with the counterfeiting for this long if he wasn't so wily.'

He felt guilty as he sat opposite her, at her fireside, with a cup of tea in his hand. He knew he'd let her down badly. Grace, too. They would both be in danger again when Harper was set free tomorrow, as he surely would be.

'Did you not explain to the magistrate that the man was lying?' she asked.

'I tried,' Sidney told her, 'but he wouldn't listen to me.'

'What evidence would you need to make him listen?' Kitty asked. 'Would it help if I went to the court and told the magistrate about finding the coins and Harper attacking me because they were his?'

'I won't let you do that,' said Sidney. 'There's a chance the magistrate might find you guilty of handling counterfeit coins. It's too risky.' He put down his tea and considered reaching for her hand, but quickly thought better of it.

'Is there anyone else who would give evidence against him?' Kitty asked. 'What about the landlord at the Spread Eagle?'

'He couldn't say anything that would convict him. He only knows the counterfeits are in circulation. And Harper is cunning. He doesn't pass them himself.'

'No. He uses Grace,' agreed Kitty.

'And she's the only one who could testify against him for that.'

'Don't involve Grace. Please,' begged Kitty, looking alarmed at the prospect. 'What would happen to her mother and Nancy if she was imprisoned? I think I'd rather see David Harper remain on the street than let them be taken into the workhouse.'

'Will you go and talk to her and explain what's happened?' Sidney asked, knowing that he was taking the easy way out. 'She's more likely to open up to you than to me. Try to find out if there's anything else she knows that might help us.'

Kitty agreed, and when the constable had gone she put on her shawl and walked up to Moore Street.

Grace greeted her eagerly at the door. She knew that Harper had been taken before the magistrate that morning.

'How long have they locked him up for?' she asked.

'Can I come in?' Kitty said, hating to be the bringer of bad news. She followed her friend through to the kitchen where Mrs Dewhurst was dozing in the chair and Nancy was stretched out asleep on the stone floor with a thin shawl over her. The empty medicine bottle was on the hearth with a spoon beside it.

'I needed some peace,' Grace confessed. 'I hate to keep giving it to her, but she was carrying on so much I was afraid I might slap her.' She looked distraught. Kitty hadn't had to say a word for her to understand that the news was not good.

'Harper told the magistrate the die had been planted on him by Constable Westwell and he believed him. He's said that Elijah Ratcliffe is the coiner responsible for all the counterfeits and it looks like the magistrate will let him go free in the morning.'

'That bastard!' Grace exclaimed.

'I know. I'm sorry. It wasn't what Constable Westwell expected.'

'He'll find me if they let him out,' said Grace with a fearful catch in her voice. 'It wouldn't surprise me if he already knows where I live. What am I going to do? He'll kill me if I don't pay him.'

Kitty could see that Grace was terrified. She reached out to comfort her but it was nothing more than a gesture. She wished she could have come up with a solution. There had to be something that she could do, but she knew that she couldn't ask Grace to go in front of the magistrate. There was only one thing to be done, she decided as she held her weeping friend. Despite Constable Westwell's advice, she must be brave and go to the court herself and tell this magistrate everything she knew about David Harper.

Whilst she was still feeling determined to do the right

thing, Kitty left Grace with a promise that she would try her best to make everything right and walked straight down to the police station to speak to the constable before she thought better of it and changed her mind.

'I could say that I was just poking them with my stick when Harper came along and attacked me,' suggested Kitty. 'Or I could say that I'd just picked them up to see if they were anything of value and that I recognized them as counterfeits straight away. I don't have to say that I took them home. That way I couldn't be accused of handling them.'

'I won't let you do that,' Constable Westwell told her. 'Harper was so charming in that courtroom this morning and the magistrate seemed to believe everything he said. What if he spins some tale about your involvement? No,' he repeated. 'I won't let you take that risk.'

'But what about Grace?' she pleaded. 'If I do nothing, then Harper will be free to hurt her again.'

'Grace is not your responsibility,' he reminded her. 'What about your own family? Your children need their mother. You can't risk your own freedom to help someone you barely know.'

'But I feel so sorry for her.'

'I do too,' said the constable. He reached out and took hold of her hand. His was warm and comforting and seemed so big. It seemed such a long time since she'd held hands with a man. She was more used to the feel of little Peter's hand in hers, and the idea of someone protecting her rather than her always having to be the protector was strange, but reassuring. 'I need to do this without involving either you or Grace,' he said. 'And maybe finding this Elijah Ratcliffe is the best way forward. Constable Milne and I are going to look for him tonight, and if we're lucky he will give enough evidence against Harper to see them both go to trial. Try not to worry,' he told her. 'It may be all over very soon.'

34

After Sidney had seen Kitty safely home, he'd left the little cottage reluctantly. Although it was only small and he often felt like he filled the place, it was clean and cosy, and he enjoyed being with Kitty and her children more than he could ever have anticipated. When he was with them he felt the loss of Susan less keenly, even though, at times, he couldn't help imagining what it would be like to still be married to her and for them to have the baby they'd hoped for with them. But that was all a dream. Kitty Cavanah was real and she'd had her share of tragedy, too. Sidney was determined to find a way to make things better for her.

'Shall we go after Ratcliffe now?' he asked Andrew Milne when he arrived back at the station. 'It won't be completely dark for an hour or two yet.'

Milne nodded. 'There was a nearly full moon coming up over the horizon not long ago. It'll light our way sufficiently to bring the prisoner back with us.'

Sidney was cheered by his colleague's optimism. After he'd sat for a few minutes and drunk a pint mug of tea and eaten a stale slice of bread and butter, he and Milne left Bleasedale lying on his bed with his boots off and went out.

Shaw raised an eyebrow as they passed but they didn't

pause to explain to him where they were heading. The man probably presumed they were going out to a public house or to call on some woman friend. Sidney knew that his opinion of them was very low.

They walked down to Penny Street, past the Spread Eagle and then out into the fields beyond. A lane led down to the village of Little Harwood and beyond that the land rose steeply towards Sunny Bower. The old manor house stood on the hillside. It was said to have been built in Tudor times, and it certainly looked old with its narrow, mullioned windows and low lintel over the front door.

Sidney put out an arm to restrain Milne.

'Wait a minute,' he said. 'We need a plan.'

It had almost gone dark and Sidney turned to appreciate the spectacular sunset that was still glowing pink and yellow on the horizon behind them. The moon had fully risen now and where the sky was darker the first stars were just visible as the daylight faded. The sight did him good.

'Do you think there's a way out at the back?' he asked Milne.

'Probably. Do you want me to go and look?'

'Yes. Wait there if you find a door. I'll approach from the front.'

As Milne made his cautious way towards the back of the house, Sidney walked towards the front door. He felt slightly anxious. There was no way of knowing how many people were in the house and he would have preferred to come with more constables than just Milne.

But he hoped that the element of surprise would give them an advantage. If they managed to secure Ratcliffe it would be a start.

He could see figures moving about inside as he came nearer, although it was impossible to tell if they were men or women, young or old; the glass of the windows was thick and distorted the shadows. There were voices talking and he thought there were at least two men and a woman, but he couldn't be certain.

He drew his truncheon and fixed his hat more securely before knocking on the door. Silence fell inside for a moment until he heard a voice ask, 'Who's that?' The tone sounded worried and Sidney hoped he would be lucky enough to catch the coiners at their work.

'Police!' he shouted. 'Open the door!'

He saw a flurry of activity as the figures moved quickly about the room and Sidney suspected they were hiding their equipment. He banged on the door again. 'Open up!'

No one obliged, and Sidney decided to take the matter into his own hands. As he hoped, the door was unlocked, and he ran into the narrow passageway and through a door into the room he had seen through the window.

There were two men and a woman. The fire was blazing hot even though the evening was still warm, and the oppressive atmosphere hit Sidney like a physical barrier. One of the men was holding a small crucible in a thick cloth, as if he had just snatched it from the fire. On the hearth there was a sand mould and the second man was clutching a pair of shears and a couple of metal objects Sidney took for dies.

He remained standing in the doorway to block any escape, wishing that Milne would come. He would need to put his truncheon down to handcuff the men, leaving him vulnerable to attack with his own weapon.

'What have you there?' he demanded as he played for time.

'Where?' asked one of the men.

'In your hands!'

''Tis nothing, sir.'

'It doesn't look like nothing to me. Hand it over.' Sidney stretched out a hand and noticed that a child, a young girl, had slunk out from a makeshift bed in the corner of the room and was clinging to the woman who must be her mother. He heard a noise behind him and glanced over his shoulder, concerned that there could be others in the house and that he might be overpowered.

He was relieved to see Milne.

'Arrest them,' he told him.

'On what charge?'

'Coining,' replied Sidney as Milne came in with his handcuffs in his hand. 'You can see all the equipment they have,' he added. He wanted to be certain that his friend would speak up in court. He saw the men glance towards the window. 'Don't think of running,' Sidney bluffed. 'There are more constables outside, surrounding the house. You'll not get far.'

He was surprised by how easily the men accepted their fate. He'd expected them to put up more of a fight, but Milne soon had one in cuffs and came to take Sidney's from his belt to secure the other.

'Where are you taking them?' asked the woman.

'To the lock-up in Blackburn,' Sidney told her, hoping that they wouldn't lose their prisoners on the way and that there were no accomplices outside waiting to attack them. He considered arresting the woman as well, but he knew three prisoners were too much to handle, and the fear on the child's face softened him a little.

'Stay here,' he instructed her as he bent to retrieve the evidence from the hearth. Then he and Milne grasped a man each and pushed them to the door.

It was a long walk back to the police station in the dark, and Sidney was glad of the moonlight. The men grumbled and tried to pull away from them, but with their hands secured behind their backs, it didn't take more than a tap or two from a truncheon to keep them moving in the right direction.

Shaw was still on duty when they got back and his face was a picture of surprise.

'What's this? I didn't think you two were working,' he complained, as if he thought they'd done something wrong. Sidney prayed he wouldn't find some excuse to let their prisoners go free.

'Constables are always on duty,' he replied, echoing Shaw's often spoken words. 'Go and find Sergeant Watkins, will you? Tell him we have the coiners.'

Sidney found it hard to read the sergeant's expression when he came down to the cells where he and Milne had locked up the men. He looked partly bemused and partly cross. Harper, on the other hand, was beaming in delight as his competitors were locked in. And Ratcliffe and his accomplice, who said he was his brother, were silent and surly when they saw Harper, suspecting, rightly, that he had informed on them. Sidney hoped it was enough to encourage them to tell the magistrate everything they knew about him.

'We caught them with these, sir,' Sidney explained to the sergeant back upstairs where he'd spread the crucible, mould and dies on the table. 'This one is for a florin and this for a half-crown,' he explained as he studied them. They looked crude, he thought, and the coins they would make would be much inferior to the shillings that Harper was producing. No wonder Ratcliffe was keen to appropriate the better die.

Sergeant Watkins picked up each object in turn. 'Did you find any coins?' he asked. Sidney felt annoyed that the man never seemed satisfied. It would kill him to admit that he and Milne had done a good job.

'No, sir. But we weren't able to search everywhere.'

'There was a woman, too, and a child,' explained Milne. 'But we thought it more important to bring in the men.'

The sergeant nodded. 'She'll have hidden any they've made by now,' he observed, as if he thought they should have arrested her as well. 'Still, you've done all right,' he admitted grudgingly. 'They can go before the magistrate tomorrow and we'll see what he says.'

35

Kitty lay in bed, between her two daughters. She couldn't sleep. She was already having second thoughts about going before the magistrate and telling him about the bag of coins. Would it be too much of a risk? She'd worked so hard to make a home for herself and her children in this town, and she couldn't bear the thought of being found guilty of some crime and sent away, leaving the children to manage without her. Agnes would probably be all right. She had her shop. Timothy was approaching adulthood, too, and he had his job. But if she was sent to prison, he wouldn't be able to afford to pay the rent on the cottage. Would Mr and Mrs Anderton take pity on him and Maria and Peter and allow them to stay? It would be a lot to expect. And what about Maria? Perhaps she could help in the shop? That only left Peter. What would happen to him? Perhaps Aileen and Michael would take him in? Surely they wouldn't allow him to be sent to the workhouse.

She sighed and turned over, disturbing her daughters.

'What's the matter? Are you poorly?' whispered Agnes.

'No. I'm just trying to think what's the best thing to do – about David Harper. I'm wondering about giving evidence against him, but I'm scared of being accused of handling those coins.'

'Constable Westwell said he wouldn't ask you to do that.'

'I know. But I'm worried about Grace Dewhurst. I want to see the man sent away.'

'I know. He deserves it for what he did to you. Why not just give evidence about the attack and not mention the coins?'

'That's what I wanted to do in the first place. But Constable Westwell persuaded me not to. He thought if he could find evidence against him for coining then he was sure to be locked up for good or transported, and I wouldn't need to be involved.'

'He cares about you,' her daughter whispered.

'I think he does,' Kitty agreed. She was becoming fond of him, too, but she knew that any consideration of marriage would raise its own problems.

'You could try encouraging him a bit more,' Agnes said.

'What do you mean? I'm perfectly nice to him.'

'I know. You're polite to him, but never warm, and that may be making him wary of saying too much.'

'But what about your father? What if he were to come and find me living with another man? I've no proof that he's dead,' Kitty said. The thought of Peter, lost in those rolling grey waves, brought tears to her eyes. She always wanted to cry when she thought of him. It wasn't like losing somebody who was old, who'd lived their life. He had been young and strong and vibrant. He'd been so enthusiastic about the life they were going to have in America. It was hard to believe that she'd never see him again. And even though she'd almost accepted that he was drowned, she knew that she could never be absolutely certain, and without seeing his body, a small part of her clung to the hope that he was alive somewhere and would one day find his way back to her.

Was this why she was hesitating to encourage Constable Westwell? Agnes could clearly see that the policeman enjoyed his visits to the house and that his reasons for coming were more than just his desire to do his job. And Kitty had seen the question in his eyes sometimes. Every time, she had turned away and spoken of something else. She dreaded him professing feelings for her because she wouldn't know how to answer him. She wasn't even sure that she was free to marry. She didn't know what the law was on missing husbands. She could ask Father Kaye. But she knew that if she did that, it would be as good as declaring her intention of becoming the constable's wife.

Nothing more was said, and when Kitty woke the sun was shining in through the window and it was time for her to get up. At least she could go about her work for one more morning without worrying about Harper waiting for her down some back alley, she thought, as she gathered her sack and stick and set off in the welcome chill of the early morning. The heatwave, which had been so welcome at first, was becoming tiresome now with the sun beating down relentlessly all day. Her cheeks felt sore and the backs of her hands were brown in comparison with the pale white of her arms when she took off her clothes at bedtime.

The chimneys had begun to belch their filth and the workers had hurried into the mills by the time Kitty decided she had gathered everything there was to find that morning. She and Maria and Peter turned to go back to Mary Ellen Street to sort out the finds and wash the white cloth to weigh in at the warehouse.

As they turned into King Street, she heard people booing and hissing. She stopped to watch what was happening and saw Constable Westwell, almost a foot taller than most of the crowd in his policeman's hat. He and another constable were escorting three prisoners towards the Sessions Room, and her stomach lurched as she recognized David Harper. One of the others must be the mysterious Ratcliffe.

Some of the crowd seemed to be jeering at the prisoners, but others were berating the constables as they forged a path through. Kitty saw that Constable Westwell had his truncheon drawn and his face looked fierce. She felt sorry for him. The police were not well liked by some, and she wished that those who were shouting abuse at him really knew what the man behind the uniform was like. He was kind and generous and had a huge sense of justice. Besides, she knew that at least one of the men he was escorting was guilty.

Eager to learn what the magistrate would decide, Kitty called to her two children to follow her and they tagged on to the end of the crowd who were walking with the constables and prisoners towards the court. Most of the crowd dispersed when they reached the door, but Kitty followed the constables in.

'No children!' the usher told her, holding out a hand to stop Maria and Peter.

'Go home with the barrow,' Kitty told them, handing her pointed stick to her daughter. 'I won't be long.'

'You can sit on that bench at the back. Don't make a sound,' the usher told her. Kitty could see that he wasn't keen to let her in, but she didn't let that daunt her. The court was public.

Everyone stood as the magistrate came in. Once he was sitting down, Kitty lowered herself on to the bench again and leaned forward with her elbows on her knees, eager to see how justice was done.

The first man brought to the dock was one of the two she hadn't seen before. He was asked his name.

'Elijah Ratcliffe,' he replied. So it was him. He didn't look anything like Kitty had imagined. She'd expected him to be well dressed and apparently prosperous like Harper. But this man was dirty and dishevelled and looked as thin and underfed as many of the out-of-work Irish who lived down at Butcher's Court.

'You are accused of coining – of the making and circulation of counterfeit coins. How do you plead?' he was asked.

'Not guilty,' he said, although his voice was barely a whisper and Kitty had to strain her ears to hear him.

'Constable Westwell? What evidence have you to offer?' asked the magistrate.

Kitty watched as the constable stepped forward. He had removed his hat and a strand of his hair was sticking up. She longed to smooth it down for him to make him look smart. He put his hand on a bible that an usher held in front of him and swore an oath to tell the truth before describing how he and Constable Milne had gone to the manor house at Sunny Bower and caught Ratcliffe and his accomplices making counterfeit coins.

She watched as a small cauldron, some tongs, a mould and two dies were presented to the magistrate. Mr Thompson barely glanced at them before he declared he considered Ratcliffe guilty and said he would be sent to Preston to await trial by jury there. The second man was brought up and he was Amos Ratcliffe, the brother of Elijah. He was also sent to Preston.

Then David Harper was called to the dock. Kitty crossed her fingers, hoping that he would meet the same fate.

'Mr Harper,' said the magistrate. 'You kept your word and played a part in the arrest of these two men.'

'I did indeed!' Harper smiled up at the magistrate as if he considered the man his best friend. 'I'm pleased to say that justice has been done.'

The magistrate turned to Constable Westwell. 'Constable, have you any new evidence to present against this man?'

'Both Elijah Ratcliffe and Amos Ratcliffe will testify that this man is a coiner.'

'To get their revenge?' asked the magistrate.

'No, sir,' replied Sidney. He seemed uneasy. 'They told me that they worked with him in the past until there was a falling-out. If you call them back to the witness stand, they'll tell you everything they know about David Harper.'

'He's guilty, all right!' shouted Elijah Ratcliffe. 'He's a coiner right enough!'

The magistrate frowned and beckoned to Constable Milne. 'Take these men back to the cells. I will not have my court disrupted in this way.'

Kitty saw that David Harper was smirking as the two prisoners were led out.

'Now,' resumed the magistrate. 'The evidence against this man is purely circumstantial, constable, but Mr Harper made a promise to help bring these coiners to justice and he has done just that, so I am inclined to err on the side of caution. Mr Harper.' He turned to address the man in the dock. 'I can find no clear evidence against you here today so I am going to dismiss the case against you. You are free to go.'

'No!' Kitty cried, attracting the wrath of Mr Thompson.

'Remove that woman from my court!' he instructed.

The usher grasped her arm, none too gently, and pushed her towards the door and out into the hall where she stood, barely able to comprehend what she had just witnessed. Harper was to go free.

'Mrs Cavanah.' She turned at the sound of Constable Westwell's voice. 'I'm so sorry,' he said.

'Will they let me go back in?' she asked him, desperately seeking to remedy the situation. 'I'll tell them that he attacked me. We can get him locked up for that at least, can't we?'

'Not today,' he replied. 'We would need to bring a new case against him.'

'But they can't just let him go, can they?' she asked. Her question was answered by the sight of David Harper walking out through the court's door. He saw her and the constable, and paused as he brushed a speck of dirt from his hat before putting it on.

'No hard feelings?' he said to Constable Westwell, offering an outstretched hand. The constable declined to take it and Harper turned his attention to Kitty, looking her up and down with disdain before turning away and walking out into the sunshine.

'That can't be it. There must be something you can do,' she pleaded with Constable Westwell.

'Don't worry.' He tried to reassure her, but Kitty could see that he was both disappointed and furious to watch the man walk away. 'I'll make sure that he goes to prison if it's the last thing I do,' he told her. 'Where are your children?' he asked, glancing about the room where a few people remained in groups chatting to one another.

'The usher wouldn't let them in. I sent them home.'

'Perhaps you should go home too,' he suggested. 'I'll walk with you.'

Kitty didn't have to ask if he thought she might be in danger. His grim face said it all. He replaced his hat and they walked down the outside steps together. She scanned the crowded street, hoping that Harper wasn't lying in wait for her somewhere. There was no sign of him.

'I really think you should stay at home until I can get Harper off the street again,' Constable Westwell told her as they walked to Mary Ellen Street.

'Do you think you can do that?' she asked, her hopes rising.

'I can if you're willing to make a complaint against him for assault,' the constable replied. 'I hate to ask you,' he went on. 'I really didn't want you to be involved. But now it may be our only way.'

'Then I'll do it,' said Kitty. She tried to sound brave and confident but, having seen the courtroom and the magistrate sitting up on his fancy chair, she felt more afraid than she had before. He hadn't hesitated to send the Ratcliffe brothers to prison, even though there was scarcely any more evidence against them than there had been against David Harper. The magistrate was obviously charmed by the man, and Kitty worried that even if she were to give evidence he might not believe a word she said.

'Will you come in for a moment?' she invited Constable Westwell when they reached her door. 'I'm sure we could both do with a cup of tea.'

'Just for a moment,' he agreed. She could see that his show of reluctance was a barely disguised sham.

Inside she took off her bonnet and was pleased to see that Maria and Peter had sorted the morning's finds and that there was tea brewing in the pot. She poured a cup for the constable and he sat down in the chair by the hearth, even though the inside of the house was unusually warm.

'What about Grace Dewhurst?' she asked as she sipped her tea.

'I'll call round to check on her,' he promised.

'It might be better if I go,' Kitty suggested. 'It might frighten her if you go.'

'I'd rather you stayed here,' he said. She thought he was going to say something about her being in danger, so she gave a slight gesture towards the children and shook her head. She didn't want them to be afraid.

'Did they lock that man up?' asked Maria.

'Not yet,' Constable Westwell told her. 'But they will soon. Don't you worry.'

Maria seemed to accept his assurance, but Kitty was less convinced. She knew that Constable Westwell would do everything he could to bring Harper to justice, but it wasn't easy when the magistrate refused to listen. She knew that next time he appeared in the court the evidence must be incontrovertible.

36

Kitty was restless after the constable had gone. Maria kept asking if they were going to the warehouse and she had to keep making excuses that seemed less and less plausible. In the end she told her daughter that she had an urgent errand to run first. She made Maria promise to lock the door after her.

'Why? Is it because of that man?' Maria asked fearfully. 'Might he come here?'

'No, of course not,' Kitty replied. 'I just think we should get into the habit of keeping the door locked. Living in a town is different from when we lived in Ireland.'

She could see that Maria was unconvinced, but she was relieved to hear the key turn once she was out on the street.

'I won't be long!' she called before hurrying away in the direction of Moore Street to find Grace and give her the bad news.

The house looked just the same, but there didn't seem to be anyone about. She listened at the door before knocking to try to ascertain if anyone was at home. Then she heard a gasping sound as if someone was crying.

'Grace!' she called. 'Grace. Are you there? It's me, Kitty.' She knocked and called again, more urgently as her anxiety grew. 'Grace! Open the door!'

Eventually the door was opened slowly. Kitty looked in horror at the sight that met her. If she'd thought that Grace had been badly hurt before, this looked a hundred times worse. The woman seemed barely alive. Her face was swollen beyond recognition and she was clutching her side, blood oozing through her fingers.

'Dear God!' Kitty exclaimed, reaching out her arms. Grace toppled forward into them and Kitty managed to support her whilst she got inside and closed and locked the door. She didn't need to ask who had done this.

'Has he gone?' she asked, suddenly fearful that Harper might still be in the house.

'Yes,' Grace whispered. 'But he threatened to come back.'

'How did he get in?'

'I opened the door. I didn't think it would be him. I thought it might be you or the policeman come to tell me he was locked up for good.'

'Oh, Grace.' Kitty wished that she'd come sooner. Harper must have come here straight from the courtroom.

She helped Grace to sit down on one of the boxes, wondering how on earth she was going to sort this out. Old Mrs Dewhurst was sitting on the chair staring at empty space and Nancy was curled in a ball in the corner, watching fearfully from behind her hands.

'Did he touch them?' asked Kitty.

'No. I'm thankful for that at least. He just came for me.'

'Did he want money?' Kitty was wondering if Harper intended to run.

'He knew I had none. He just wanted to punish me. He kept shouting that it was me who told the police where he lived. He was hitting me and hitting me and I pleaded with him to stop because I had no idea where he lived. But he was so angry. He wouldn't listen. I thought he was going to kill me. Why wasn't he locked up?' she sobbed. 'I thought he was going to be sent to prison.'

'The magistrate decided the evidence wasn't enough,' Kitty explained. 'He let him go. Do you think he's broken any bones?' she asked as she tried to assess Grace's injuries.

'I don't know. Everything hurts.'

'You need to see a doctor,' Kitty told her. 'I'll find Constable Westwell. You can't let him get away with this.'

'But he got away with the other,' Grace pointed out.

'He won't this time,' Kitty replied. She hoped that she was right.

She filled a bowl with water and found a rag to bathe what she could of Grace's injuries, but there wasn't much she could do, so she told Grace that she was going to get help. She thought her friend might ask her not to, but Grace was too badly hurt to argue.

Kitty wondered where to find Constable Westwell. She wasn't sure if he would be at the police station or out walking his beat, and although she didn't want to go to the station and speak to any of the other constables, she decided that it would be the most sensible thing to do.

When she reached the police station her heart sank when she saw Constable Shaw behind the main desk. He recognized her but waited for her to speak first.

'I'm looking for Constable Westwell. Is he here?'

'Don't bring thy sordid affairs into this station,' he told her. He looked pleased to have the chance to abuse her again.

Kitty looked the odious man in the eye and stood up straight, trying to make herself as tall as he was, which wasn't difficult.

'I'm here to report a crime,' she said. 'And I'd prefer to speak to Constable Westwell.'

'He's not here. So if tha's a genuine crime to report, then tha'll have to deal with me.' It was obvious he didn't believe there was a crime and Kitty hated the thought of explaining Grace's injuries to him. She doubted it would elicit much sympathy.

He stood watching her with a smirk on his face, but Kitty was determined not to walk away from him.

'A woman has been badly beaten. She says it was David Harper that did it – the man who was freed from the court this morning.' A flicker of uncertainty crossed Shaw's face. 'Are you not going to write it down?' Kitty asked him, pointing to the pile of paper on the desk.

'Aye. Aye, of course.' He took a sheet from the pile and dipped a pen into the inkwell. 'Name?'

'She's called Grace Dewhurst. She lives at six Moore Street. She needs a doctor.'

'Tha'll have to go to the dispensary about that. Now, I need thy name.'

'Kitty Cavanah,' she replied, knowing that he was well aware of who she was. He seemed to have an unhealthy fascination about the relationship she had with Constable Westwell, even though they had done nothing wrong.

She watched as he wrote a few sentences and then set the pen down and blotted the ink before adding the page to a wire tray on the other side of the desk.

'Are you going to send someone round?' she asked him.

'Eventually,' he replied. 'It's not urgent, is it?'

'Of course it's urgent. The man has almost killed her and he's on the loose somewhere.'

Shaw was shaking his head. 'Those types are always fighting,' he replied dismissively. 'She'll probably withdraw any complaint if I go up there, and I'm far too busy to be bothered with such petty matters.'

Kitty felt her anger and indignation rising, but she knew that he was just trying to draw her into an argument and she tried not to rise to his bait. Instead, she walked out without another word, although she thought she heard Shaw laughing as she banged the door closed behind her. Constable Westwell must be out on his beat, and she decided the best course of action now was to try to find him and hope that Grace would be all right until she got back.

She knew from what Timothy had said that the constable's beat now covered Eanam and the surrounding area, so she set off quickly in that direction, hoping that she wouldn't miss him. Not that he was easy to miss with his imposing height and his tall hat.

She was crossing Salford Bridge when she saw him in the distance, strolling towards her, and she called out to him. 'Constable! Constable Westwell!'

He came up to her quickly, looking concerned.

'What is it? What's the matter?' he asked.

'It isn't me,' she reassured him. 'It's Grace. Harper got into her house and he's hurt her badly. I went to the police station, but Shaw was on the desk.'

His face took on a look of anger. 'You don't need to explain,' he muttered. 'I'll come with you now.'

Together they hurried to Moore Street, Kitty having to run to keep up with the constable's long strides. But she was glad that he didn't temper his pace on her account. It would have been harder if he had dawdled.

'She's a mess. She needs a doctor,' Kitty explained, trying to get her breath back as they waited for Grace to open the door.

When Grace appeared, she looked even worse and could barely stand. She was holding on to the walls, and the injury to her side seemed to be bleeding more heavily. Constable Westwell's eye was drawn to it immediately.

'That looks like a stab wound!' he said.

'He had a knife,' Grace confirmed.

'Run for the doctor,' the constable told Kitty, taking a shilling from his pocket and pressing it into her hand. 'Tell him it's a knife wound and it's bleeding profusely. Make sure he comes back with you.'

'No, don't leave me with the policeman,' pleaded Grace, even though she looked so weak, Kitty was sure she would faint to the floor at any moment.

'Go!' instructed Constable Westwell. 'I'll stay here and look after them.'

Kitty saw the sense in it. If Harper came back, there

was little she could do to stop him, but with the constable in the house, Grace and her family would be safer.

'Lock the door behind me,' she said before she began to run towards King Street.

It was a long time since she'd run so far, and she wondered if she was getting too old for it. She was drawing attention to herself as well, she realized, but she was so afraid for Grace that she didn't care, although she was too breathless to speak when she finally reached the dispensary.

After a moment she managed to tell Dr Skaife what the problem was and where he was to go. He packed some supplies into his bag, put on his coat and hat and she showed him the way, wishing that he would hurry.

Back at Moore Street, Constable Westwell came to the door immediately in answer to her knock and almost pulled the doctor inside. He had Grace lying on the floor with her feet on one of the boxes and a rag pressed tightly against her side. She seemed to be unconscious and her breathing was shallow. Kitty was terrified that she was going to die.

As the men tended to Grace, Kitty tried to reassure old Mrs Dewhurst that everything would be all right. But the woman was bewildered and there was fear in her eyes, and Nancy had shuffled into the furthest corner and covered her ears with her hands. She simply mewled like a kitten when Kitty went near her.

'I'll get the hospital to send a cart for her,' said Dr Skaife after a while.

'She hasn't gone, has she?' Kitty asked. Her friend was very still and she feared she had died.

'No. She's living, but she needs care.'

'What about her mother and sister?'

The doctor got up from his knees and assessed the situation. 'If there's no one to care for them they'll have to go to the workhouse.'

Kitty knew how hard Grace had tried to prevent that happening. It was the reason she was in debt to David Harper in the first place. She couldn't allow them to be taken to that place. She made her decision.

'I'll care for them,' she said. 'They can come home with me.'

'Are you sure?' asked Constable Westwell. He looked doubtful. 'It's a big responsibility.'

'I'm sure,' Kitty told him, although she was far from certain. She had no idea how she would manage, especially if Grace didn't survive.

37

Sidney helped to lift Grace Dewhurst and carry her to the cart that was drawn up in the street outside. He felt profoundly guilty. It was all his fault. If David Harper had been sent to prison, he wouldn't have been able to attack Grace like this. He had failed again – as a policeman and as a man. The only consolation was that it wasn't Kitty who had been hurt, although he knew that was a selfish thought. And now Kitty had volunteered to care for the dependent old woman and the incapable sister without considering how she could possibly earn her living at the same time. It was all a mess. And he was to blame.

'I'll stay here with them tonight,' Kitty told him when the cart bearing Grace to the hospital had rumbled away. 'Nancy is too distraught to be taken somewhere strange. I'll spend the night and maybe she'll be easier to persuade tomorrow.'

'You've taken a lot on,' he observed. 'It would be understandable if you changed your mind. No one will hold you to your promise.'

'It's the least I can do,' she told him. 'I feel like it's my fault.' He understood that feeling.

'There was nothing else you could have done,' he said, trying to comfort her.

'There was,' she replied. 'I could have stood up in that

court and told the magistrate that I know David Harper is a coiner. I could have told him about the coins I found and the threats he made against me. If I'd been braver, he would have been in prison and this would never have happened.'

'You could have been in the prison yourself,' he reminded her.

'I should have taken the risk,' she told him. 'I could have stopped this, and if poor Grace dies then it will be on my conscience.'

'She won't die,' he reassured her, even though he knew the words sounded hollow. Grace was badly hurt and her survival was not certain.

'I'll fetch some coal for the fire and some food,' he said. 'It's the least I can do. What about your children?'

'They'll manage for one night. Agnes is sensible. Would you call at the cheese shop and tell her what's happened?' she asked him. 'I'm sorry to be a nuisance.'

'You are never a nuisance!' he told her. 'You're one of the most selfless people I know.' He longed to put his arms around her and kiss her. He wanted to take all her worries and fears and make them his own. He wanted to tell her that he loved her. But the moment wasn't right and he went out to take her message and make the necessary purchases. He could at least help out practically.

Sidney went to see Agnes first. She looked anxious when she saw him.

'It's not my mother, is it?' she asked.

'No. Nothing has happened to your mother, but Grace Dewhurst has been hurt.' He explained what had happened and saw the colour drain from her cheeks.

'It could have been my mother,' she said. 'Where is Harper now?'

'I don't know,' Sidney admitted. 'But I'll not rest until he's caught. He'll not get away a second time,' he promised.

Agnes told him that she would shut the shop early and go home to care for her siblings.

'Tell my mother not to worry,' she said. 'We'll manage.'

When he returned to Moore Street with the sack of coal, some candles, tea, sugar and hot pies from the market stall, he found Kitty on her hands and knees cleaning the bloodstains from the floor. She stood up and went to empty the bucket of dirty water into the street.

'I'm not sure this bucket is fit to use for drinking water now,' she told him. 'But it was the only one there is. I have a spare one at home if you could go and fetch it for me and fill it with fresh water from the pump. I'll light a fire and then when you come back we can make some tea.'

Glad to make himself useful, Sidney went to Mary Ellen Street and was able to reassure Maria and Peter that their sister would be home soon to care for them and that their mother was safe but helping some less fortunate folks.

'I can make our tea,' Maria told him. 'Tell her not to worry about us.'

They were such resourceful children, thought Sidney. Well used to fending for themselves and making the best of things. He was growing fond of them all.

He returned to Moore Street and fetched the water. Kitty had broken open the pies to let them cool and had given one to old Mrs Dewhurst. She was picking at it with her fingers but didn't seem hungry.

'I've tried to explain things to her, but she doesn't seem to understand,' Kitty said. 'And Nancy is so afraid she won't come out of the corner at all. I'm not sure what to do.'

'Best leave her,' he advised. 'Put a pie on a plate and leave it beside her.'

'I don't think there are any plates,' Kitty told him.

Sidney saw it was true. The Dewhursts had hardly anything. There was a pan in which Kitty had put some water to boil and three cracked cups, but apart from that the shelves were empty. There didn't seem to be beds or bedding either, and he wondered how they would manage to keep warm when winter came.

Kitty brewed tea and they sat, each on a wooden box, to drink it.

'I think old Mrs Dewhurst must sleep in her chair,' said Kitty. 'I went to look upstairs but the room's empty. If they had beds then they must have been sold to repay their debts. Grace and Nancy must sleep on the floor.'

'Will you be all right, alone with them?' he asked her, worried about how she would cope if Nancy became agitated. He knew that he ought to go back to the police house. There was a curfew of ten o'clock for the constables who weren't on duty – designed to keep them out of the public houses and brothels. Staying out without permission was a serious offence, but he doubted that Sergeant Watkins would give his permission even if he went to ask. It was better to take the risk, he decided.

'I'll stay if you'd like me to,' he offered.

The relief on Kitty's face was clear.

'Would you? I'd be grateful,' she replied, and he saw that she was worried that she might not be able to manage. Tomorrow he must try to make other arrangements, he decided. It was asking too much to expect Kitty to care for Mrs Dewhurst and Nancy. Goodness knows how Grace managed.

Just before it became too dark to see the way, Kitty walked Mrs Dewhurst down to the privy at the end of the street and he stayed with Nancy. The girl had eaten her pie and drunk some tea, but she still wouldn't come out of the corner or look at anyone. She was like a frightened animal and Sidney wished he knew what was going on inside her head. He tried to talk to her, to explain what had happened, but she didn't respond and he wasn't sure whether she understood or not.

When Kitty came back, she settled Mrs Dewhurst on to the chair and looked in vain for a blanket. The evening had turned chilly and the old woman looked cold, so she draped her shawl over her and she dozed off to sleep.

Sidney wished that he'd brought some straw mattresses and blankets. He had the money, but there were no shops open now, so they would have to make do with the bare earth.

He offered to go to Mary Ellen Street to fetch something for Kitty but she said no, she would be all right.

He lit a candle and placed it between them. Nancy, exhausted by the events of the day, had fallen asleep in her corner and there was nothing more to be done until morning.

'I'm glad you stayed,' Kitty told him as they heard footsteps pass by in the street outside. 'I would have been terrified of Harper coming back if I'd been alone.'

'I wouldn't have left you here on your own,' he said.

'Will you get in trouble?' she asked. 'At the police station?'

'No. Of course not,' he replied, even though he knew he would. 'They'll understand that it was an emergency.'

She seemed satisfied with his answer and he was glad. He didn't want her to feel responsible. It was his decision. Whatever the sergeant and the superintendent said, he would deal with it tomorrow.

It was a long time since he'd sat with a woman by candlelight and he felt shy and tongue-tied. Kitty yawned.

'You're tired,' he said. 'Why not sleep for a while? I'll keep watch over these two.'

She looked grateful. 'Do you not mind?' she asked.

'No. Get as comfortable as you can by the hearth. Don't worry. I'll be here.'

He watched as she settled herself as best she could. She put her head on her arm and tucked a hand under her chin. She closed her eyes and she looked so fragile and so pretty by the light of the flickering flame that all he wanted to do was gather her close and hold her in his arms to keep her from harm. He sat and watched as her breathing slowed and he thought that she was sleeping. He was warmed by the realization that she trusted him and needed him. It was a long time since he'd been needed, and he enjoyed the feeling of it.

38

Kitty didn't know where she was when she woke. The ground was hard beneath her and her neck was stiff. She looked around the room and wondered if she was dreaming, but it was real, and after a moment she remembered that she was in Grace Dewhurst's house.

She heard a sound behind her and sat up, alarmed, but it was only Constable Westwell. He was coaxing a fire into a blaze.

'Good morning,' he said when he saw that she was awake. 'I'm about to make some tea.'

'Thank you. Are they all right?'

She got to her feet to check on her charges. Nancy was still asleep in the corner. Mrs Dewhurst was in the chair, but she was very still and her jaw had dropped open. Kitty's heart raced in fear as she approached the woman, fearing that she was dead, but when she touched her hand she gave a little gasp and opened her bewildered eyes.

'Hello,' she said gently. 'Would you like a cup of tea?' The woman nodded and Kitty knew that it would be easy to care for her until Grace was better, but she dreaded Nancy awakening because she had no idea how she would react. Looking after Nancy was going to be a challenge, but she was determined to do it rather than see her taken to the workhouse.

'I'll have to go in a while,' said Constable Westwell. 'It'll be time for my beat. Will you be all right?'

'Yes.' She was determined to reassure him. He'd done so much to help her already, far more than she could have expected. It wouldn't be fair to detain him any longer, and once she had Mrs Dewhurst and Nancy at Mary Ellen Street they should be safe from Harper, because he had no idea where she lived – or so she hoped.

'How will you get them home?' he asked. 'Do you want me to help you?'

Kitty hated to beg one more favour, but she knew it would be much easier if he came with them.

'Do you have time?' she asked.

He consulted his pocket watch and nodded. 'Plenty of time,' he told her.

Mrs Dewhurst was amenable. That made it easier to help her. Kitty took her to the privy then put her shawl around the woman's head and shoulders. Nancy was more of a challenge.

'Would you like to come and visit my house?' Kitty asked her, holding out a hand. Nancy looked at her from between the fingers that were covering her face. 'Just for a little bit,' she told her. 'Until Grace comes back.' Nancy shook her head and Kitty looked to the constable for support. 'I don't want to force her,' she said. 'She seems so frightened.'

'It's not surprising given what she had to witness yesterday,' he said. 'I could carry her,' he offered.

'No. That'll frighten her even more. Perhaps she'll come if she sees us leave with her mother. Can you give Mrs Dewhurst your arm and go ahead? I'll try to coax her.'

Kitty watched as the constable took Grace's mother out of the door. She was surprisingly agile, which was a relief. It was just her mind that seemed damaged.

'Come on, Nancy,' she said. 'You can have some toast when you get to my house. You'd like that, wouldn't you?'

'Man hurt Grace,' she replied.

'I know.' Kitty's heart went out to the childlike woman. 'But Grace will be better soon and the man won't come back. That policeman is going to catch him and lock him up,' she promised, not sure how much of what she was saying Nancy understood. 'Come and stay with me for a day or two. Just until Grace comes home. Where's your doll?' she asked, remembering the bundle of cloths that she'd seen Nancy nursing. She looked about for it and saw that it had been piled up with the rags she'd used to bathe Grace's face. She retrieved it and held it out to Nancy.

'Baby!' she cried out, reaching for it. Feeling cruel, Kitty held it out of her reach.

'Let's take baby to my house as well,' she said, walking towards the door. As she hoped, Nancy got up from the floor and followed her.

'Baby!' she demanded.

When she was out of the door and Kitty had locked it behind them, she gave Nancy her doll. She clung to it and held it close as if it was a real child.

'Come on,' Kitty said, getting hold of one of Nancy's hands and holding her tightly. 'Let's go.'

She was frightened that Nancy would pull away from

her and run, but she seemed subdued and walked along beside her, crooning to the doll she held in her free arm. Kitty hoped that she would remain compliant. She remembered the bottle of medicine that Grace used to calm her and wished that she'd thought to look for it. She would send Agnes or Maria to the dispensary with sixpence to ask Dr Skaife for another, she decided. It seemed wrong to drug Nancy, but it might be the only thing she could do if she had one of her fits.

They caught up with Constable Westwell and Mrs Dewhurst before they reached Mary Ellen Street. They must have made an odd sight, Kitty thought, walking through the early morning street like the raggle taggle gypsies. She was relieved when they all got inside.

Agnes was up and making the breakfast. She welcomed their visitors and sat Mrs Dewhurst down by the fire and offered the other chair to Nancy. But Nancy shook her head. Her eyes darted around the small room until she saw the corner in the scullery by the sink and she scuttled towards it and sat down, clutching the doll and staring about wide-eyed.

'Is she all right?' Agnes asked.

'She's frightened,' explained Kitty. 'She'll probably come out in a little while.'

Agnes offered the constable more tea and he accepted a cup and sat down opposite Mrs Dewhurst.

'Thank you for your help, constable,' Kitty said. 'I don't know what I would have done without you.'

'Will you not call me Sidney?' he asked her. 'Constable seems so formal.'

'Sidney,' she replied. She hadn't known his name before, but it suited him and she liked it.

'What will you do about your work?' he asked her.

Kitty knew it would present a problem. Grace must have left her mother and sister alone when she went to her cleaning job, but Kitty was unsure how safe they would be in a different place.

'I'll stay at home today,' she said. 'We'll manage.' She tried to make it sound as if it was of no consequence, although the truth was that every day she didn't bring in some money made it harder to afford everything they needed. Yesterday she'd felt so guilty about what had happened to Grace that she'd been compelled to step in and care for her family, but now, as she began to take stock of her situation, she wondered whether she really could manage.

'I'll call round as soon as I've finished my shift,' Sidney promised. Kitty turned to him and smiled. It was a relief to know that she wouldn't have to face this alone, that he would continue to offer his help.

'I'll send Maria to bring some potatoes from the market,' she said. 'I'll make a pie. You can eat with us.'

'I'll look forward to it,' he said. 'Home cooking is one of the things I miss.'

Kitty didn't ask what else he missed. She could easily guess. They were the things she missed too: companionship, security and the knowledge that someone had her best interests at heart.

39

As soon as Sidney walked into the police station he sensed the atmosphere. The other constables shifted their gaze when he looked at them and he realized that his empty bed had been noted.

'The sergeant wants you,' Constable Milne warned him.

Sidney decided to go and face Watkins at once. He knew that he could have gone out on his beat without speaking to him, but it would only have been putting off the inevitable.

The sergeant looked annoyed when he tracked him down in the kitchen where he was enjoying a mug of tea and a bacon sandwich.

'I heard you wanted a word with me,' he said.

'Westwell.' The sergeant put down his tea and stared at him. 'I presume you know what it's about.'

'I presume it's because I didn't return to the station last night.'

'Damn right!' replied the sergeant. 'Would you care to explain where you were?'

'I was helping to care for the family of the woman who was beaten by David Harper.'

'And who asked you to do that?'

'No one asked me,' Sidney replied, feeling irritated at the sergeant's manner. 'It just seemed the decent thing to do.'

'And were you alone caring for these women?'

'No. Mrs Cavanah was there as well.'

The sergeant snorted and brushed crumbs from his tunic. 'And there's the crux of it,' he said. 'You spent the night with a woman. You do know that's a sackable offence?'

'I don't think your interpretation of "spending the night with a woman" is quite what happened,' said Sidney, standing straight as he towered over the sergeant.

'And what do you think my interpretation is?' enquired the sergeant with a leer.

Sidney wondered whether to spell it out to him, but decided it wasn't worth the bother. The man had probably already made his decision and nothing he could say would make any difference. He kept silent and waited for the sergeant to speak again.

'I'll have to inform the superintendent,' he warned.

'Yes, sir,' Sidney replied. The words were hard to say, but he was anxious that he was going to be dismissed before he'd finished his work. He wouldn't be satisfied until he had David Harper on a ship to the other side of the world.

Sidney went upstairs to tidy himself. He put on a clean shirt and then splashed some water on his face and brushed his hair. He decided that he had neither the time nor inclination to shave, so he pulled on the arm band that showed he was on duty, straightened his tunic and went to the door. He was tired. He'd hardly slept all night, preferring to let Kitty rest instead. She had a difficult day ahead of her with the responsibility she'd taken on.

He began to walk towards Penny Street. The shops and businesses were just opening. He saw a dray loaded with beer barrels coming out of the brewery gates and it put a thought into his head. He walked briskly towards the Spread Eagle, hoping that the fresh air might revive him and that Billy Yates might have some news concerning the whereabouts of David Harper.

The pub was still closed at this time of the morning and Billy Yates was probably still abed, but Sidney was eager to make progress in his pursuit of the coiner, so he banged on the door with his truncheon until the landlord, bleary-eyed and sleepy, came to open it.

'Oh, it's you,' said Billy. He looked resentful at being disturbed and Sidney wondered whether his action had been altogether sensible. He needed the man's co-operation.

'I'm looking for David Harper. Do you know where he is?'

'Come in,' said Billy. 'It's your lucky day.'

The landlord led him through the bar into the kitchen and pointed to a prone body, snoring on the stone floor near to the back door.

'He owes me eighteen shillings,' he complained. 'He came in here just after noon yesterday, swaggering and boasting that he had a new best friend in yon magistrate. He ordered a round of drinks for everyone and sat in the bar telling his story to anyone who cared to listen. And they were all willing to listen for the price of a drink. He's never not paid before so I kept on serving, thinking of the profit that was adding up. But by closing time he was drunk and refused to pay his bill. He turned nasty, saying he couldn't possibly owe that much and that I was a cheat and a thief. Then he took a swing at me. But as I say, he'd had a bellyful and was fairly wide of the mark. I warned him I'd send for a constable if he didn't settle up and he swore at me and pulled out a knife. I was scared,' Billy admitted, 'but he was swaying about like a line of washing in the wind as he came towards me, so I took my chance and punched him. Landed a lucky blow. He went down like a felled tree. So I dragged him there and locked him in. He's all yours,' ended the landlord. 'We'll see what sort of a friend this magistrate is when I tell him what he owes me.'

With a feeling of elation that swept his tiredness away, Sidney took out his handcuffs and secured Harper's hands.

'Fetch a bucket of water,' he instructed Billy, and when the landlord brought it he tipped it over Harper, drenching him through but at least rendering him conscious. 'You're under arrest,' he told him enthusiastically, before hauling him to his feet. 'Come with me.'

Harper moaned and threatened Sidney all the way through the streets of Blackburn. It caused quite a stir, with townsfolk turning out to take sides for and against the police force. Although Sidney would have liked to lecture them on Harper's crimes, he kept his focus on getting his prisoner back to King Street where he could do no more harm. He flung the coiner into a cell and saw him stagger and hit his head as he lost his balance. Sidney's fists were itching to add to the bruising that was already visible from Billy Yates's blow the previous evening, but he restrained himself, reminding himself that he was a better person than that and this time the magistrate would deal with it fairly. The evidence was overwhelming for the assault, and he hoped that Grace Dewhurst would speak up and get Harper convicted for the coining as well. He knew that Kitty would do it if Grace couldn't, but he hated the idea of her taking that risk. He would never be able to live with himself if she was sent to prison. Of course that fate might await Grace, but he was determined to do everything he could to plead for lenience. The woman needed help, not punishment, although not every judge and jury saw it like that.

'What's this?' asked Constable Milne, coming down the steps. 'Our friend Harper again?'

'Aye. And this time he'll not go free,' Sidney said.

'The superintendent has asked to see you.'

Sidney's mood plummeted. But at least, even if he was about to be dismissed, he had Harper in the cells, he told himself, hoping fervently that the superintendent wouldn't take it upon himself to let the man go.

He climbed the stairs, his legs leaden with weariness, and went to the room where Superintendent Marshall was sitting behind the desk with a frown furrowing his brow.

'Shut the door,' he instructed. Sidney did as he was told and stood rigidly to await his fate.

The superintendent read out a list of his supposed misdemeanours and asked him for an explanation. Sidney's eyes were heavy and his head was throbbing. He wanted to sleep, not to have to answer these questions, and his impatience got the better of him as he rallied himself to speak.

'I have just arrested the man who almost killed Grace Dewhurst yesterday,' he said. 'I'm hoping she will live, not least to give evidence of the assault, but also to give evidence that this man, David Harper, is the coiner who is responsible for flooding this town with counterfeit coins. I spent last night helping to care for Grace Dewhurst's elderly mother and her invalid sister. If that contravenes some rule in your police handbook then I'm sorry. Not sorry for what I did, but sorry that this police force that you've set up has such bloody stupid rules!'

Superintendent Marshall stared at him, rendered speechless. Sidney regretted his words immediately, but there was no taking them back.

'I take it I'm dismissed,' he said, wondering where he would go now that he had no home. He couldn't possibly impose on Kitty. She had enough to deal with.

'No.' Sidney realized that the superintendent had repeated the word. 'What you've just told me puts a very different slant on the matter,' he went on. 'I was given to understand that you'd been conducting an affair with a prostitute rather than attending to your duties.'

'Who told you that?' growled Sidney. 'The woman who has been helping me with this enquiry is a respectable widow. And I have not been conducting an affair with her!'

'Please calm down. Sit down,' invited the superintendent, and Sidney felt so weary that he acquiesced. 'I was surprised by what I was told,' he admitted. 'When I first interviewed you for this job, I concluded that you were a reliable and mature applicant, not given to dereliction of your duties. Have you any explanation for why these allegations were made?' He looked perplexed and Sidney decided to enlighten him.

'Constable Shaw hates me,' he replied. 'Probably because he knows I'm a better policeman than he will ever be.' He stifled a yawn and watched as the superintendent shuffled his papers.

'Take the rest of the day off,' he said at last. 'You'll need to have your wits about you when you bring Harper in front of the magistrate tomorrow. And make sure that you are back here before evening curfew every day,' he added.

40

'Will you be able to manage, Mam?' Agnes asked Kitty after they'd eaten their breakfast. Timothy had already gone, but her elder daughter was lingering, clearly concerned about leaving her alone with the Dewhursts.

'I'll be fine,' she said. 'Mrs Dewhurst won't move from that chair and I don't think Nancy will come out of her corner anytime soon. You could do me a favour if you get a moment, though. Could you call into the dispensary and ask about the medicine that they give Grace for her sister? I may not need it, but it could be useful if she becomes too restless.'

Kitty reached for her purse and gave sixpence to her daughter to pay for it.

'I'll get it as soon as Jonas comes,' she promised. 'He can mind the shop whilst I run back with it.'

Kitty was grateful.

'Are we going gathering?' asked Maria when Agnes had gone. 'It's getting late,' she observed.

'I can't leave our guests this morning,' Kitty told her. 'We'll have a day off.' She tried to make it sound like a treat. 'And later you can go to buy some potatoes for a pie. Constable Westwell is coming for his tea so we'll need to make plenty.'

Kitty counted the money that was left in her purse.

There was enough for a big bag of potatoes and an onion, and she had flour and a little lard to make a pastry crust. But if she couldn't go out to work she would struggle to buy food tomorrow. She could send Maria and Peter out gathering, but the thought of David Harper still being on the loose worried her. It was more important to keep her children safe.

'Can I play out?' asked Peter.

'All right. But don't go off the street,' she warned him. 'And try not to get dirty.'

With Maria gone to the market and Peter playing in the dust with a few sticks and stones, lost in some imaginary game, Kitty washed up the pots and took the opportunity to tidy the room and sweep the floor. Mrs Dewhurst watched her and Kitty chatted as she worked, inconsequential talk about how hot the weather was and what they were going to eat later and how she worried that cooking a pie would make the room even warmer. All the while she kept an eye on Nancy, who watched her but glanced away every time Kitty looked at her. It was sad, she thought. Nancy was so pretty, although she looked a mess at the moment with her hair tangled and her face dirty. She longed to wash her and brush her hair and make her look respectable, but she knew Nancy wouldn't stand for it. The doll she held was filthy too. It would benefit from a wash, but Kitty had no intention of trying to take it away from her. It was the only thing that seemed to give her some comfort.

Kitty admired the way Grace cared for her, refusing to allow her to be taken away to one of the sordid institutions where such unfortunates were often left by their families. It was a huge burden on her. And how could she ever marry and raise a family of her own? What man would be prepared to take on her sister as well? No wonder she had been duped by David Harper.

Midway through the morning, Agnes came in with the medicine.

'How is she?' she asked.

'Still quiet. What did it cost you?'

'Dr Skaife wouldn't take any money for it,' Agnes said, handing the sixpence back to Kitty. 'He told me to tell you that he visited Grace at the hospital this morning and they've stitched up her wound. He said it wasn't as bad as he feared and she should be able to come home in a day or two as long as no infection sets in.'

'Well, that's good news. She'll still need help, though,' Kitty said, wondering how it could all be managed without either family going hungry.

The potato pie was making the house smell appetizing by the time Timothy and Agnes came home that evening. Kitty had added the pastry crust and it was browning nicely. Even Nancy had come closer to the table, obviously hungry, and Kitty wondered if she could coax her up on to a stool to eat with them.

'That's Constable Westwell – Sidney,' Kitty corrected herself when she heard him at the door. 'Go and let him in,' she said to Timothy. 'Tell him there's no need to knock.'

A moment later he was standing by her fire, warming

his hands – probably out of habit, because it was so stifling in the crowded kitchen that she'd risked leaving the back door ajar. Even if Nancy did run out there, she couldn't escape the small yard unless she managed to climb the six-foot wall.

'I've got good news.' He was beaming. 'Harper is in the cells and up before the magistrate again tomorrow. He'll not let him go this time.'

'Will I have to give evidence?' she asked, feeling anxious. 'Dr Skaife sent a message to say that Grace is getting better, but she's still in the hospital so she won't be able to appear in court.'

'I'm relieved she's going to be all right,' said Sidney, 'and you don't need to worry about giving evidence. I can describe what I saw and what Grace told me when I arrived at her house yesterday. I'm going to argue that it wasn't simply a common assault, but an assault with the intention to kill. It's a far more serious charge and it means the magistrate will have to send him to Preston for trial by jury rather than giving a sentence himself. I did want to see him convicted for the coining, but perhaps it's for the best if he isn't. It will protect Grace from being accused of passing the shillings and being found guilty herself.'

'I'll speak up if it's necessary,' Kitty told him, trying to sound braver than she felt. 'What he's done to Grace is far worse than what he did to me, and I'm determined that justice should be done this time.'

'We'll see,' Sidney told her. It was clear that he was doing his best to protect her and Kitty was grateful for it, but when she thought about poor Grace she knew that she must give evidence since her friend couldn't.

Kitty dished out the pie and tried to fit everyone around the small table. It was quite a squeeze, so she handed Mrs Dewhurst hers in a dish and told her to stay sitting in the chair. She called to Nancy to come and join them, but she looked overwhelmed by the noise and the crowd of people she didn't recognize and retreated into her corner with her doll. So Kitty took her food to her and was relieved when she accepted it and picked up the spoon.

'Blow on it,' she warned her. 'It's hot!'

'Grace certainly has a hard time, with her family,' whispered Sidney as he watched Nancy. 'Such a shame. She's a pretty lass, too. It makes me wonder what will become of her.'

'Grace is determined to care for her and for her mother, even though it cost her a job at the mill.'

'I can see why she got sucked into helping David Harper,' he admitted. 'Crime isn't always as black and white as Sergeant Watkins and the superintendent seem to think. I'd be sorry to see Grace go to prison for what she's done.'

'Do you think there's a danger of that?' asked Kitty.

'No,' Sidney reassured her. 'Harper will be charged with the attack and hopefully that will be enough to see him sent away to New South Wales.'

Kitty felt relieved. She knew how much it meant to Sidney to see Harper found guilty of coining and she was glad that he seemed content to let that matter go unpunished if Harper could be tried for the assault. She would have hated seeing Mrs Dewhurst and Nancy taken to the stark stone building on the edge of the moorland if Grace was sent to prison, or worse. She knew that women had been transported for less than what Grace had done.

'Would you like me to stay the night again?' he asked after a while.

'You don't have to,' she told him. 'I have Agnes to help me if Nancy becomes restless. I don't want to impose on you or get you into any bother.'

'Don't worry about that,' he said.

'You'd have to sleep in the chair,' she said. 'And I've barely enough blankets to make a bed for Nancy – although I don't know if I can persuade her to lie down. I was thinking of sleeping in the chair myself so I could keep an eye on her.'

'You go to bed,' he told her. 'I'll sleep in the chair. I really don't mind,'

'All right,' agreed Kitty. She could tell that he didn't want to go back to the police house and she wondered why.

41

Next morning, Kitty decided to give Nancy a spoon of her medicine to make her sleep whilst she went to the courtroom to see David Harper brought before the magistrate. Not wanting to leave Maria and Peter alone with the Dewhursts, she took them with her and gave them strict instructions to sit on the steps and not move until she came back out.

The same usher was at the courtroom door, but he let her through and Kitty found a space on the end of a bench. Word had got around the town that the coiner had been arrested again and quite a few folk had turned out to see him.

They all stood up as the magistrate came in. Kitty saw that it was the same man as before – the one called Thompson. He looked grave and she thought he seemed disappointed when David Harper was brought to the dock.

'What is this man accused of now?' he asked Sidney with an air of irritation. 'I hope it isn't the coining again.'

'No, sir,' Sidney replied calmly, taking the witness stand. 'David Harper is accused of assault with the intent to kill.'

Kitty heard a woman gasp and a ripple of excited murmurs filled the room until the magistrate called for silence.

'Come now, constable. That's quite an accusation,' Mr Thompson said, clearly startled. 'I think you probably intend this as an accusation of common assault.'

'No, sir,' Sidney replied. 'If you care to hear the evidence, I'm sure you will agree that the more serious charge is appropriate on this occasion.'

'Then get on with it.' Mr Thompson waved his hand as if he were swatting away one of the annoying bluebottles that were plaguing the town. He sighed and tried to get comfortable on his hard wooden chair.

Kitty saw Sidney take a breath to steady himself before giving his short speech. He looked nervous and she willed him to explain it as well to the magistrate as he had to her the day before.

'After leaving this court yesterday, the accused, David Harper, went directly to the home of one Grace Dewhurst and attacked her with a knife, leaving her so badly wounded and beaten that she is currently in the hospital.'

Sidney paused to let his words resonate. Mr Thompson looked unimpressed.

'And you, Mr Harper,' the magistrate said, turning his attention to the prisoner. 'What have you to say?'

'I'm not guilty, sir,' declared Harper. His expression was one of astonishment that he could be accused of such a thing. 'I admit that I did visit Grace Dewhurst,' he continued. 'She owes me a substantial amount of money and I was keen that she should repay her debt to me, as I had made up my mind that I would leave Blackburn in light of the false charges that were brought against me yesterday. But I was never violent towards her, even though she told me that she did not have my money.'

'And what did you do when she told you she couldn't repay you?' asked the magistrate.

'There wasn't a lot I could do, sir. I'd tried to help the woman when she came to me in great distress. She promised me that she would find work and pay me back when she was able, but it seems that she has only worked as a part-time charwoman and has been unable to set anything aside.'

'Did it not make you angry when she refused to pay her debt to you?' Mr Thompson asked him.

'No, not angry,' Harper replied. 'I was disappointed because I needed the money, but I could see that she was impoverished.'

'So what transpired?'

'I went on my way, sir, cursing myself for having been taken in by her pleading and resigned to the fact that my money was lost. It was a lesson learned the hard way.' Harper sighed theatrically and gazed around the courtroom, trying to catch the eye of anyone who might be sympathetic. Kitty looked down when his gaze reached her. She wanted to shout out that he was a thief and a liar, but people around her were whispering that he seemed such a pleasant and charming man that he couldn't possibly be guilty.

'Can you give any plausible explanation for why she is now in the hospital with a knife wound?' the magistrate asked him.

'I can, sir,' Harper told him, and Kitty exchanged a

worried glance with Sidney as she wondered what he was going to say in his own defence. 'Grace Dewhurst has an idiot sister who lives with her. They call her Nancy. She's prone to outbursts of extreme temper and I myself have witnessed such a tantrum on one occasion when she picked up several items and threw them about the room. It occurs to me that the injuries inflicted on Grace were at the hand of this sister and I think it's probable that, having been stabbed by Nancy, Grace Dewhurst saw an opportunity to blame me for the attack and so rid herself of the obligation of repaying her debts.'

The courtroom erupted into cries of those who believed David Harper and those who claimed that it couldn't possibly be true and that there was no evidence to support it. The magistrate banged his fist on the table and called for silence, threatening those on the benches that they would be removed from the room if they interrupted the proceedings again.

'Have you any evidence that Mr Harper was the perpetrator of this supposed crime?' Mr Thompson asked Sidney. 'Were there any witnesses?'

'Grace Dewhurst's mother and sister were present, sir.'

'And are they here to give their evidence?'

'No, sir,' Sidney admitted.

'And why is that?' the magistrate demanded. Kitty was uncertain who looked more smug – him or David Harper.

'The mother is very elderly and her mind wanders,' explained Sidney. 'And it's true that the sister is . . .' He hesitated to use the medical term.

'An imbecile?' asked the magistrate bluntly.

'Yes, sir.'

'Given to violence?'

'I couldn't say, sir.'

The magistrate drummed his fingers thoughtfully on his desk as he weighed up what he had been told. Silence fell as people awaited his decision. Kitty felt her mouth go dry. What would she do if Mr Thompson decided to let Harper go again? She knew that there was only one thing she could do – if she could control her shaking legs enough to stand and steady herself to speak.

'This is a very flimsy case, constable,' said the magistrate at last. 'It makes me wonder whether there is some other reason that you've brought this man before me again.'

'What other reason?' asked Sidney, clearly bewildered.

'Well, Mr Harper did make rather a fool of you yesterday and it makes me wonder whether you are simply trying to save face by arresting him again on a charge that has no more substantial evidence to support it than the last one.'

Kitty saw a flush of either anger or embarrassment rise on Sidney's cheeks. He seemed at a loss as to what to say and she knew that she must speak out – both to save his reputation and to ensure that Harper did no more harm.

She pushed herself to her feet and tried to call out. The first time she went unheard, so she stepped down into the well of the courtroom and spoke again.

'Excuse me, sir!'

'What is that woman doing there?' the magistrate demanded when he caught sight of her. He gestured to the usher. 'Remove her immediately. I'll not have my court reduced to a circus by these onlookers!'

'But David Harper *is* a coiner!' she told him. 'I know, because I found a bag of his shillings!'

The magistrate held up a hand to prevent the usher grasping Kitty by the arm. 'A moment,' he said. 'I will hear this out. Where did you find these shillings?' he asked Kitty. 'Speak up!'

Even though her legs were trembling and she could feel her heart thudding in her chest, Kitty told her story as best she could, describing the bag she had found and how David Harper had attacked her in the alley behind King Street when she was trying to put it back. 'He had a knife then,' she said.

'And what makes you so sure this money was counterfeit?' demanded the magistrate.

'I took it to Mr Reynolds at the rag warehouse and he weighed it and it was found wanting,' she explained.

'So you found a bag of shillings and you took them?' asked the magistrate. Panic hit Kitty with its full force as she realized what she'd said. The magistrate was twisting her words and had made it sound like she had stolen them. She was terrified that she was going to be accused of a crime and that Harper would walk free. 'Why did you not take them to the police station?' he asked.

'She did!' interrupted Sidney. 'After she had finished her work at the warehouse she brought the bag straight to us.'

He shot her a warning look and Kitty knew that she must agree with his version of events. She realized that he was trying to save her and she was so grateful that she wanted to fall to her knees and thank him there and then.

'Is this true?' asked the magistrate.

'Yes, sir,' replied Kitty. She knew it was wrong to tell a lie, but she hadn't sworn on the Bible like Harper had, so she hoped that God would forgive her on this occasion.

The magistrate looked perplexed by the turn of events. He looked from Kitty to Harper and back again and frowned.

'Shillings, you say?'

Kitty nodded. 'Yes, sir.'

'Why was this evidence not brought before me yesterday when Mr Harper was on trial for coining?' the magistrate asked Sidney.

'Mrs Cavanah did not want to give evidence,' he replied. 'She was too afraid of David Harper – with good reason as it turns out.'

Mr Thompson drummed his fingers again and then shrugged. 'This is too complex a matter for this court,' he announced after a moment. 'David Harper, I'm sending you for trial at the quarter sessions at Preston for the crimes of coining and assault with intent to kill. Let a judge and jury there decide.'

Without looking at Kitty, Sidney stepped forward to secure his prisoner and return him to the cells until he could be taken to Preston. Harper's face had taken on a look of shock and bewilderment. He began to protest, but the magistrate was already rising from his chair and everyone else in the court was getting to their feet. It was a good result, thought Kitty. It meant Harper would be kept under lock and key until his trial. But the thought that she might have to stand up in a bigger court and swear on the Bible that she would tell the truth worried her. She didn't want to be sent to prison herself, but neither did she want to risk her immortal soul by telling a lie.

42

The heat was even more intense outside than it had been in the courtroom. It confronted Kitty with its full force, leaving her feeling dazed by what had happened, and it took her a few moments to remember where she had left Maria and Peter.

'Are you all right?' asked Maria.

'Yes. Just a little faint. It was airless inside,' she said. 'Come on. Let's go home.'

David Harper might be secured, but she was aware of many conversations going on around her and not everyone believed that what she had said was true.

Grasping the hands of her children, she walked towards Mary Ellen Street, relieved to get away from the crush. As she approached the door she began to worry about Mrs Dewhurst and Nancy. She hoped that they were all right and that she hadn't given Nancy too much, or too little, of the medicine.

She turned the key in the lock with trembling fingers and entered with trepidation, but everything was calm. Mrs Dewhurst was dozing in the chair and Nancy was sitting beside her with her head resting in her mother's lap. They looked so peaceful and Kitty was relieved, but as she began to prepare the dinner she found herself wondering about David Harper's version of events. She glanced across at Nancy. She was still sleepy and quiet, but it was only because of the medicine. She remembered the first time she'd seen her, when she'd been on the street in her shift, and although she'd never seen her be violent towards Grace, Kitty knew that her sister struggled sometimes to keep her calm – hence the bottle of medicine. Was it possible that what Harper had said was true? Could it have been Nancy who had stabbed Grace? No. She was sure he'd only said it to try to save himself, but even so, when she saw Nancy watching her she turned away to hide the sharp bread knife in the oven. She had her children to think of as well as herself, and she had to admit that she was slightly afraid of having Nancy in the house whilst Sidney wasn't there to help her. She hoped that he would come again after his shift. She needed his company and his protection, and she needed to talk to him about what she'd said in the courtroom and ask whether he thought she'd put herself in danger.

After dinner, she sent Maria and Peter to play outside and she gave Nancy another spoonful of the medicine. It seemed slightly cruel to keep her sedated with the liquid, but Kitty told herself that she mustn't take any risks until Grace came home.

The afternoon dragged as she looked around the kitchen for jobs to do. Normally she was busy for every moment and it was strange to have time on her hands. She took Mrs Dewhurst out to the privy, locking Nancy inside whilst she was gone. She watched her two younger children playing a game with some sticks. It was a holiday for them and they looked happy to be at leisure for once, but worries about what the future held loomed like a dark shadow over Kitty as she walked the old woman back to her door. What she'd said that morning could never be taken back and she had to face the consequences it would bring.

Towards teatime she heard someone try the door handle and then knock repeatedly. She peeped out of the window and saw that it was Sidney. She hurried to let him in, and as soon as he was through the door, he gathered her into his arms and held her close for a moment before setting her at arm's length and demanding to know what had possessed her to speak out.

'What were you thinking?' he asked. 'I was so shocked and I had to think quickly about what I could say to save you from condemning yourself. You ought to have kept quiet.'

'But Mr Thompson was about to let Harper go. I had to do something,' she told him.

'Oh, Kitty.' He hugged her to him again. 'I'm so sorry. I was so pleased to get Harper into court again that I never considered he would find any excuse for what he'd done. It seemed watertight with Grace so injured and Dr Skaife's evidence. Who could ever have imagined he would turn it all about and blame poor Nancy?'

'But he'll be sent to Preston for trial now,' Kitty reminded him. 'If I hadn't said anything, he could have been walking free again tonight.'

'I know. But it's you I'm worried about,' Sidney told her. 'You'll be expected to give evidence at the sessions now, and they'll ask you all sorts of questions to try to catch you out. We need to talk about exactly what you're going to say.'

He looked so serious and concerned that Kitty was frightened.

'Please don't let them send me to prison,' she whispered.

'I won't,' he promised. 'Whilst there's breath in my body I'll make sure that doesn't happen.'

He sounded reassuring, but Kitty knew that any decision was not his to make. There was danger ahead and she wondered if she had done the right thing after all.

Once he was sure that she was all right, for the time being at least, Sidney went to buy some food. He fetched some sliced meat, a lettuce, some fresh tomatoes and bread and butter.

'It's too hot for you to be cooking anything,' he told her as he set the food on the table. 'So I thought we would have a salad.' Kitty was grateful for his thoughtfulness. She felt suddenly exhausted.

After they'd brewed tea, they let the fire burn down. Now that Nancy had come out from the corner, Kitty was worried about her getting close to it. The flames seemed to fascinate her. She sent Maria and Peter to wash themselves at the sink. They were filthy from playing out and she would have loved to bath them, but baths were rare and luxurious things and she didn't even have a tin tub to hang on her back wall. After they'd gone to bed, she sat with Sidney and her elder children and talked about David Harper.

Agnes was horrified to discover that Kitty had spoken up in court.

'I wish you hadn't,' she told her.

'So do I,' Sidney replied, 'but we can't change it now, and as long as we prepare what your mother is to say at Preston, I'm sure it will be all right.'

'It's getting late,' Kitty said, to change the subject. 'Do you need to get back?'

'I'll stay again if you want me to,' he offered.

'Would you?' she asked. 'I'd feel better if you did – just until Grace comes home.'

'I'll stay down here and watch them,' he offered. 'You go upstairs and have a good night's sleep. You look all in.'

'I am,' she admitted. 'Thank you.'

Next morning, after Sidney had gone to walk his beat and Timothy and Agnes had gone to work, Kitty helped Mrs Dewhurst wash her hands and face and then she tried to coax Nancy into having a wash and allowing her to brush her hair. She didn't want Grace to come home and think that she hadn't attempted to keep her sister clean and tidy.

Thankfully, Nancy was in an amenable mood and when her face and hands were clean she sat on a stool and let Kitty begin to untangle her hair. She cried out in protest when Kitty teased at the worst of the knots, but she didn't lash out, and Kitty felt guilty that she'd given credence to Harper's words even for a moment. She was certain that it was him and not Nancy who had attacked Grace. Nancy seemed soothed by Kitty's rhythmic brushing of her hair. Once it was smoothed and Kitty was tying it at the nape of her neck with a piece of string, she heard a knock at the door. She answered it to find Grace standing on the step looking worried.

'Come in,' she said, taking Grace's arm and drawing her inside. 'How are you?' she asked, although she could see that Grace was pale and tired. The swelling on her face had gone down a little, but the bruises covered every inch of her skin and she held a hand to her side, obviously in pain.

'Are they all right?' asked Grace, looking at her mother and sister.

'Yes. They're just fine,' Kitty reassured her as Nancy jumped up and ran towards her sister and threw herself at her. Grace staggered and almost fell and Kitty grasped hold of Nancy to try to pull her off.

'Be careful now,' she warned her. 'Your sister's been hurt. You must be gentle.'

'Have you seen David Harper?' Grace asked and Kitty realized that the reason she was afraid was because she didn't know that he was locked up. She must have been terrified every step of the way from the hospital, expecting him to jump out on her at any moment.

'It's all right,' she reassured her. 'Come and sit down. Constable Westwell found Harper at the Spread Eagle and arrested him. He's going to Preston for the quarter sessions.'

She explained what had occurred in the courtroom and saw Grace's appalled expression when she got to the part about Harper blaming Nancy for the attack.

'What kind of man blames a poor innocent woman for something they've done?' she demanded. 'I hope they didn't believe him. They won't come for her, will they?' she asked, grasping her sister's hand with a look of dismay.

'No, of course not,' Kitty told her. 'Once Harper is convicted everyone will know he's a liar and a cheat.'

'Will I have to give evidence about the coining?' Grace asked. 'If I admit to passing the coins they'll send me away.'

'No. Don't worry,' Kitty reassured her. 'I'll tell them about the bag of shillings I found. That will be enough to condemn him, I'm sure. And if he's convicted for that crime, there may not need to be a trial for the assault, so you might not have to give evidence at all. I'll speak to Constable Westwell about it,' she promised. 'I'm sure there's no risk to you.' She tried to sound certain, though the truth was that she was far from sure. All she knew was that she must speak up herself, because she couldn't stand by and risk Grace being sent to prison or transported if she could prevent it.

43

Sidney wasn't surprised that Superintendent Marshall was waiting for him when he finished his shift. He just hoped that the man wouldn't dismiss him before he had given evidence against David Harper at the sessions.

'Well, you got your way with Harper,' the superintendent began with a begrudging manner. 'Milne has taken him by coach to Preston this morning and the case is to be heard next week. I suppose you'll have to remain in uniform until then,' he went on, 'but you've severely tried my patience. I thought I'd made it clear to you last time we spoke that you must return to the police house before curfew each evening.'

'I've been assisting Mrs Cavanah with the care of Grace Dewhurst's relatives,' Sidney explained. 'We have her to thank for Harper being sent for trial at all. If she hadn't spoken up about the coining, I think the magistrate might have been inclined to release him again after he told his story about Grace's sister.'

'You think it was nonsense?' the superintendent asked.

'I do. I've met Nancy Dewhurst. She wouldn't hurt a fly.' Sidney didn't know if it was true. He'd seen that Kitty was wary of the girl, but he wasn't going to admit that.

'Yet you saw the need to assist Mrs Cavanah in the care of the girl.'

'The girl and her mother. They both need a lot of care. I felt it was my duty to be there.'

'And do you not care that people talk?' asked the superintendent. 'You'll be judged by your actions.'

'I don't believe I've done anything wrong,' Sidney told him. He was about to say that he didn't care what people were saying, but he did care. Not for himself, but for Kitty. He hated to think that her reputation was being besmirched. 'Besides,' he went on, unable to stop himself, 'I intend to marry Mrs Cavanah.'

His words rendered the superintendent speechless for a moment and Sidney enjoyed the small triumph.

'You would need to ask for permission. From me,' he blustered.

'Would you refuse?' Sidney asked.

'Well. No. Probably not. In principle. She's a widow, isn't she? But there would be the matter of accommodation. I'm not sure a house would be available – and you would have to live in a police house. Are you aware of that?'

'I am,' Sidney admitted. He knew that Constable Shaw lived in a very pleasant three-bedroomed terraced and he was hoping for something similar. He wanted Kitty to have a much nicer home than the tiny cottage she and her family were living in now.

'I'd have to make enquiries,' the superintendent said, shuffling some papers on his desk. 'I take it Mrs Cavanah understands the limitations of being a policeman's wife?'

Sidney hesitated before answering. He regretted blurting out his intentions. He should have spoken to Kitty about it first to see if she was agreeable. He would look a complete fool now if she turned him down.

'All right. You can go,' Superintendent Marshall said without pressing him for an answer, and Sidney left the small office wondering what he had committed himself to. He'd sworn to himself that he wouldn't even consider another marriage until he'd seen Harper and the other coiners punished. He owed that to Susan, but having declared his intentions to Mr Marshall, he thought that perhaps it would be prudent to sound out Kitty on the matter sooner rather than later.

Grace told Kitty that she would prefer to go home now that she knew she was safe from another attack and Kitty walked with the family back to Moore Street, holding Mrs Dewhurst by the arm whilst Nancy danced along beside her sister, relishing being outside.

'She loves to walk,' Grace told Kitty after she'd pleaded with Nancy to slow down. 'I try to take her out as much as I can, but between work and caring for my mother, I don't always have the time. I think it's why she gets frustrated. I know it's not good for her being cooped up all the time.'

When they got Nancy inside, Kitty saw that there was nothing for them to eat and she offered to go and fetch some food. Grace shook her purse and a few coppers fell out.

'That'll be enough,' Kitty said, gathering them into her hand. She knew the money wouldn't buy much and that she would have to add the sixpence that Dr Skaife had refused to take for the medicine, but decided to do it secretly rather than make Grace feel awkward. 'I won't be long.'

She bought a loaf and some potatoes, and then went to Agnes's shop to beg some cheese. It was for a good cause and she would pay her daughter back the next day now that she could get back to her rag gathering.

As she was leaving she saw Sidney coming towards her. He looked determined and serious and she hoped that nothing was wrong. Her worst fear was that Harper would somehow escape justice once more.

'He's gone on the coach to Preston prison,' Sidney reassured her when she asked about him. 'But I need to talk to you about something else. Something important.'

'What is it?' she asked, worrying that he had some new concerns about her giving evidence at the trial.

'Not here,' he said. 'I need to talk to you alone. Can we go to your house?'

'I need to take this shopping to Grace first. She's out of the hospital.'

'How is she?' he asked.

'In pain and very weak. But she insisted on going back to Moore Street.'

He nodded and walked beside her. He was quiet and seemed preoccupied. Kitty wanted to ask him what was the matter, but he seemed determined to hold his tongue until her errand was completed and they were back at Mary Ellen Street. She feared it was something serious and that he had some bad news to impart to her about the evidence she'd given against Harper. She worried that he'd been sent to arrest her.

They took the shopping to Grace, and Kitty was pleased to see that Mrs Dewhurst was settled back in her own chair and that Nancy looked calm. She'd given Grace the rest of the medicine and told her to give some to Nancy at bedtime so that they could both get a good night's rest.

'How did you manage to buy all this?' asked Grace as Kitty piled the items on her shelf. 'I must owe you something?'

'No.' Kitty shook her head. 'It was going cheap,' she told her. 'And the cheese is a gift.'

'I can't let you do that. You've done so much already, looking after my mam and Nancy. I don't want to be obligated to you.'

'Gifts don't come with any obligations,' Kitty told her. 'I want you to have it. One day, when things have improved for you, you may find yourself able to help someone less fortunate. And that's all the thanks I need.'

'If you're sure,' replied Grace. Kitty could see that she hated being in debt, even to a friend.

'I'm sure,' she told her.

'I'd offer you both a cup of tea,' Grace began.

'No. Thanks, but we can't stay,' Kitty replied. 'We just wanted to drop off this shopping.'

She looked at Sidney and he nodded. He was still distracted and Kitty began to fear the worst.

They left Grace's house and headed towards Mary Ellen Street. The silence between them was taut and Kitty felt like crying. She supposed that if Sidney had been told to arrest her, he didn't have much choice, and she wished he would just tell her and get it over with. Although she couldn't blame him for not wanting to do it publicly in the street. It must be why he had asked to go to her house.

'I understand that you have no other option. I'll go with you to the police station. I won't make a scene,' she said as soon as they were in her kitchen.

'What are you talking about?' He put his hat down on the table and stared at her.

Kitty felt herself blush. Had she made a mistake? 'I thought you were going to arrest me,' she told him.

'Arrest you?' Suddenly his serious face dissolved into laughter. 'Of course I'm not going to arrest you. Whatever made you think that?'

'Well, something's the matter,' she said, feeling embarrassed by his reaction. 'You were so quiet and stern, I couldn't think what else might be wrong. You did say that you needed to talk to me.'

'Oh, Kitty, I'm sorry.' His laughter vanished as he saw that he'd hurt her feelings. 'Have you been thinking that all the time we were with Grace? I'm so sorry. I wish I'd known. I would have said something sooner. It wasn't my intention to worry you.' He looked crestfallen now.

'What do you want to talk about, then?' she asked. She couldn't think what else it might be. 'It's not Timothy, is it? Or Agnes? Or . . .'

'No. No, there's nothing wrong.'

'What, then?' she asked as she watched him unbutton his jacket. His face was flushed and she hoped he wasn't unwell.

'Sit down,' he told her. 'But it isn't bad news.'

'What, then?' she asked again, wishing he would stop prevaricating and just tell her what was wrong.

'Sit down,' he repeated, pulling out a chair from under the table. Kitty obliged, but he remained standing and it was making her neck ache looking up at him as he tried to find the words to say whatever it was that he needed to tell her.

'You know I was married,' he began.

'Yes. You told me about Susan.'

'I loved her.'

'I know you did. And I know you feel guilty about what happened to her. But it wasn't your fault.'

He nodded. 'I knew you'd understand,' he said. 'And you know that I wanted to get these coiners convicted as a sort of reparation for what happened to Susan.'

'I know,' Kitty said, wondering what this was all leading up to. 'And it looks like the Ratcliffes and David Harper will all be found guilty. I hope it helps you to feel better. I hope it brings you some peace of mind. Oh, do sit down,' she implored him.

'In a minute. I have something to say first.' Kitty almost told him to get on with it, but she saw that he was struggling. She knew it was hard for him to speak about Susan. It was clear he'd loved her very much. 'I was going to wait until I'd seen Harper convicted,' he went on, 'because I thought it might be premature to say something to you sooner, but the superintendent had me in his office this morning and he was giving me a hard time for not returning to the police house these past few nights.'

'He hasn't dismissed you, has he?' asked Kitty. He must have done. Nothing else would account for how distressed Sidney appeared to be.

'No! Not yet, anyway,' he admitted. 'But he was saying that people would judge me, and worse, that they would judge you for allowing me to be in your house overnight. And I couldn't bear to hear him questioning your reputation so I told him that we were going to be married.'

Kitty stared at him. 'I see,' she said after a moment. 'Well. I suppose you can always say you changed your mind. Or that I changed my mind. I understand that you were just trying to protect me and stop people talking –'

'No!' Sidney interrupted her. 'Not that. Well, not just that.' Kitty was taken by surprise as, without warning, he fell down on one knee beside her and grasped her hand. 'I meant it,' he explained. 'I always meant to ask you, but now I need to do it sooner than I'd planned to. Kitty, will you marry me?'

She stared down at his earnest face and with all her heart she wanted to say yes. But it was impossible.

'I'm sorry. I wish I could say yes, but I don't think I can,' she said, feeling so sad as she watched his face change to an expression of disappointment.

'But I thought . . .' he began, looking as if he might cry. 'I thought . . .'

'You were right to think it,' Kitty assured him, holding his hand tightly in her own. 'If I could say yes, then I would. Really I would. But I can't.'

He seemed puzzled. 'Why not?'

'Because I think I may still be married to Peter.'

'But I thought your husband was drowned on the ship from Ireland.'

'I think he was,' Kitty explained. 'But the truth is I can't be certain. His body was never found, so there was no death registered. I tell everyone that I'm a widow, but I can't be certain. I don't think I can be married again without proof. I don't think the law would allow it.'

Sidney got up from the floor and pulled out another chair to sit on whilst he digested what she'd told him.

'I don't know what the law says,' he admitted after a moment. 'We would need to ask. But I'm sure we can sort it out, Kitty. I'm sure we can. And if it turns out you are free to marry, then would you say yes?'

She nodded. 'Yes, of course I would,' she assured him, reaching out to touch his face. 'I'd love to be married to you,' she admitted. 'But I didn't want to encourage you because I knew I'd have to turn you down. Even Agnes and my friend Aileen Walsh have been wanting me to encourage you, but I knew it couldn't end happily if there's a chance that my Peter is still alive.'

'It's not likely though, is it?' he asked. He sounded hopeful.

'No,' Kitty agreed. 'I used to hope he was alive, but in the end I had to accept that he probably wasn't. But it doesn't change the law. I think I would need a death certificate before I could remarry.'

Sidney reached out and took both her hands in his. 'Don't worry,' he told her. 'I'll find out if it's possible for you to get a certificate. Then we can decide what to do next. But I'll tell you this, Kitty Cavanah, wedding or no wedding, I'm not going to let you go.'

Kitty smiled into his sincere eyes. It was clear that he loved her. She could see it on his face. And she realized that she loved him too. She'd come to look forward to hearing his footsteps, to seeing his face, to sitting beside the fire talking to him. And it was such a relief to know that someone cared for her, wanted to help her, to make her life easier.

By the time Agnes came home from her shop, Kitty and Sidney were sitting companionably by the hearth, drinking cups of tea. The back door stood open to let out the worst of the heat and there was a spread of food on the table that resembled a feast — cold ham, bread and butter, salad, a fruit cake and fresh apples.

'What are we celebrating?' asked her daughter.

'Grace being home from the hospital. David Harper being in Preston prison.'

'And?' persisted Agnes with a knowing look.

'Sidney has asked me to marry him.'

'Oh, Mam! I'm so pleased!' Her daughter hugged her tightly and Kitty was thankful for her approval.

What was to come would mean changes for all of them — not least, having to find somewhere larger to live. Kitty didn't want to share a bedroom with any of her children once Sidney was living with them.

'So when is the wedding?' asked Agnes.

'Not just yet,' Kitty told her.

'There are some complications to iron out first,' said Sidney.

'Because you're a policeman?'

'Partly,' he replied. 'And partly because your mother needs to get a death certificate.'

'Because of what happened to my father?' asked Agnes.

'Don't fret. We'll sort it out,' Sidney told her.

They waited for Timothy to come home and then called Maria and Peter to wash their hands and they sat down around the table. A family, thought Kitty. They were a family. She wouldn't allow her misgivings and worries to spoil that. Her children all seemed pleased at the suggestion of a marriage between her and Sidney – both the older ones and the younger ones who couldn't really remember what it was like to have a father. Having Sidney sitting at the table made them smile and Kitty hoped the smiles would continue. She knew that it wouldn't be easy for any of them to adjust to the new situation, but she hoped that the willingness to make it work would see them through.

'Do you want to stay?' she asked Sidney when he'd helped to wash up the pots and told Peter a story about a highwayman that Kitty hoped wouldn't give the boy nightmares. All the children had gone up to bed and they were alone. 'You'd have to sleep down here again.'

'Well, much as I'd love to, I think I'd better go back to the police house,' he told her. 'I have no real excuse to stay. It's not that I don't want to,' he added with a smile.

'I understand,' she said.

'It'll be different when we're married,' he told her. 'I'm going to move you all out of here. We'll get somewhere bigger.'

'A police house?'

'Maybe.' He looked doubtful for a moment. 'I'm sure they'll find us something,' he went on after a moment. 'Do you think Agnes will want to come?'

'Of course. Why wouldn't she?'

'Well, I thought it might be a good time for her and Jonas Marsden to think about getting together as well. They seem to like one another. Is there a problem?' he asked when she didn't reply eagerly.

'He's not a Catholic,' she told him.

'Does it matter?' Sidney asked, looking perplexed.

'Of course it matters.'

'Why?' he asked. 'You haven't refused them permission, have you?'

'They haven't asked,' Kitty admitted. 'I don't think Jonas wants to marry her.'

'Don't talk nonsense!' Sidney replied. 'From what I've seen, I would say he very much wants to marry Agnes. But maybe he's afraid to ask because he thinks you'll refuse.'

'But Jonas wouldn't want to be married at St Alban's. They would have to marry in the parish church and Father Kaye says it wouldn't be a real marriage so it would be like Agnes was living in sin. And I couldn't let her do that.'

'Oh, Kitty.' Sidney said it with a sigh and Kitty saw he was trying to hide a smile, trying not to laugh at her.

'There's no reason for them not to marry if they love one another. Maybe Jonas will agree to a wedding at St Alban's. You don't know for sure he would refuse. And what could be better for Agnes than to be his wife? He's a hard-working young lad with a growing business. She'd not find anyone better.' He hesitated when he saw the look of confusion on her face. 'You never even asked me which church I go to,' he reminded her.

She hadn't, thought Kitty. It hadn't seemed important. She'd just known that she wanted to be with him.

'It isn't that I wouldn't want Agnes to live with us if that's what she preferred,' he reassured her. 'I know that I'm taking on your children as well as you. I'll treat them as my own – and maybe . . .' A gleam lit his eyes as he changed the subject. 'Maybe there'll be more?' he said, and Kitty knew from the sadness that momentarily clouded his face that he was thinking of the child he and Susan had lost. She reached out to take his hand.

'God willing,' she said as the image of her own baby, lost in the sea, swam before her eyes. Another child could never replace the ones that were gone, and Sidney would never replace Peter, but a new chance and a new life would help to heal the hurt. She and Sidney could rediscover the happiness that they had both taken for granted before it had been so tragically snatched away from them.

44

'Constable Westwell has asked my mother to marry him!' exclaimed Agnes as soon as Jonas walked into the shop the next morning.

'Really?' He almost dropped the cheese he was carrying. 'What did she say?' he asked, putting it down on the counter and turning to her.

'She said yes. She has to get a death certificate for my father first. But once she has that, they're going to be married and live in a police house.'

'Well,' Jonas said. 'That's good news. Isn't it?' he added. 'You're happy for her, aren't you?' he asked, looking unsure about how he was expected to react.

'Of course I am. I like him. And she deserves to be happy after everything that's happened to her.'

Jonas looked thoughtful. 'And what about you?' he asked. 'Will you live with them in the police house?'

Agnes suddenly realized the implications that the news had for her. She'd been so excited that she hadn't considered it yet.

'I don't know,' she admitted. 'I suppose so.'

'It might be a good time to consider your future as well,' Jonas told her. He went and closed the door as he saw a customer approaching. 'We're not open yet,' he told them. 'Come back in ten minutes.'

'Jonas! It is opening time!'

'They can wait,' he said.

'I know what you're going to ask,' Agnes told him.

'But do you know what you're going to answer?' he challenged her. 'You're a grown woman, Agnes. And now that you don't need to worry about your mother being alone, there's nothing stopping you from agreeing. Agnes Cavanah,' he said as he went down on one knee. 'Will you marry me?'

She hesitated and almost told him to stop being so silly and to get up. But his face was earnest.

'I love you,' he went on. 'And I'm willing to be married at your church. I know my father wouldn't have allowed it, but my mother isn't so prejudiced. She'll be pleased. She likes you.'

'Jonas.' Agnes looked at the growing line of customers who were gathering outside the window, nudging one another and watching excitedly.

'I'm not moving or opening this shop until you say yes,' he told her.

Agnes saw she had no choice. She'd always intended to agree eventually, and the worries she'd had about leaving her mother alone had been resolved.

'You can still come to the shop,' he cajoled. 'Lizzie will help my mother in the dairy. I'll buy another pony and trap so you don't have to walk. We can afford it. Just say yes,' he implored her.

'Yes,' she replied, suddenly relieved that she'd made a decision.

He got up and pulled her into his arms. And as he

kissed her, Agnes heard the applause from the waiting customers.

'I suppose I'll have to speak to your mother and ask her permission,' Jonas said later that morning when the shop was momentarily empty. He sounded anxious.

'We'll go when we've shut up the shop, before you go home,' Agnes told him. 'She's in such a good mood at the moment with her own proposal that I'm sure she'll agree. Don't worry,' she added. 'I think you've grown on her. It's not like that first time when you came to the house and she shouted at you and sent you away.'

'I remember that,' he replied. 'She was angry with you for buying so much cheese.'

'She thought I was going to plunge her into debt. She was so worried,' recollected Agnes. 'But we've done well, haven't we?'

'We have,' he agreed. 'I can assure her she need have no worries about me providing for you.'

'She'll agree. I'm sure she will,' Agnes reassured him.

She did have some doubts, though. She knew how much her mother wanted her to marry someone from their own community and how upset she'd been about Patrick Ryan. But Jonas was a better prospect. Surely her mother would see that? He was a businessman and he had so much ambition. Soon he would have cheese shops all over the county.

Still, when the day was over and the shop closed, Agnes felt a quiver of trepidation when Jonas took her hand in his and they walked to Mary Ellen Street.

When they went in Agnes was pleased to find Constable Westwell sitting by the hearth. She hoped he would prove to be an ally.

Her mother looked up at them. 'Hello,' she said to Jonas. She didn't seem surprised to see him and her glance towards Sidney betrayed that they may have already discussed such a development.

'Jonas has something to ask you,' Agnes told her before he could say a word.

Her mother nodded and put down the cloth she was holding and reached to smooth her hair. Agnes nudged Jonas and he cleared his throat, twisting his hat in his hands.

'Mrs Cavanah,' he began hesitantly. 'I'd like to marry Agnes. May I have your permission?'

Agnes closed her eyes and then realized that she was holding her breath as she waited for her mother's response.

'Yes,' she heard her mother say. 'As long as you marry her at St Alban's and it's a proper wedding, then yes, I'll give it my blessing.'

'Thank you!' Agnes rushed forward to embrace her mother. 'I was so worried you would refuse.'

'Well, I might have done at one time,' her mother admitted, 'but I talked about it with Sidney and he made me realize that it's for the best. And now that I've agreed to marry him, how could I say no?' she asked with a smile as she hugged Agnes again. 'All I ever wanted was for you to be happy and secure – and now that you and Jonas are doing so well with the cheese selling, then I think you will be.'

'Thank you,' said Agnes to Sidney. 'Thank you for whatever it was you said to her.'

'I know love when I see it,' he replied, reaching for her mother's hand. 'We've double the reason to celebrate now,' he declared. 'Put the kettle on, Kitty, and make us all a cup of tea. Young Jonas there looks like he needs one!'

45

On his beat the next morning, Sidney thought he would call in at the Spread Eagle and give Billy Yates the good news about David Harper, if he hadn't already heard it. The door was locked, but he risked knocking, hoping that he wasn't dragging the man from his bed again. But when the door was opened he saw that Billy was up and dressed.

'Oh, it's you,' he said. 'I was expecting a delivery and wondered why they were knocking at the front instead of coming round the back.' He scratched his head and yawned. 'I suppose you'd better come in.'

'I came to ask if you'd heard about Harper?'

'Aye. Gone to Preston in handcuffs. I saw Constable Milne getting on the coach with him. They should have made him walk, lazy good-for-nothing.'

'Well, I don't think Andrew Milne would have been keen on walking. And the sergeant said there was less chance of Harper making a run for it on the coach.'

'Aye. I suppose so.' Billy picked up a cloth and began to wipe down the bar. 'Still, I hope he gets locked up for a long time after what he did to Grace Dewhurst. Coining is one thing, but to do that to a woman is unforgivable.' He began to gather some of the tankards that had been left over from the night before and took them to be washed.

'Do you run this place alone?' Sidney asked him.

'Aye. I had a wife, but she wasn't one for hard work. She ran off with a chap from Darwen who promised her a life of leisure, though I suspect he was all talk. I've not seen her since.'

'No children, then?'

Billy shook his head. 'No. I think she considered it a bit beneath her – same as waiting on in here. She had notions above her station, did our Fanny.'

'You might meet someone else.'

'Happen so. Not here, though.' Sidney raised an eyebrow. 'I've had my fill of it,' Billy told him. 'I've decided to move on. There's a place out Chorley way, on the turnpike road where the coaches stop off. It has stables and room for overnight accommodation and they're looking for an ostler and a handyman. I'm hoping it'll suit me better.'

'So this'll be up for lease?' asked Sidney, looking around with a renewed interest. 'It's a nice little place.'

'Not that little,' Billy told him. 'There's three bedrooms upstairs as well as a small sitting room. I fair rattle around on my own since the wife up and left. It needs a man and wife, really. There's potential for cooking dinners and such, and it's near enough the coach stops to attract travellers and businessmen if there were a dining room as well as a bar. And there's room for it. When I first took it on, I considered partitioning that side of it off for tables and chairs, but I never got around to it, and it's too late now.'

Sidney reassessed the space. It was larger than the

beerhouse he'd run in Manchester and it would need hard work to put the changes Billy suggested into place, but he saw what could be done and he felt a moment of envy for the new landlord. It was a challenge he wouldn't have minded taking on himself if things had been different.

'I wish you well,' he told Billy and shook him by the hand. 'I'm grateful for your assistance. It isn't always easy to come by.'

After his shift was finished, Sidney walked reluctantly back to the police station. He would much rather have gone to Mary Ellen Street and spent his leisure time with Kitty, but he was reluctant to take any risks with his employment until David Harper was convicted.

Sergeant Watkins was on duty when he went in. He didn't greet him. Sidney went through to the kitchen to see if there was any tea in the pot. There wasn't. So he filled the kettle and put it on to boil whilst he sat down and wished he could be with Kitty.

Before he could brew his tea, the superintendent put his head round the door and Sidney stood up, reaching for the jacket he'd hung over the back of the chair.

'It's all right, Westwell. I won't keep you a moment. I just wanted to update you on the housing situation. There's a two-up two-down on Halliwell Street becoming available in a few weeks that might fit your needs. I wondered if you'd set a date for your wedding.'

'Not yet, sir,' Sidney told him. 'There's a slight complication.'

The superintendent frowned and came further into the room.

'She's not turned you down, has she?'

'No, sir! Nothing like that. It's just that Mrs Cavanah needs to get a death certificate for her late husband.'

'Does she not have one?' Mr Marshall sounded suspicious. 'She is a widow, isn't she?'

'Yes. Her husband was lost at sea.'

Mr Marshall was thoughtful for a moment. 'Do you have proof of it?' he asked.

Sidney felt anger rise in him and tried to quell it. It would do no good to lose his temper.

'I have no reason to disbelieve it,' he replied.

'Mrs Cavanah will need to provide a death certificate for the wedding to go ahead.'

'I know. That's the slight complication,' said Sidney. 'She's unsure how to go about procuring one.'

'You couldn't have the house without a wedding,' Mr Marshall warned him. 'There's no question of you simply moving a woman in. You do understand that?'

'Yes. I do, sir,' Sidney replied. He felt irritated by the man and his rules.

'Well. Let's hope she can get the certificate then,' he said. 'It looks like I may have to let this particular house go, but I'm sure we'll find you something else once the wedding can be arranged.'

He nodded briefly and went out. Sidney sat back down. He was beginning to hate the many restrictions of this job – the need to account for his whereabouts at all hours and the requirement to wear his uniform at all times. He longed to dispense with the heavy serge jacket and trousers, the thick boots and the ridiculous hat. He thought longingly of his own clothes, stowed upstairs in his trunk. They would be cooler and more comfortable in this relentlessly hot weather. He wanted to dress in them and go to sit in Kitty's kitchen and watch her prepare food whilst enjoying a cooling breeze from her open back door. He wanted her company and the company of her children – Agnes with her serious face, Timothy with his tales of the things he'd seen on his postal round, sweet Maria who reminded him of Susan in so many ways, and little Peter with the stories he made up about the meagre, broken toys which were all he had to play with. He wanted to take them all away from Mary Ellen Street and give them a home where they would have room to blossom and grow, away from the hardships that had beset their lives ever since they'd arrived in this town.

Instead, he got up to brew his tea. He picked up the milk, sniffed it and recoiled at the sour stench. His tea would have to be drunk black. His meal would be badly cooked and greasy, and his evening would be long and spent without company. It wasn't what he'd imagined when he'd joined the police. Did he regret it? He wasn't sure. If Harper was convicted then he would have kept his promise to himself to avenge his late wife. He knew that he'd done something good by taking the coiner off the street, but was it enough now that the real disadvantages of the job were becoming clear? His thoughts strayed back to the Spread Eagle as he wondered whether the police force really was the place for him.

46

Kitty had hoped that Sidney might come after his shift was finished. She'd listened for his footsteps as she peeled potatoes and sliced them, but as the afternoon wore on she realized that he wasn't coming. She knew that he was expected to return to the police house but she'd hoped he might defy the superintendent again. She'd come to miss him when he wasn't there, and the rules he was forced to live by seemed ridiculous to her. It was as if the police force owned him, body and soul, rather than it just being a job of work.

If they were married and living in a police house he would be allowed to return home after his shifts. She wished that it could be arranged quickly, but she knew that without a death certificate for Peter it was impossible for them to be married, and she had no idea how to go about getting one.

She wondered if Mr Anderton might know. He knew lots of things, so it might be worth asking him. As she slid the potatoes into her pan of boiling water she decided that she would go to see him later that evening and ask him.

Not wanting to knock at the front door of the Andertons' house, Kitty went around the back to the kitchen. She could see Dorothy through the window, washing up the pots, and she tapped gently, not wanting to startle her.

'Mrs Cavanah! Is everything all right?' she asked when she'd wiped her hands on a towel and opened the door.

'I just wanted a word with Mr Anderton, if he's in. I want to ask him about something.'

'I'll go up and tell him you're here. Sit down.'

Kitty perched on the edge of a chair whilst she waited for Dorothy to come back. She hated to take up Mr Anderton's time, but she didn't know who else to go to.

'I'm sorry to intrude on your evening,' she said after Dorothy had taken her up the stairs and showed her into the parlour.

'Nonsense. You're always welcome. Come and sit down. Has Dorothy offered you tea?'

'Yes. She said she'd bring another cup from the kitchen.'

'How are you?' Mrs Anderton asked her. 'I heard that the man who attacked you was sent off to the prison at Preston this morning.'

'Yes. And I'm thankful for it. It's a relief to Grace Dewhurst too. She was very frightened.'

'I'm sure she must have been. She's in a difficult situation. I wish there was something we could do for her.'

'She's reluctant to accept help because she worries about her sister and mother being taken to live in the workhouse.'

Mrs Anderton nodded. 'I can understand that,' she said.

'So what brings you to see us this evening?' Mr

Anderton asked when Kitty had been supplied with tea and cake.

'Well, it's partly good news,' she began. 'Constable Westwell has asked me to marry him.'

'And you've accepted him?' burst out Mrs Anderton excitedly. 'That's wonderful news! Isn't it, Joshua?'

'But there's a problem,' Kitty told them. 'I need a death certificate for Peter. I never got one, but now I need it or I can't marry Sidney. I wondered if you knew anything about them.'

'I don't really,' Mr Anderton admitted. 'I've never had to deal with a death. I think the best person to speak to is Coroner Hargreaves.'

'Who's that?' Kitty asked.

'He's the town clerk,' Mr Anderton explained. 'But he also serves as the coroner. That means he investigates deaths, so he should know how you could go about getting a certificate. He has his offices on Shorrock Fold. Go and ask to speak to him. I'm sure he'll be able to help you.'

'Thank you,' Kitty said, feeling relieved. If Coroner Hargreaves could tell her how to obtain the certificate she needed, then her wedding to Sidney would be able to go ahead after all.

She left the Andertons' house a while later feeling that a huge weight had been lifted from her shoulders. She wanted to share the news with Sidney straight away, so she turned down towards the police station to ask for him. She hated going there, but this wouldn't wait until tomorrow.

Sergeant Watkins came to the desk when she rang the small handbell. Kitty saw his face turn sour when he saw her.

'I need a word with Constable Westwell,' she said. 'I have something important to tell him. It's personal,' she added in case the sergeant began to insist she told him instead.

'Wait there,' he said and went back through the inner door. A few moments later Sidney came out looking alarmed.

'What's wrong?' he asked.

'It's all right. It's good news,' she said and explained what Mr Anderton had told her.

Sidney nodded. 'That's a very sensible idea. I'm sorry I didn't think of it myself,' he told her. 'We'll go tomorrow, as soon as my shift is finished. I'll come round to the house and call for you.'

He glanced over his shoulder to check the sergeant wasn't watching then he bent to quickly kiss her.

'Shall I walk you home?'

Kitty was about to agree enthusiastically but Sergeant Watkins came back through the door.

'Westwell. I've a job for you,' he said.

Kitty thought that he'd done it deliberately and she could see that Sidney was undecided about whether to refuse him or not.

'I'll be all right,' she assured him. 'I'll see you tomorrow.'

'Are you sure?'

'Yes. The sergeant must have something very important that he needs you to do.' She glared at the man. He infuriated her and she knew that Sidney was off duty, but she also knew he didn't want to risk being dismissed. He was determined to give his evidence against David Harper at the Preston sessions.

The next day, Sidney came as he'd promised. Kitty was ready and waiting, having had a good wash after going out gathering and sorting through the finds. She'd dressed herself in her Sunday best, wanting to make a good impression with the coroner. Sidney always looked so smart in his uniform and she didn't want to let him down.

They left Maria minding her little brother and walked to Shorrock Fold. Kitty put her hand on Sidney's arm. She wanted the world to see that they were a couple.

'I'm sorry about last night,' he said.

'What did the sergeant want with you?'

'Nothing really. I think he just wanted to prevent me seeing you home.'

'I thought so too,' Kitty replied. 'I know he doesn't like me, but there's nothing he can do to prevent our marrying so he'll just have to get used to it.'

They found the offices and Kitty went in eagerly. Sidney had called earlier and requested an appointment and Coroner Hargreaves was expecting them.

He was a slight man, dressed in a black coat and waistcoat with a white cravat. His hair was already thinning and he wore it brushed forwards in a style that had gone out of fashion some years ago.

'Sit down,' he invited and Kitty perched on the edge of the chair she was offered. She was anxious but excited. This man in his splendid mahogany office could tell her how to get the certificate she needed and she could barely wait to hear what he had to say.

She listened as Sidney briefly explained their situation, but the frown on the coroner's face worried Kitty. He didn't look like a man who was about to give her good news.

'When did you last see your husband, Mrs Cavanah?' he asked her.

Kitty told him what had happened on the boat from Ireland. 'The last time I saw Peter he was going across the deck to help the boy who'd been trapped by the fallen mast,' she explained as unexpected tears assailed her. She thought she'd come to terms with her husband's death, but having to tell the story of his loss again had made her anguish raw.

The coroner nodded. 'How long ago did this happen?' he asked.

'Four years,' she replied.

'I see.' He frowned again. 'According to the law, a person must have been missing for seven years before they can be presumed dead.'

Disappointment hit Kitty. She'd been so sure that this man would be able to help them, but now he was telling them they must wait another three years before they could be married.

'Unless there are extenuating circumstances,' the coroner added.

'What does that mean?' asked Sidney as he reached for Kitty's hand to comfort her.

'Well, in this case, when someone is lost at sea a

court may rule that they are dead before the seven years have passed.'

'A court?' asked Sidney.

'Yes. You would have to take your case before a judge to explain the circumstances. It is possible that in this case you would receive a verdict of death by drowning and a certificate would be issued.'

'So you couldn't issue one?' Sidney asked.

'I'm afraid not. It's out of my jurisdiction. You would probably have to go to court in Liverpool. I would need to check.'

'I see.' Sidney sounded as deflated as Kitty felt.

'I'm sorry I can't be of more help,' said Coroner Hargreaves. 'Do feel free to come and see me again if you have any further questions.'

It was clear to Kitty that their interview was over and she stood up on trembling legs and almost forgot to thank the coroner before she hurried out of his office. Sidney followed her and caught up with her on the street where she was fighting to control her tears. She'd been so sure that they would come out with the certificate they needed to go ahead with the wedding, and now everything seemed hopeless once more. But it was the law, she reminded herself, and it was reasonable for the law to need proof.

Sidney was quiet too.

'What are we going to do?' whispered Kitty after a moment.

'We could try to go to court, but it might be very expensive. We would be expected to pay a fee. I should have asked,' he said, glancing back towards the closed door.

All Kitty's earlier optimism was gone and she just felt miserable. The thought of marriage to Sidney had filled her with such joy, and the prospect of not being allowed to go ahead with it was making her wretched. 'Three years is a long time,' she said, wondering if he would have found someone else by the time it had passed. She doubted he would stay single that long. It was too much to expect of him to ask him to wait.

'I'll think of something,' he said, even though he looked as shocked and defeated as she felt. 'There has to be a way,' he said, more to himself than to her.

Kitty didn't answer. She had no idea what other solution there might be.

47

The trial of David Harper for coining had been called for the following week. Both Sidney and Kitty were being called as witnesses and Kitty was terrified.

'What if I say the wrong thing?' she kept asking Sidney. 'What if they lock me up?'

'Just tell the story that we've agreed,' he said. 'Everything will be all right. Don't worry.'

But Kitty did worry. She lay awake at night worrying, and as the days passed and the trial grew nearer she was unable to think of anything else.

On the morning of the trial, Sidney came to collect her from the house. She'd been up at her usual early time but hadn't gone out gathering and had spent an hour or more pacing the small room, rehearsing in her head the words that she must say. By the time Sidney came, Agnes had gone to open her shop, Timothy to deliver his letters and Maria had taken Peter to help Aileen sort out her morning's finds. Kitty wished that she could take her children with her. She worried that she wouldn't be allowed to come back and that she might never see them again.

'Are you ready?' asked Sidney. He seemed excited and Kitty knew he was looking forward to seeing David Harper found guilty. She just hoped that today things would turn out as they anticipated.

They walked to the White Bull where the coach to Preston was waiting. Kitty felt fearful. She'd never ridden in a coach before and had never considered that she might. She'd expected to walk, but Sidney had insisted that she travel with him and had paid for her ticket.

He offered his hand to help her on board, and as she settled into her seat he climbed in after her, making the carriage rock on its springs. He'd taken off his tall hat as there was no headroom to keep it on and he held it on his knee, brushing flecks of dust off it now and again. Other people got in, including Sergeant Watkins who sat opposite them and put paid to any conversation that they might have had as they travelled. Others climbed the ladder to the roof and once the coach was so full that Kitty could hardly breathe, never mind move her arms, the driver cracked his whip and they lurched forward, making her glad that she was wedged in so securely.

The heat was intense, even though it was still early in the morning, and Kitty felt her gown grow wet under her arms and knew that her face was probably bright red under her Sunday hat.

'Is it far?' she managed to whisper to Sidney after a while. She didn't like to confess that she was feeling quite faint. She wished that someone would open one of the windows, but it seemed it wasn't allowed.

By the time they reached Preston she was feeling nauseous as well as overheated, and it was with relief that she climbed down from the coach and looked around at the busy town.

'This way,' said Sidney, taking her by the elbow. 'It's only a short walk.'

He led her towards a square building with long windows and an open porch held up by columns of stone. He urged her through the doors into the interior, which was at least cooler than outside in the sun. With his imposing height increased by his policeman's hat, Sidney found it easy to cut a way through the crowd and Kitty followed him closely, worried about being left behind.

'Wait here,' he said at last, taking her to a long wooden bench that was already almost full. 'Make way for this lady,' he instructed those who were already sitting there, and they obligingly shuffled up to make space for Kitty.

'I have to go through there,' he told her, pointing to a set of double doors that she thought must lead to the courtroom. 'Listen for your name. They'll call you when it's your turn.'

She nodded and watched him walk away from her. She felt so alone and vulnerable in this strange place, but she told herself that she must be brave for Grace's sake as well as her own. She must remember to say all the right things so that they could both be free from the menace of David Harper.

When the usher called her name, Kitty stood up and followed him to the door. He opened it for her to pass through and she found herself in a courtroom quite different from the one in Blackburn. This one was panelled in dark wood and her eyes were immediately drawn to David Harper as he stood in the brass-railed dock. He looked smaller than she remembered and less sure of himself, although she glanced away before he could lock his eyes with hers.

The usher led her to a lectern where he asked her to place her hand on a bible and repeat some words after him – 'I promise to tell the truth, the whole truth and nothing but the truth. So help me God.'

A shiver ran through Kitty. She knew that she was supposed to tell the truth and her eyes sought Sidney's. He gave her a warning look, with an imperceptible shake of his head, and she turned to the judge who asked her if she knew the man in the dock. Kitty affirmed that she did and went on to describe the day that she had found the bag of coins in the alley behind the Andertons' house.

'You say that you were in possession of this bag of shillings?'

'That's right, sir. I found them as I was going about my business as a rag gatherer.'

'And what did you do with these shillings?' he asked.

'I took them to Mr Reynolds at the rag warehouse. He said he thought they weren't real, that they were counterfeited.'

'And what did you do with them then, Mrs Cavanah?'

Kitty's heart quickened and her mouth felt dry. She longed for a drink of water. It seemed to her that she was the one on trial here and she was scared that she might say something to condemn herself. She glanced at Sidney but couldn't read his face.

'I went to the police station,' she said after a moment. It was the truth and she'd taken an oath to speak the truth, but she knew it wasn't the whole truth. She hadn't told the judge that first she'd taken the coins home and that she'd been tempted to keep some of them. She didn't say that she'd decided to put the coins back rather than go to the police and that it was only after the attack that she'd spoken to Constable Westwell.

'And what transpired there?' the judge asked her.

Kitty hesitated again. Sidney had told her what to say. He'd told her that she must corroborate the story he'd told in the court at Blackburn. But Kitty knew it wasn't true and she was afraid. She thought that something terrible would happen if she told a lie – that she would be instantly struck down by God in His anger that she had broken the vow made on the Bible.

'What happened at the police station?' the judge asked again.

'Constable Westwell suggested I put the coins back where I had found them so that he could keep watch for whoever came to retrieve them,' she blurted out as fast as she could. She braced herself for the punishment that would be unleashed on her, closing her eyes and balling her hands into tight fists. Nothing bad happened. When she opened her eyes she saw the judge writing something down then he nodded at her, thanked her and told her she could go.

Kitty was trembling all over as she followed the usher out of the courtroom.

'Do you think I could have a drink of water?' she asked when he instructed her to sit back down on the bench. 'I don't feel well.'

'It'll be the heat,' he replied, not unkindly. 'I'll get someone to fetch one for you.'

Kitty lowered herself to the seat and took deep breaths to steady herself. She would have to go to confession and tell Father Kaye what she had done. He would be angry, she was sure, even when she explained that it had been done with the best of intentions. Sidney had been insistent that this was what she should say to prevent any chance of her being accused of theft and to ensure that David Harper was found guilty of coining today.

Someone came with a cup of water and Kitty sipped it thankfully. The trembling was abating now. She hoped that the priest would intervene on her behalf and God would understand why she had done it. Besides, even though she'd been tempted, she hadn't kept the shillings. She'd done nothing wrong.

Kitty waited for a long time. She wasn't sure if she could go back into the courtroom to watch the proceedings and she could find no one to ask, so she was forced to wait until the doors opened and people began to come out. She got to her feet and looked for Sidney. He was easy to spot and she threaded through the crowd towards him.

His face broke into a huge smile when he saw her.

'Did you hear? Seven years' transportation!' he cried. For a moment Kitty thought he was going to pick her up and swing her around in celebration, but he contented himself with a brief kiss, even if it did draw looks of disapproval.

'And what about the charge of assault?'

'It will be dropped unless Grace Dewhurst decides to pursue it, but I doubt she will if it means her having to appear in court. And there wouldn't be much point because the sentence wouldn't be any longer.'

'She'll be relieved,' Kitty said. 'Can we go now?' The courthouse was making her feel uneasy. She still felt guilty about what she'd said.

'Yes. Of course. Sergeant Watkins has told me I have to go straight back anyway.'

48

Sidney escorted Kitty back to the coach stop. She looked weary and even though he'd been told to return immediately by the sergeant, who he could see was seething with anger, he took her into the Golden Lion and bought her a half-pint of ale to drink before the return journey.

'You did well. I was proud of you,' he told her. For a moment he'd been afraid that she wasn't going to stick to the words he'd taught her, but would blurt out the truth that she had taken the coins home rather than to the police station. He'd been terrified that she might be accused of stealing them and planning to keep them.

She nodded but seemed far less pleased at the verdict than he'd expected. He wondered what was wrong.

'David Harper will never bother you or Grace again,' he said, trying to reassure her. 'He's been taken back to a cell and before long he'll be on a ship to New South Wales. I thought you'd be more pleased.'

'I am pleased,' she replied. 'It's a huge relief.'

'Then what's wrong?'

She glanced about the room and drew closer to him to speak confidentially. 'I broke the oath that I swore,' she told him in a trembling voice. 'I'm frightened that something bad will happen to me.'

'Oh, Kitty!' He took her hand and found that she was

shaking. 'You were brave and courageous. What you did today was a good thing. God will understand that.'

'Do you think so?' she asked.

'I'm sure of it,' he told her. 'Don't give it another thought.'

She nodded, although he could see that she wasn't fully convinced. For a moment he regretted asking her to perjure herself, but when he considered the risk of the truth he knew that he had done the right thing.

'Come on,' he urged. 'Let's go home. I'm sure Grace will be anxious to hear the news.'

Once back in Blackburn, he offered to take Kitty home, but she said she would go straight to Moore Street to speak to Grace. He wanted to go with her, but the sergeant's angry voice was still ringing in his ears and he knew that he would only make things worse by delaying the inevitable interview.

He kissed Kitty and told her that he would call round to see her later. Then he turned towards the police station to hear what Sergeant Watkins had to say.

'Oh, there you are, at last,' the sergeant greeted him when he went in. 'Where have you been? I've been back over an hour.' He didn't wait for an answer. 'I've told Superintendent Marshall what you did. He's waiting to see you in his office.'

Sidney went in to see Mr Marshall looking grim.

'Watkins tells me that you stood up in the court and told some cock and bull story about telling Mrs Cavanah to return those counterfeit shillings to where she found them so that you could spy on the man who came to get them.'

Sidney decided to be honest. 'Yes. It's what I said,' he agreed.

'Is it true?' he demanded.

'Not entirely,' Sidney admitted.

'I thought I'd made it quite clear that investigating is not part of your job here.' Sidney saw the superintendent was furious with him.

'I wanted to protect Mrs Cavanah,' he explained. 'If I'd told the court that she didn't bring the coins straight to us I was afraid that she would be accused of stealing them.'

'Did she steal them?'

'She was in the process of putting them back when Harper attacked her. She'd done nothing wrong.'

'Then why not simply say so?'

'It didn't seem worth the risk, sir.'

'It won't do, Westwell,' Mr Marshall told him. 'You must see that. I can't have members of my police force taking it upon themselves to lie in court, no matter how well meaning they consider themselves. You took an oath – both here and in the courtroom – to serve loyally and to speak the truth. You've broken both those oaths.'

'Yes, sir. I'm sorry,' Sidney said, although he felt far from sorry because he knew he'd done the right thing.

Mr Marshall frowned at him. He could see that Sidney had no regrets.

'You leave me with no choice,' he told him. 'I have to dismiss you.'

'Yes, sir,' Sidney replied. He'd suspected it would end like this all the way back from Preston. If only Watkins hadn't come to court as well, he'd have got away with it. And there was no real reason for him to be there, except to pretend that he was the one responsible for bringing the coiner to justice.

'You've let me down,' Mr Marshall went on. He sounded regretful. 'I had such hopes for you. Still, you'd best get out of the uniform and gather your belongings. Do you have somewhere to go?'

'I'll find somewhere.'

'I suppose you'll move in with Mrs Cavanah and her brood. That's what you've always wanted to do. It's a shame. It's getting mixed up with that woman that's brought you to this juncture. You could have had a good job here,' he said. 'You could have risen through the ranks and done well for yourself.'

'Perhaps it wasn't right for me,' Sidney told him calmly, although his own temper had flared at the superintendent's words and he longed to say more.

'Maybe so,' replied Mr Marshall and waved a hand to indicate he was dismissed. 'Make sure you leave everything you were issued with,' he called after him as he walked out.

Sidney saw Watkins grinning when he came out. It was clear the man had been listening and had heard everything. He ignored him, suppressing the urge to punch him and change his expression. He went up to the dormitory, shedding his jacket as he went. He flung it on to the bed and pulled off the boots and trousers, taking a moment to cool himself as he stood in his underwear. Then he pulled out his trunk and found the things he'd worn the day he went to look for Harper at Old Dadds. He felt relieved as he dressed in his own clothes and packed what few things he owned into the trunk. It had been a mistake, he thought. He wasn't cut out for this life with its restrictions and hierarchy of tyrants. He'd always been used to working for himself before and that's what he would do again. He would need to speak to Kitty about it first, but if she was agreeable it might be the answer to all their problems.

He locked the trunk with a padlock and told Andrew Milne that he would send a cart for it later. Then he walked out into the cooling air. There were clouds gathering from the west and a freshening breeze had sprung up. Thunder was in the air and it seemed that before nightfall the heatwave would break and there would be rain.

49

After she'd parted from Sidney at the coach stop, Kitty went straight to Moore Street. Grace must have been watching out for her because she opened the door at her approach with an eager face.

'Seven years' transportation!' Kitty called before she even reached her friend. She saw the anxiety melt from Grace's face.

'Oh, heaven be praised!' she exclaimed. 'Seven years, did you say?'

'Yes, but he'll not come back. He's gone for good. Your debt is cancelled.'

'Thank God!' said Grace and as she began to cry, Kitty put her arms around her to comfort her.

'You're safe now,' she told her, rubbing her back as she sobbed.

They went inside and Kitty was pleased to see Nancy sitting on the floor with her doll. She was dressed and her hair was brushed and she seemed calm.

'Hello Nancy,' she greeted her and was rewarded with a shy smile of recognition. 'She looks well,' she told Grace.

'Yes. I took her out walking. She was a good girl. Will you take some tea with us?'

'If you have some, then I'd be grateful. It's been a tiring day,' Kitty admitted.

'It's been a good day,' replied Grace. She put one spoonful of tea into her pot.

'Did you get to your work?' asked Kitty.

'I did. But it's not a solution,' Grace told her. 'It doesn't pay enough to keep us. I need to do more, but how can I?' Her worries seemed to beset her again and her customary expression of anxiety returned. 'I can't be in two places at the same time.'

Kitty knew how hard it was for her, but she could think of nothing helpful to say.

'I spoke to the Andertons,' she told Grace, 'but they say the parish will probably only help if you send Nancy away.'

'I know. They pretend to care, but they're cruel. And then when you get into debt they blame you.'

'I wish there was something I could do,' Kitty said.

'Aye, well, it's not your fault. You've done more than enough already by ridding me of David Harper. I'll manage,' she said. 'Somehow.'

They drank tea together, weak and black, but it was welcome and Kitty enjoyed it.

'Will you come again?' asked Grace when it was time for her to go. 'I don't have many friends.'

Kitty knew she had none. 'Yes, of course,' she said warmly. 'I'd be glad to come again.'

As she walked home she wracked her brains for some way that she could help Grace, but she could think of nothing. The trouble was that people like Nancy were not always considered important by the men who made up the committee of Poor Law guardians. Their only concern was to get people into work, and it was clear that Grace couldn't work whilst she had to care for her sister and mother – so it was cheaper to remove them to the workhouse than pay Grace to stay at home to look after them. Kitty hoped it wouldn't come to that, but she could see no other option and it made her so sad.

She hadn't expected Sidney to come until much later, so she was surprised to find him sitting on her doorstep and even more surprised to see he was dressed in his own clothes. The checked shirt looked like it hadn't seen a flat iron in a long time and she wished she could press it for him. He had on a waistcoat over it that was flapping loose and a neckerchief around his throat. He looked much younger now that he was out of the police uniform – and less stern. It surprised her how different he seemed. Even his demeanour was more relaxed.

He stood up slowly as she approached.

'You're early,' she said when she reached him. He ran a hand through his hair and then grinned at her.

'I've been sacked.'

'What? I don't understand.'

'They've dismissed me from the police. I'm a free man.'

'Why?' she asked. 'Was it because of me?'

'No, it isn't your fault. It was because of what I said in court, which was my idea. The superintendent was furious with me, even though it got Harper convicted. Still, it could have been worse.'

'How could it be worse?' asked Kitty. All sorts of things ran through her mind: if he had no job he had no wages; the house he'd promised her was lost; there was no room for him to move in with them and she was afraid he might decide to move on, seeing as there could be no wedding.

'They might have had me back in court for perjury,' Sidney said.

'But you did it to protect me, and Grace.'

'I know. And I don't regret it. It was the right thing to do.'

'What will you do now?' she asked. He didn't seem at all troubled and it was so unlike him not to be concerned about something as serious as this. She suddenly wondered if she'd misjudged him.

'Don't look so worried. I have a plan. Let's go inside.'

He followed her in and Kitty turned to hear what he had to say, hoping that he wouldn't tell her he was leaving.

'You know that Susan and I ran a beerhouse in Manchester,' he began. She nodded. 'Well, I think I might do the same again.'

'In Manchester?' she asked, feeling bereft. She was convinced now that he was planning to go away.

'No! Here in Blackburn. Billy Yates told me the Spread Eagle is coming up for rent. I thought nothing of it at the time because I was so set on proving myself in the police and us marrying and getting a nice house. But now everything's changed. I won't do anything unless you agree,' he assured her. 'But I think it might suit us.'

'Us?' asked Kitty, bewildered by what he was telling

her. 'Do you want me to help you run a public house? I know nothing about them.'

'You'd soon learn,' he said. 'It isn't hard – and you can cook. You can turn even the cheapest ingredients into something tasty. I know. I've tasted your Irish stew.'

She stared at him. 'You want me to cook for customers?' she asked.

'I'd need help to run it to its full potential,' he explained. 'There's room to open a dining room and you're such a good cook. I'm sure it would be popular.'

'I'd have to give up the gathering.'

'I was hoping you'd give that up anyway,' he said. 'Look, I promised that I would take care of you and find somewhere better for us to live, and if I take on the Spread Eagle I can do both those things. I've run a pub before. It's hard work, but I know what I'm doing and I'm sure we can make a good living from it.' He paused. 'But I won't do it if you don't want me to.'

'What else would you do?'

'I'm not sure. Work in a mill, maybe, or a printing works again.' She could see he wasn't enthusiastic.

'What about us not being a married couple?' she ventured, unsure if them being unwed would make a difference to his plans.

'There's no rule about us having to be man and wife to take on a pub,' he reassured her. 'We'll marry after the seven years are up, when you can get the death certificate. If it's still what you want,' he added. 'Because in the end it's all about pieces of paper, isn't it? Does it really make a difference whether we have a marriage certificate or not? I love you, Kitty. I want to be with you and I swear that I'll stand by you and care for you and the children whether we've been legally joined or not.'

Kitty sat down on a chair. She was finding it difficult to think clearly. It had come as a surprise, but one which she could see held possibilities for a better future for both of them – if only she was free to marry him.

'I don't know,' she said. 'I'll have to talk to Father Kaye. I couldn't do it without his blessing.'

'Kitty.' He knelt down beside her and took her hand. 'You know he'll set you against the idea. This is a decision you must make for yourself. What if we had separate rooms until we were married?' he asked. 'Would that make you feel better?'

'I couldn't ask you to do that.'

'I'm offering to do it. I'm willing to wait. Please say yes.'

Kitty longed to say yes even though she was afraid of committing such a sin. But then she remembered that she'd already taken one chance today with God's wrath and nothing bad had happened. And she loved Sidney and she wanted to be with him. Surely it couldn't be wrong if they loved one another and the only reason they couldn't marry right away was because she couldn't get a certificate?

He was looking up at her imploringly with his earnest brown eyes and in that moment she found it impossible to refuse him. She nodded. 'Yes,' she whispered. 'Yes. Let's do it.'

'Father Kaye can like it or lump it!' declared Agnes when she came home and heard the good news. Kitty had to smile. Her daughter had never been much of a church-goer. Agnes hugged her. 'I'm so pleased. You deserve some happiness,' she told her mother. 'Don't allow anything to stand in your way.' She hesitated and Kitty could see something was bothering her. 'Will there be room for all of us at the pub?' she asked.

'Of course there'll be room for you!' Sidney exclaimed. 'You and Timothy and Maria and Peter. You're all my children now. I'll care for all of you.'

Kitty took his hand and squeezed it. 'I'm so lucky to have found you,' she said. 'I can't believe how lucky I am.'

'Not as lucky as me,' he told her. 'I never thought I could be happy again until I met you.'

Agnes rolled her eyes. 'I may have to ask Jonas to bring our wedding forward if you're going to be like this all the time,' she complained.

'You should,' Kitty told her. 'I want to see you as happy as I am.'

'Maybe it is time,' Agnes agreed. 'I can work in the shop some days so I'll still see you.'

'And I can come to help,' Maria volunteered.

'It's a solution,' said Kitty. 'It would be a better place for you than the rag warehouse.'

'Well, we're getting a bit ahead of ourselves,' Agnes reminded her. 'You haven't even seen this public house yet.'

'Come and see it tomorrow,' urged Sidney. 'Leave the barrow and the rags for once. I want to show you your new home.'

*

'Will you stay?' Kitty asked Sidney later. 'You'll have to make do with the floor again. Or maybe you'd be more comfortable if you got a bed at a lodging house?'

'I'd rather not go to one of those places,' he said. 'Your floor is clean at least.'

'I can't invite you upstairs.'

'I know. I wouldn't expect it. The bedroom's scarcely big enough for all of you anyway. There'll be much more space at the Spread Eagle.'

Suddenly, lightning lit the kitchen, making Kitty gasp. Almost immediately after there was an ominous roll of thunder and huge drops of rain began to fall on the yard beyond the open door.

'I'd better shut it,' she said as it groaned on its hinges in the freshening breeze.

'Leave it a moment,' said Sidney as he got up and went to look outside. 'I enjoy a good thunderstorm. Nothing like it to clear the air.'

'It makes me nervous,' Kitty admitted, as another bright flash lit up the sky. She wished he would close the door and come in.

'Come and watch it,' he said. Reluctantly, she went to join him and he put an arm around her shoulders and held her against him so that she felt safe. 'The weather will be cooler now,' he said, 'but I pity whichever constables are walking their beats tonight.'

'Will you miss it?' she asked him. 'Being a policeman?'

'No. I don't think I will. I don't think it's where I belong. Being a landlord will suit me better.'

Kitty lay in bed that night and thought about Sidney

downstairs, on the hard floor. She was tempted to go down and join him, but she didn't want to risk waking any of the children.

The latest turn of events had taken her completely by surprise. She'd thought that his job as a policeman was secure. She knew he was paid a good wage, and even with the complication of them having to wait to be married she'd never suspected that he was unhappy with it or wanted to give it up. Taking on a public house was something she'd never considered. Even though she knew he and Susan had run a beerhouse, they'd left it to come to Blackburn and she'd always thought that Sidney hadn't enjoyed it. But his enthusiasm for running the Spread Eagle had been infectious and he'd assured her that it could make them more money than his job with the police. She hoped he was right and that he wasn't simply clutching at straws. If it failed then she would blame herself, because the only reason Sidney had been dismissed was because he had protected her.

When Kitty went down the stairs the next morning, Sidney was still sleeping. She watched him for a moment as he lay on his back, breathing slowly. The blanket she'd given him was cast aside and he looked cold. She bent to cover him with it but he awoke and looked puzzled until he remembered where he was.

He got stiffly to his feet as she filled the kettle.

'That was quite a storm last night,' he said. 'It went on for hours. Did it keep you awake?'

'For a while,' she admitted.

'Well, it's brightening now, thank goodness. You're not thinking of going gathering, are you?'

'No. I'd rather stay here with you. And I thought you were going to show me the pub.'

'I will, but Billy Yates won't be up yet. We'll have to wait a while.' He sat on one of the chairs and ran a hand over his chin. 'I left all my things in a trunk at the police station,' he told her. 'I was going to send a cart to collect them and I forgot all about it. I'd better do it this morning. I can't shave or change my clothes.'

'You can have a wash in the sink,' Kitty told him. 'I'll find a towel for you.'

He was splashing his face with cold water when Agnes came down and she smiled when she saw him.

'It feels strange, but it feels right,' she told her mother. 'I think it was meant to be.'

'And I won't forget your father,' Kitty assured her. 'I'll never forget him.'

'Neither will I,' said Agnes, 'but he's gone and you deserve to be happy again. Go and look at this public house and say yes to Sidney's idea. Promise me you will?'

'I will,' Kitty said.

When Agnes and Timothy had gone to work and Sidney had fetched his trunk from the police station, they set off for the Spread Eagle. Maria and Peter walked with them, Peter splashing in the puddles left by the storm and Maria determined not to be left out of this important decision.

The door of the pub was open and Sidney went in first. Kitty followed him. She didn't know much about public houses. She'd never had the money or the inclination to go into them and she was surprised by how nice it was – clean and tidy, with tables surrounded by stools and chairs and a long bar with a marble top that Billy Yates was washing down with hot soapy water.

'What can I get for you?' he asked and then looked startled as he recognized Sidney. 'Constable Westwell! Sorry, I didn't realize it was you.'

'Not *constable* any more,' Sidney told him. 'Like you, I've decided to move on to pastures new. Is this place still up for rent, do you know?'

'Aye. It is. Why? Might you be interested?'

'I am interested,' Sidney told him. 'Me and Mrs Cavanah here are keen to take it on. I've been thinking about what you said about making a dining room, and I think it's a viable idea. Mrs Cavanah makes the best Irish stew. It's bound to be popular.'

'Well, I'd be glad to see it in your capable hands,' Billy told him.

'Could Mrs Cavanah see the kitchen, and the upstairs?' Sidney asked.

'Of course.' Billy threw his wet cloth into a bucket and opened a door for Kitty. 'This way,' he said.

They went through into a room that was at least twice the size of Kitty's own kitchen on Mary Ellen Street. There was a range with two ovens and a hob, a scrubbed wooden table for preparation and plenty of cupboards. It all seemed well kept.

'Upstairs is this way. You'll have to excuse me if it's a bit untidy.'

Kitty and Sidney followed him up the stairs and they came to a small landing.

'Sitting room,' said Billy, pushing open a door, and she looked in at a cosy room with paper on the walls, thick flowered curtains, a nice rug and two armchairs. 'It's a bit bare. My wife took a lot of things with her when she left, but what there is can stay. I'll not be needing any furniture in my new job. I'll leave the bed as well,' he said, showing her the bedroom which also looked out on to Penny Street. 'You'll need to bring bedding, but that's all, and I can let you have the washstand and the chest of drawers.'

Kitty looked around. It wasn't as plush as the Andertons' house, but it was certainly a step up from the little cottage where she was living now.

She turned to Sidney, who'd followed them up. 'Can you really afford to take this on?' she asked him. 'It's huge.'

'It makes money,' Billy told her. 'I'm only going because it's too hard for me to run it alone. With a dining room as well, it'll make a good living, and with help from your youngsters it'll be a thriving family business.' He hesitated. 'Are you gettin' wed?' he asked Sidney.

'In time,' he replied as he exchanged a smile with Kitty. 'So? What do you think?' he asked her.

'It's nice,' she agreed. 'I've never done anything like it before, though.'

'It's easy enough if you're willing,' Billy replied. 'And Const— Mr Westwell told me he's run a beerhouse before.'

They all went back downstairs and Billy poured them a drink, even finding some lemonade for Maria and Peter.

'On the house!' he told them. 'I think there's cause for a celebration.'

Sidney raised his cup and touched it to Kitty's in a toast. 'So you're agreeable?' he asked.

'I am.' She sipped her drink and looked around, barely able to believe that this place was to become her new home. Sidney looked so pleased that she wanted to hug him, but she was shy to make the first move in such a public place. Some of the regulars were drifting in and Billy introduced them to Sidney as the new landlord. Then, when they'd finished their drinks, Sidney went off to speak to the owner of the building about the rental and Kitty took Maria and Peter home. Billy Yates had agreed to move out as soon as the new agreements were signed, and Kitty thought that she would need to see Mr Anderton again to give him notice on Mary Ellen Street.

As they went in, Kitty looked at her barrow propped up against the wall. Agnes had first bought it to transport her cheeses home, but she had no use for it now and Kitty was using it to gather her rags. She wouldn't need it in the future either, and she was wondering whether or not to keep it when an idea struck her.

'Stay here,' she told Maria and Peter. 'There's something I must do.'

She grasped the barrow by the handles and manoeuvred it through the door, then filled it with the sharp sticks and sacks that they used to gather anything valuable and pushed it along the puddle-filled streets to Moore Street, where she knocked on Grace's door.

'I've brought this for you,' Kitty told her. Grace stared at the barrow.

'Why?' she asked.

'You can use it to go rag gathering,' said Kitty. 'I don't need it any more because I'm going to help Sidney run the Spread Eagle.'

'Rag gathering?' asked Grace, looking dubious.

'Yes. Help me get it into your kitchen and I'll explain.'

Once the barrow and its contents were safely inside, Kitty told Grace how she'd managed to earn enough from gathering rags to support herself and her children.

'I'll take you out and show you what to do,' she said. 'And I'll introduce you to Mr Reynolds at the rag warehouse. But the best thing is that you'll be able to take Nancy out with you. She might even be able to help. Peter learned to pick things up when he was only small, so it shouldn't be beyond Nancy. I'm sure she could learn to look for shiny things on the ground. Then once you've finished you can come home to sort out your finds, so you wouldn't have to leave your mother alone all day. I don't know why I didn't think to suggest it before.'

Grace smiled. 'Thank you!' she said and then hugged Kitty fiercely. 'Thank you! It's such a good idea.' Then she drew back and looked at the barrow. 'I can't afford to give you anything for it.'

'I don't want anything! It's a gift,' Kitty insisted.

'Are you sure?'

'Completely sure. I'm so lucky to have found Sidney, and even if we can't be married straight away, I know he'll look after me. You have no one to care for you, but you've sacrificed so much to look after your family that you deserve some help – and it isn't much. I wish I could do more for you.'

'It's more than I ever expected,' Grace told her. 'And I'm thankful. I really am.'

'And when you call in at the Spread Eagle there'll always be a welcome,' Kitty told her. 'I'm going to be making big pots of my stew and you're always welcome to come and share a plate.'

'I couldn't impose on you,' protested Grace.

'You wouldn't be imposing,' said Kitty. 'You're my friend.'

As Kitty walked to King Street to see Mr Anderton and give him her news, she suddenly understood what he'd meant when he'd spoken about the rewards of paying favours forward. She hadn't realized how good it would make her feel until she'd seen how grateful Grace had been for the help she'd given her.

Dorothy answered her knock on the door. For once she'd gone to the front.

'I've come to give notice on my house,' she said, 'and to thank Mr and Mrs Anderton for everything they've done for me and the children. I want them to know how much I appreciate it,' she said, hoping that the same warmth would flood through them at her gratitude. She knew how lucky she'd been to receive their help and to meet Sidney Westwell. She was one of the fortunate ones, even though at times it had seemed that nothing but bad things were happening to her.

I did it, she told Peter and hoped that wherever he was he could hear her. *I found a better life for me and the children.*

When she got back to Mary Ellen Street, Sidney was there waiting for her.

'It's all arranged,' he said. 'We can move in next week. Are you happy?' he asked.

'Happier than I've been for a long time,' she told him as she hugged him tightly. 'I can't believe that I used to be so afraid of you,' she confessed. 'That first time you knocked on my door I was convinced you were going to lock me up.' She felt him laugh as he held her tight. 'And are you happy?' she asked. 'I know it's not been easy. I know I can't replace Susan.'

'I wouldn't want you to,' he said, setting her at arm's length. 'I loved Susan. I still do. But I love you just as much, and what I felt for Susan doesn't diminish what I feel for you. Love is infinite,' he told her. 'There's always more to give and to receive, if you know where to look for it.'

Kitty felt comforted by his words. It meant she didn't have to explain that although she felt more love for Sidney with every day that passed, her love for Peter was still strong as well. She was lucky, she knew, to have found not just one, but two men who cared for her so much. Her years as a widow had been challenging and she was glad that now she had someone to share future trials with – because there would be hardships ahead as well as good times, she knew. But with Sidney by her side she was ready to face them.

Acknowledgements

Thank you to my editor Hannah Smith for all her hard work and input. Also to Clare Bowron, to my copy-editor Sarah Bance and my proofreader Jill Cole, to Katya Browne and all the editorial management team, and to everyone at Penguin Michael Joseph.

SIGN UP TO OUR SAGA NEWSLETTER

Penny Street

The home of heart-warming reads

Welcome to **Penny Street**, your **number one stop for emotional and heartfelt historical reads**. Meet casts of characters you'll never forget, memories you'll treasure as your own, and places that will forever stay with you long after the last page.

Join our online **community** bringing you the latest book deals, competitions and new saga series releases.

You can also find extra content, talk to your favourite authors and share your discoveries with other saga fans on Facebook.

Join today by visiting
www.penguin.co.uk/pennystreet

Follow us on Facebook
www.facebook.com/welcometopennystreet

He just wanted a decent book to read ...

Not too much to ask, is it? It was in 1935 when Allen Lane, Managing Director of Bodley Head Publishers, stood on a platform at Exeter railway station looking for something good to read on his journey back to London. His choice was limited to popular magazines and poor-quality paperbacks – the same choice faced every day by the vast majority of readers, few of whom could afford hardbacks. Lane's disappointment and subsequent anger at the range of books generally available led him to found a company – and change the world.

'We believed in the existence in this country of a vast reading public for intelligent books at a low price, and staked everything on it'
Sir Allen Lane, 1902–1970, founder of Penguin Books

The quality paperback had arrived – and not just in bookshops. Lane was adamant that his Penguins should appear in chain stores and tobacconists, and should cost no more than a packet of cigarettes.

Reading habits (and cigarette prices) have changed since 1935, but Penguin still believes in publishing the best books for everybody to enjoy. We still believe that good design costs no more than bad design, and we still believe that quality books published passionately and responsibly make the world a better place.

So wherever you see the little bird – whether it's on a piece of prize-winning literary fiction or a celebrity autobiography, political tour de force or historical masterpiece, a serial-killer thriller, reference book, world classic or a piece of pure escapism – you can bet that it represents the very best that the genre has to offer.

Whatever you like to read – trust Penguin.

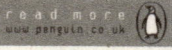